"Marked by wise-cracking humor, eccentric characters, and a gritty urban New Jersey setting . . . Evanovich's 'Stephanie Plum' series attracts an ever-increasing number of fans with each book."

—*Library Journal*

"Loads of fun . . . with laughs on every page."

—*USA Today*

"Evanovich continues . . . her successful formula . . . [she] provides a beginning that illustrates all that is right with this series and an ending that ties the story together, gives us a dose of reality, and leaves us with a cliffhanger."

—*Chicago Tribune*

When the god calls
you must answer...

The old man whispered in her ear, "You were born to free the gods—but you are not yet worthy. You are flawed—and must be tempered. I will be your forge.

Karah fell forward onto her bedroll, and groaned, "You will be my death."

"Only if you prove unworthy.

Karah squinted up at the madman, who sat cross-legged, and stared blindly off into nothingness. As she watched, he became more translucent with every passing second.

She closed her eyes, and murmured. "Please, just kill me now."

First Captain Morkaarin's voice said, "If you aren't out of that tent in five seconds, I just might. You've slept through call."

Karah's whole body jerked, and she opened bleary eyes. Two legs in high boots stood framed by her tent opening. "Oh, godsall, no. I can't get up," she groaned. "I'm dying."

The First Captain's face peered into her tent. Karah noted that what had been an expression of annoyance on his face became one of—shock? Fear? Incredulity?

"What happened to you?" he asked.

"I couldn't sleep last night," she said. And then she considered what she had been through, and decided a lie would be safest. "Nightmares."

He cleared his throat. "Nightmares..."

She nodded.

He gnawed thoughtfully on one side of his bottom lip, then sighed. "We're packing and moving out today, but you can sleep for the moment. And go to the infirmary when you wake."

He walked away.

Karah rolled on her side, ready to let herself drift into sleep. However, she noticed an odd glow in her tent. She looked down at her legs, and then at her hands and arms

Then she rolled onto her belly and pressed her face into the coarse blanket of her bedroll. She started to cry.

Her body glowed with a soft, pale light.

HARD EIGHT

JANET EVANOVICH

St. Martin's Paperbacks

HARD EIGHT

Copyright © 2002 by Evanovich, Inc.

ISBN: 0-312-98894-X

Printed in the United States of America

St. Martin's Press hardcover edition / June 2002
St. Martin's Paperbacks International Edition / January 2003

St. Martin's Paperbacks are published by St. Martin's Press, 175 Fifth Avenue, New York, NY 10010.

10 9 8 7 6 5 4 3 2 1

Here's to the great teams of the world:
Betty and Veronica, Stephanie and Lula, Ralph and Alice,
and me and Jennifer Enderlin, my St. Martin's editor.
Thanks Jen . . . you're the greatest.

*Thanks to Ree Mancini
for suggesting the title for this book.*

ONE

LATELY, I'VE BEEN SPENDING A LOT OF TIME ROLLING on the ground with men who think a stiffy represents personal growth. The rolling around has nothing to do with my sex life. The rolling around is what happens when a bust goes crapola and there's a last ditch effort to hog-tie a big, dumb bad guy possessing a congenitally defective frontal lobe.

My name is Stephanie Plum, and I'm in the fugitive apprehension business . . . bond enforcement, to be exact, working for my cousin Vincent Plum. It wouldn't be such a bad job except the direct result of bond enforcement is usually incarceration—and fugitives tend to not like this. Go figure. To encourage fugitive cooperation on the way back to the pokey I usually persuade the guys I capture to wear handcuffs and leg shackles. This works pretty good most of the time. And, if done right, cuts back on the rolling around on the ground stuff.

Unfortunately, today wasn't most of the time. Martin Paulson, weighing in at 297 pounds and standing five feet, eight inches tall, was arrested for credit card fraud and for being a genuinely obnoxious person. He failed to show for his court appearance last week, and this put Martin on my Most Wanted List. Since Martin is not too bright, he hadn't been too hard to find. Martin had, in fact, been at home engaged in what he does best . . . stealing merchandise off the Internet. I'd managed to get Martin into cuffs and leg shackles and into my car. I'd even managed to drive Martin to the police station on North Clinton Avenue. Unfortunately, when I attempted to get Martin *out* of my car he tipped over and was now rolling around on his belly, trussed up like a Christmas goose, unable to right himself.

We were in the parking lot adjacent to the municipal building. The back door leading to the docket lieutenant was less than fifty feet away. I could call for help, but I'd be the brunt of cop humor for days. I could unlock the cuffs or ankle shackles, but I didn't trust Paulson. He was royally pissed off, red-faced and swearing, making obscene threats and horrifying animal sounds.

I was standing there, watching Paulson struggle, wondering what the hell I was going to do, because anything short of a forklift wasn't going to get Paulson up off the pavement. And just then, Joe Juniak pulled into the lot. Juniak is a former police chief and is now mayor of Trenton. He's a bunch of years older than me and about a foot taller. Juniak's second cousin, Ziggy, is married to my cousin-in-law Gloria Jean. So we're sort of family . . . in a remote way.

The driver's side window slid down, and Juniak grinned at me, cutting his eyes to Paulson. "Is he yours?"

"Yep."

"He's illegally parked. His ass is over the white line."

I toed Paulson, causing him to start rocking again. "He's stuck."

Juniak got out of his car and hauled Paulson up by his armpits. "You don't mind if I embellish this story when I spread it all over town, do you?"

"I do mind! Remember, I voted for you," I said. "And we're almost related."

"Not gonna help you, cutie. Cops live for stuff like this."

"You're not a cop anymore."

"Once a cop, always a cop."

Paulson and I watched Juniak get back into his car and drive away.

"I can't walk in these things," Paulson said, looking down at the shackles. "I'm gonna fall over again. I haven't got a good sense of balance."

"Have you ever heard the bounty hunter slogan, Bring 'em back—dead or alive?"

"Sure."

"Don't tempt me."

Actually, bringing someone back dead is a big no-

no, but this seemed like a good time to make an empty threat. It was late afternoon. It was spring. And I wanted to get on with my life. Spending another hour coaxing Paulson to walk across the parking lot wasn't high on my list of favored things to do.

I wanted to be on a beach somewhere with the sun blistering my skin until I looked like a fried pork rind. Okay, truth is at this time of year that might have to be Cancún, and Cancún didn't figure into my budget. Still, the point was, I didn't want to be *here* in this stupid parking lot with Paulson.

"You probably don't even have a gun," Paulson said.

"Hey, give me a break. I haven't got all day for this. I have other things to do."

"Like what?"

"None of your business."

"Hah! You haven't got anything better to do."

I was wearing jeans and a T-shirt and black Caterpillar boots, and I had a real urge to kick him in the back of his leg with my size-seven CAT.

"Tell me," he said.

"I promised my parents I'd be home for dinner at six."

Paulson burst out laughing. "That's pathetic. That's fucking pathetic." The laughter turned into a coughing fit. Paulson leaned forward, wobbled side to side, and fell over. I reached for him, but it was too late. He was back on his belly, doing his beached whale imitation.

. . .

My parents live in a narrow duplex in a chunk of Trenton called the Burg. If the Burg was a food, it would be pasta—penne rigate, ziti, fettuccine, spaghetti, and elbow macaroni, swimming in marinara, cheese sauce, or mayo. Good, dependable, all-occasion food that puts a smile on your face and fat on your butt. The Burg is a solid neighborhood where people buy houses and live in them until death kicks them out. Backyards are used to run a clothesline, store the garbage can, and give the dog a place to poop. No fancy backyard decks and gazebos for Burgers. Burgers sit on their small front porches and cement stoops. The better to see the world go by.

I rolled in just as my mother was pulling the roast chicken out of the oven. My father was already in his seat at the head of the table. He stared straight ahead, eyes glazed, thoughts in limbo, knife and fork in hand. My sister, Valerie, who had recently moved back home after leaving her husband, was at work whipping potatoes in the kitchen. When we were kids Valerie was the perfect daughter. And I was the daughter who stepped in dog poo, sat on gum, and constantly fell off the garage roof in an attempt to fly. As a last ditch effort to preserve her marriage, Valerie had traded in her Italian-Hungarian genes and turned herself into Meg Ryan. The marriage failed, but the blonde Meg-shag persists.

Valerie's kids were at the table with my dad. The nine-year-old, Angie, was sitting primly with her hands folded, resigned to enduring the meal, an almost perfect clone of Valerie at that age. The seven-year-old, Mary Alice, the kid from hell, had two sticks poked into her brown hair.

"What's with the sticks?" I asked.

"They not sticks. They're antlers. I'm a reindeer."

This was a surprise because usually she's a horse.

"How was your day?" Grandma asked me, setting a bowl of green beans on the table. "Did you shoot anybody? Did you capture any bad guys?"

Grandma Mazur moved in with my parents shortly after Grandpa Mazur took his fat clogged arteries to the all-you-can-eat buffet in the sky. Grandma's in her midseventies and doesn't look a day over ninety. Her body is aging, but her mind seems to be going in the opposite direction. She was wearing white tennis shoes and a lavender polyester warm-up suit. Her steel gray hair was cut short and permed to within an inch of its life. Her nails were painted lavender to match the suit.

"I didn't shoot anybody today," I said, "but I brought in a guy wanted for credit card fraud."

There was a knock at the front door, and Mabel Markowitz stuck her head in and called, "Yoohoo."

My parents live in a two-family duplex. They own the south half, and Mabel Markowitz owns the north half, the house divided by a common wall and years of disagreement over house paint. Out of necessity, Mabel's made thrift a religious experience, getting by on Social Security and government-surplus peanut butter. Her husband, Izzy, was a good man but drank himself into an early grave. Mabel's only daughter died of uterine cancer a year ago. The son-in-law died a month later in a car crash.

All forward progress stopped at the table, and everyone looked to the front door, because in all the years Mabel had lived next door, she'd never once *yoohoo*ed while we were eating.

"I hate to disturb your meal," Mabel said. "I just wanted to ask Stephanie if she'd have a minute to stop over, later. I have a question about this bond business. It's for a friend."

"Sure," I said. "I'll be over after dinner." I imagined it would be a short conversation since everything I knew about bond could be said in two sentences.

Mabel left and Grandma leaned forward, elbows on the table. "I bet that's a lot of hooey about wanting advice for a friend. I bet Mabel's been busted."

Everyone simultaneously rolled their eyes at Grandma.

"Okay then," she said. "Maybe she wants a job. Maybe she wants to be a bounty hunter. You know how she's always squeaking by."

My father shoveled food into his mouth, keeping his head down. He reached for the potatoes and spooned seconds onto his plate. "Christ," he mumbled.

"If there's anyone in that family who would need a bail bond, it would be Mabel's ex-grandson-in-law," my mother said. "He's mixed up with some bad people these days. Evelyn was smart to divorce him."

"Yeah, and that divorce was real nasty," Grandma said to me. "Almost as nasty as yours."

"I set a high standard."

"You were a pip," Grandma said.

My mother did another eye roll. "It was a disgrace."

MABEL MARKOWITZ LIVES IN A MUSEUM. SHE MARried in 1943 and still has her first table lamp, her first pot, her first chrome-and-Formica kitchen table. Her living room was newly wallpapered in 1957. The flowers have faded but the paste has held. The carpet is dark Oriental. The upholstered pieces sag slightly in the middle, imprinted with asses that have since moved on . . . either to God or Hamilton Township.

Certainly the furniture doesn't bear the imprint of Mabel's ass as Mabel is a walking skeleton who never sits. Mabel bakes and cleans and paces while she talks on the phone. Her eyes are bright, and she laughs easily, slapping her thigh, wiping her hands on her apron. Her hair is thin and gray, cut short and curled. Her face is powdered first thing in the morning to a chalky white. Her lipstick is pink and applied hourly, feathering out into the deep crevices that line her mouth.

"Stephanie," she said, "how nice to see you. Come in. I have a coffee cake."

Mrs. Markowitz *always* has a coffee cake. That's the way it is in the Burg. Windows are clean, cars are big, and there's always a coffee cake.

I took a seat at the kitchen table. "The truth is, I don't know very much about bond. My cousin Vinnie is the bond expert."

"It's not so much about bond," Mabel said. "It's more about finding someone. And I fibbed about it being for a friend. I was embarrassed. I just don't know how to even begin telling you this."

Mabel's eyes filled with tears. She cut a piece of coffee cake and shoved it into her mouth. Angry. Mabel wasn't the sort of woman to comfortably fall victim to emotion. She washed the coffee cake down with coffee that was strong enough to dissolve a spoon if you let it sit in the cup too long. *Never* accept coffee from Mrs. Markowitz.

"I guess you know Evelyn's marriage didn't work out. She and Steven got a divorce a while back, and it was pretty bitter," Mabel finally said.

Evelyn is Mabel's granddaughter. I've known Evelyn all my life, but we were never close friends. She lived several blocks away, and she went to Catholic school. Our paths only intersected on Sundays when she'd come to dinner at Mabel's house. Valerie and I called her the Giggler because she giggled at everything. She'd come over to play board games in her Sunday clothes, and she'd giggle when she rolled the dice, giggle when she moved her piece, giggle when she lost. She giggled so much she got dimples. And when she got older, she was one of those girls that boys love. Evelyn was all round softness and dimples and vivacious energy.

I hardly ever saw Evelyn anymore, but when I did there wasn't much vivacious energy left in her.

Mabel pressed her thin lips together. "There was so much arguing and hard feelings over the divorce that the judge made Evelyn take out one of these new child custody bonds. I guess he was afraid Evelyn wouldn't let Steven see Annie. Anyway, Evelyn didn't have any money to put up for the bond. Steven took the money that Evelyn got when my daughter died, and he never gave Evelyn anything. Evelyn was like a prisoner in that house on Key Street. I'm almost the only relative left for Evelyn and Annie now, so I put my house here up for collateral. Evelyn wouldn't have gotten custody if I didn't do that."

This was all new to me. I'd never heard of a *custody* bond. The people I tracked down were in violation of a *bail* bond.

Mabel wiped the table clean of crumbs and dumped the crumbs in the sink. Mabel wasn't good at sitting. "It was all just fine until last week when I got a note from Evelyn, saying she and Annie were going away for a while. I didn't think much of it, but all of a sudden everyone is looking for Annie. Steven came to my house a couple days ago, raising his voice and saying terrible things about Evelyn. He said she had no business taking Annie off like she did, taking her away from him and taking her out of first grade. And he said he was invoking the custody bond. And then this morning I got a phone call from the bond company telling me they were going to take my house if I didn't help them get Annie back."

Mabel looked around her kitchen. "I don't know what I'd do without the house. Can they really take it from me?"

"I don't know," I told Mabel. "I've never been involved in anything like this."

"And now they all got me worried. How do I know if Evelyn and Annie are okay? I don't have any way of getting in touch. And it was just a note. It wasn't even like I talked to Evelyn."

Mabel's eyes filled up again, and I was really hoping she wasn't going to flat-out cry because I wasn't great with big displays of emotion. My mother and I expressed affection through veiled compliments about gravy.

"I feel just terrible," Mabel said. "I don't know what to do. I thought maybe you could find Evelyn and talk to her . . . make sure her and Annie are all right. I could put up with losing the house, but I don't want to lose Evelyn and Annie. I've got some money set aside. I don't know how much you charge for this sort of thing."

"I don't charge anything. I'm not a private investigator. I don't take on private cases like this." Hell, I'm not even a very good bounty hunter!

Mabel picked at her apron, tears rolling down her cheeks now. "I don't know who else to ask."

Oh man, I don't believe this. Mabel Markowitz, crying! This was at about the same comfort level as getting a gyno exam in the middle of Main Street at high noon.

"Okay," I said. "I'll see what I can do . . . as a neighbor."

Mabel nodded and wiped her eyes. "I'd appreciate it." She took an envelope from the sideboard. "I have a picture for you. It's Annie and Evelyn. It was taken last year when Annie turned seven. And I wrote Evelyn's address on a piece of paper for you, too. And her car and license plate."

"Do you have a key to her house?"

"No," Mabel said. "She never gave me one."

"Do you have any ideas about where Evelyn might have gone? Anything at all?"

Mabel shook her head. "I can't imagine where she's taken off to. She grew up here in the Burg. Never lived anyplace else. Didn't go away to college. Most all our relatives are right here."

"Did Vinnie write the bond?"

"No. It's some other company. I wrote it down." She reached into her apron pocket and pulled out a folded piece of paper. "It's True Blue Bonds, and the man's name is Les Sebring."

My cousin Vinnie owns Vincent Plum Bail Bonds and runs his business out of a small storefront office on Hamilton Avenue. A while back when I'd been desperate for a job, I'd sort of blackmailed Vinnie into taking me on. The Trenton economy has since improved, and I'm not sure why I'm still working for Vinnie, except that the office is across from a bakery.

Sebring has offices downtown, and his operation makes Vinnie's look like chump change. I've never met Sebring but I've heard stories. He's supposed to be extremely professional. And he's rumored to have legs second only to Tina Turner's.

I gave Mabel an awkward hug, told her I'd look into things for her, and I left.

My mother and my grandmother were waiting for me. They were at my parents' front door with the door cracked an inch, their noses pressed to the glass.

"*Pssst*," my grandmother said. "Hurry up over here. We're dying."

"I can't tell you," I said.

Both women sucked in air. This went against the

code of the Burg. In the Burg, blood was *always* thicker than water. Professional ethics didn't count for much when held up to a juicy piece of gossip among family members.

"Okay," I said, ducking inside. "I might as well tell you. You'll find out anyway." We rationalize a lot in the Burg, too. "When Evelyn got divorced she had to take out something called a child custody bond. Mabel put her house up as collateral. Now Evelyn and Annie are off somewhere, and Mabel is getting pressured by the bond company."

"Oh my goodness," my mother said. "I had no idea."

"Mabel is worried about Evelyn and Annie. Evelyn sent her a note and said she and Annie were going away for a while, but Mabel hasn't heard from them since."

"If I was Mabel I'd be worried about her *house*," Grandma said. "Sounds to me like she could be living in a cardboard box under the railroad bridge."

"I told her I'd help her, but this isn't really my thing. I'm not a private investigator."

"Maybe you could get your friend Ranger to help her," Grandma said. "That might be better anyway, on account of he's hot. I wouldn't mind having him hang around the neighborhood."

Ranger is more associate than friend, although I guess friendship is mixed in there somehow, too. Plus a scary sexual attraction. A few months ago we made a deal that has haunted me. Another one of those jumping-off-the-garage-roof things, except this deal involved my bedroom. Ranger is Cuban-American with skin the color of a mocha latte, heavy on the mocha, and a body that can best be described as *yum*. He's got a big-time stock portfolio, an endless, inexplicable supply of expensive black cars, and skills that make Rambo look like an amateur. I'm pretty sure he only kills bad guys, and I think he might be able to fly like Superman, although the flying part has never been confirmed. Ranger works in bond enforcement, among other things. And Ranger always gets his man.

My black Honda CR-V was parked curbside. Grandma walked me to the car. "Just let me know if there's anything I can do to help," she said. "I always thought I'd make a good detective, on account of I'm so nosy."

"Maybe you could ask around the neighborhood."

"You bet. And I could go to Stiva's tomorrow. Charlie Shleckner is laid out. I hear Stiva did a real good job on him."

New York has Lincoln Center. Florida has Disney World. The Burg has Stiva's Funeral Home. Not only is Stiva's the premier entertainment facility for the Burg, it's also the nerve center of the news network. If you can't get the dirt on someone at Stiva's, then there isn't any dirt to get.

IT WAS STILL EARLY WHEN I LEFT MABEL'S, SO I drove past Evelyn's house on Key Street. It was a two-family house very much like my parents'. Small front yard, small front porch, small two-story house. No sign of life in Evelyn's half. No car parked in front. No lights shining behind drawn drapes. According to Grandma Mazur, Evelyn had lived in the house when she'd been married to Steven Soder and had stayed there with Annie when Soder moved out. Eddie Abruzzi owns the property and rents out both units. Abruzzi owns several houses in the Burg and a couple large office buildings in downtown Trenton. I don't know him personally, but I've heard he's not the world's nicest guy.

I parked and walked to Evelyn's front porch. I rapped lightly on her door. No answer. I tried to peek in the front window, but the drapes were drawn tight. I walked around the side of the house and stood on tippy toes, looking in. No luck with the side windows in the front room and dining room, but my snoopiness paid off with the kitchen. No curtains drawn in the kitchen. There were two cereal bowls and two glasses on the counter next to the sink. Everything else seemed tidy. No sign of Evelyn or Annie. I returned to the front and knocked on the neighbor's door.

The door opened, and Carol Nadich looked out at me.

"Stephanie!" she said. "How the hell are you?"

I went to school with Carol. She got a job at the button factory when we graduated and two months later married Lenny Nadich. Once in a while I run into her at Giovichinni's Meat Market, but beyond that we've lost touch.

"I didn't realize you were living here," I said. "I was looking for Evelyn."

Carol did an eye roll. "Everyone's looking for Evelyn. And to tell you the truth, I hope no one finds her. Except for you, of course. Those other jerks I wouldn't wish on anyone."

"What other jerks?"

"Her ex-husband and his friends. And the landlord, Abruzzi, and his goons."

"You and Evelyn were close?"

"As close as anyone could get to Evelyn. We moved here two years ago, before the divorce. She'd spend all day popping pills and then drink herself into a stupor at night."

"What kind of pills?"

"Prescription. For depression, I think. Understandable, since she was married to Soder. Do you know him?"

"Not well." I met Steven Soder for the first time at Evelyn's wedding nine years ago, and I took an instant dislike to him. In my brief dealings with him over the following years I found nothing to change my original bad impression.

"He's a real manipulative bastard. And abusive," Carol said.

"He'd hit her?"

"Not that I know. Just mental abuse. I could hear him yelling at her all the time. Telling her she was stupid. She was kind of heavy, and he used to call her 'the cow.' Then one day he moved out and moved in with some other woman. Joanne Something. Evelyn's lucky day."

"Do you think Evelyn and Annie are safe?"

"God, I hope so. Those two deserve a break."

I looked over at Evelyn's front door. "I don't suppose you have a key?"

Carol shook her head. "Evelyn didn't trust anyone. She was real paranoid. I don't think her grandma even has a key. And she didn't tell me where she was going, if that's your next question. One day she just loaded a bunch of bags into her car and took off."

I gave Carol my card and headed for home. I live in a three-story brick apartment building about ten minutes from the Burg . . . five, if I'm late for dinner and I hit the lights right. The building was constructed at a time when energy was cheap and architecture was inspired by economy. My bathroom is orange and brown, my refrigerator is avocado green, and my windows were born before Thermopane. Fine by me. The rent is reasonable, and the other tenants are okay. Mostly the building is inhabited by seniors on fixed incomes. The seniors are, for the most part, nice people . . . as long as you don't let them get behind the wheel of a car.

I parked in the lot and pushed through the double glass door that led to the small lobby. I was filled with chicken and potatoes and gravy and chocolate layer cake and Mabel's coffee cake, so I bypassed the elevator and took the stairs as penance. All right, so I'm only one flight up, but it's a start, right?

My hamster, Rex, was waiting for me when I opened the door to my apartment. Rex lives in a soup can in a glass aquarium in my kitchen. He stopped running on his wheel when I switched the light on and blinked out at me, whiskers whirring. I like to think it was *welcome home* but probably it was *who put the damn light on?* I gave him a raisin and a small piece of cheese. He stuffed the food into his cheeks and disappeared into his soup can. So much for roommate interaction.

In the past, Rex has sometimes shared his roommate status with a Trenton cop named Joe Morelli.
Morelli's two years older than I am, half a foot taller,
and his gun is bigger than mine. Morelli started looking up my skirt when I was six, and he's just never
gotten out of the habit. We've had some differences
of opinion lately, and Morelli's toothbrush is not currently in my bathroom. Unfortunately, it's a lot harder
to get Morelli out of my heart and my mind than out
of my bathroom. Nevertheless, I'm making an effort.

I got a beer from the fridge and settled in front of
the television. I flipped through the stations, hitting
the high points, not finding much. I had the photo of
Evelyn and Annie in front of me. They were standing
together, looking happy. Annie had curly red hair and
the pale skin of a natural redhead. Evelyn had her
brown hair pulled back. Conservative makeup. She
was smiling, but not enough to bring out the dimples.

A mom and her kid . . . and I was supposed to find
them.

CONNIE ROSOLLI HAD A DOUGHNUT IN ONE HAND
and a cup of coffee in the other when I walked into
the bail bonds office the next morning. She pushed
the doughnut box across the top of her desk with her
elbow and white powdered sugar sifted off her doughnut, down onto her boobs. "Have a doughnut," she
said. "You look like you need one."

Connie is the office manager. She's in charge of
petty cash and she uses it wisely, buying doughnuts
and file folders, and financing the occasional gaming
trip to Atlantic City. It was a little after eight, and

Connie was ready for the day, eyes lined, lashes mascara-ed, lips painted bright red, hair curled into a big bush around her face. I, on the other hand, was letting the day creep up on me. I had my hair pulled into a half-assed ponytail and was wearing my usual stretchy little T-shirt, jeans, and boots. Waving a mascara wand in the vicinity of my eye seemed like a dangerous maneuver this morning, so I was au naturel.

I took a doughnut and looked around. "Where's Lula?"

"She's late. She's been late all week. Not that it matters."

Lula was hired to do filing, but mostly she does what she wants.

"Hey, I heard that," Lula said, swinging through the door. "You better not be talking about me. I'm late on account of I'm going to night school now."

"You go one day a week," Connie said.

"Yeah, but I gotta study. It's not like this shit comes easy. It's not like my former occupation as a ho helps me out, you know. I don't think my final exam's gonna be about hand jobs."

Lula is a couple inches shorter and a lot of pounds heavier than me. She buys her clothes in the petite department and then shoehorns herself into them. This wouldn't work for most people, but it seems right for Lula. Lula shoehorns herself into _life_.

"So what's up?" Lula said. "I miss anything?"

I gave Connie the body receipt for Paulson. "Do you guys know anything about child custody bonds?"

"They're relatively new," Connie said. "Vinnie

isn't doing them yet. They're high-risk bonds. Sebring is the only one in the area taking them on."

"Sebring," Lula said. "Isn't he the guy with the good legs? I hear he's got legs like Tina Turner." She looked down at her own legs. "My legs are the right color but I just got more of them."

"Sebring's legs are white," Connie said. "And I hear they're good at running down blondes."

I swallowed the last of my doughnut and wiped my hands on my jeans. "I need to talk to him."

"You'll be safe today," Lula said. "Not only aren't you blonde, but you aren't exactly decked out. You have a hard night?"

"I'm not a morning person."

"It's your love life," Lula said. "You aren't getting any, and you got nothing to put a smile on your face. You're letting yourself go, is what you're doing."

"I could get plenty if I wanted."

"Well, then?"

"It's complicated."

Connie gave me a check for the Paulson capture. "You aren't thinking about going to work for Sebring, are you?"

I told them about Evelyn and Annie.

"Maybe I should talk to Sebring with you," Lula said. "Maybe we can get him to show us his legs."

"Not necessary," I said. "I can manage this myself." And I didn't especially want to see Les Sebring's legs.

"Look here. I didn't even put my bag down," Lula said. "I'm ready to go."

Lula and I stared at each other for a beat. I was

going to lose. I could see it coming. Lula had it in her mind to go with me. Probably didn't want to file. "Okay," I said, "but no shooting, no shoving, no asking him to roll up his pants leg."

"You got a lot of rules," Lula said.

We took the CR-V across town and parked in a lot next to Sebring's building. The bonds office was on the ground floor, and Sebring had a suite of offices above it.

"Just like Vinnie," Lula said, eyeballing the carpeted floor and freshly painted walls. "Only it looks like humans work here. And check out these chairs for people to sit in . . . they don't even have stains on them. And his receptionist don't have a mustache, either."

Sebring escorted us into his private office. "Stephanie Plum. I've heard of you," he said.

"It wasn't my fault that the funeral parlor burned down," I told him. "And I almost never shoot people."

"We heard of you, too," Lula said to Sebring. "We heard you got great legs."

Sebring was wearing a silver gray suit, white shirt, and red, white, and blue tie. He reeked of respectability, from the tips of his shined black shoes to the top of his perfectly trimmed white hair. And behind the polite politician smile he looked like he didn't take a lot of shit. There was a moment of silence while he considered Lula. Then he hiked his pants leg up. "Get a load of these wheels," he said.

"You must work out," Lula said. "You got excellent legs."

"I wanted to speak to you about Mabel Markowitz," I said to Sebring. "You called her on a child custody bond."

He nodded. "I remember. I have someone scheduled to visit her again today. So far, she hasn't been helpful."

"She lives next door to my parents, and I don't think she knows where her granddaughter or her great-granddaughter have gone."

"That's too bad," Sebring said. "Do you know about child custody bonds?"

"Not a lot."

"PBUS, which as you know is a professional bail agents association, worked with the Center for Missing and Exploited Children to get legislation going that would discourage parents from kidnapping their own kids.

"It's a pretty simple idea. If it looks like there's a good chance either or both parents will take off with the child for parts unknown, the court can impose a cash bond."

"So this is like a criminal bail bond, but it's a child who's at risk," I said.

"With one big difference," Sebring said. "When a criminal bond is posted by a bail bondsman and the accused fails to appear in court, the bondsman forfeits the bond amount to the *court*. Then the bondsman can hunt down the accused, return him to the system, and hopefully be reimbursed by the court. In the case of a child custody bond, the bondsman forfeits the bond to the wronged *parent*. The money is then supposed to be used to find the missing child."

"So if the bond isn't enough of a deterrent to kidnapping, at least there's money to hire a professional to search for the missing child," I said.

"Exactly. Problem is, unlike a criminal bond, the child custody bondsman doesn't have the legal right to hunt down the child. The only recourse the child custody bondsman has to recoup his loss is to foreclose on property or cash collateral posted at the time the bond is written.

"In this case, Evelyn Soder didn't have the cash on hand for the bond. So she came to us and used her grandmother's house as collateral for a surety bond. The hope is that when you call up the grandmother and tell her to start packing, she'll divulge the location of the missing child."

"Have you already released the money to Steven Soder?"

"The money gets released in three weeks."

So I had three weeks to find Annie.

TWO

"THAT LES SEBRING SEEMED LIKE A NICE GUY," LULA said when we were back in my CR-V. "I bet he don't even do it with barnyard animals."

Lula was referring to the rumor that my cousin Vinnie had once been involved in a romantic relationship with a duck. The rumor's never been officially confirmed or denied.

"Now what?" Lula asked. "What's next on the list?"

It was a little after ten. Soder's bar and grill, The Foxhole, should be opening for the lunch trade. "Next we visit Steven Soder," I said. "Probably it'll be a waste of time, but it seems like something we should do anyway."

"No stone unturned," Lula said.

Steven Soder's bar wasn't far from Sebring's office. It was tucked between Carmine's Cut-rate Appliances and a tattoo parlor. The door to The Foxhole was open. The interior was dark and uninviting at this hour. Still, two souls had found their way in and were sitting at the polished wood bar.

"I've been here before," Lula said. "It's an okay place. The burgers aren't bad. And if you get here early, before the grease goes rancid, the onion rings are good, too."

We stepped inside and paused while our eyes adjusted. Soder was behind the bar. He looked up when we entered and nodded an acknowledgment. He was just under six foot. Chunky build. Reddish blond hair. Blue eyes. Ruddy complexion. Looked like he drank a lot of his own beer.

We bellied up to the bar, and he found his way over to us. "Stephanie Plum," he said. "Haven't seen you in a while. What'll it be?"

"Mabel is worried about Annie. I told her I'd ask around."

"Worried about losing that wreck of a house is more like it."

"She won't lose the house. She has money to cover the bond." Sometimes I fib just for practice. It's my one really good bounty hunter skill.

"Too bad," Soder said. "I'd like to see her sitting on the curb. That whole family is a car crash."

"So you think Evelyn and Annie just took off?"

"I know they did. She left me a fucking letter. I

went over there to pick the kid up and there was a
letter for me on the kitchen counter."

"What did the letter say?"

"It said she was taking off and next time I saw the
kid would be never."

"Guess she don't like you, hunh?" Lula said.

"She's nuts," Soder said. "A drunk and a nut. She
gets up in the morning and can't figure out how to
button her sweater. I hope you find the kid fast because Evelyn isn't capable of taking care of her."

"Do you have any idea where she might have
gone?"

He made a derisive grunt. "Not a clue. She didn't
have any friends, and she was dumb as a box of nails.
So far as I can figure she didn't have much money.
They're probably living out of the car somewhere in
the Pine Barrens, eating from Dumpsters."

Not a pretty thought.

I left my card on the bar. "In case you think of
something helpful."

He took the card and winked at me.

"Hey," Lula said. "I don't like that wink. You wink
at her again, and I'll rip your eye outta your head."

"What's with the fat chick?" Soder asked me. "The
two of you going steady?"

"She's my bodyguard," I told him.

"I'm not no *fat chick*," Lula said. "I'm a big
woman. Big enough to kick your nasty white ass
around this room."

Soder locked eyes with her. "Something to look
forward to."

I dragged Lula out of the bar, and we stood blinking on the sidewalk in the sunlight.

"I didn't like him," Lula said.

"No kidding."

"I didn't like the way he kept calling his little girl *the kid*. And it wasn't nice that he wanted an old lady kicked out of her house."

I called Connie on my cell phone and asked her to get me Soder's home address and car information.

"You think he got Annie in his cellar?" Lula asked.

"No, but it wouldn't hurt to look."

"What's next?"

"Next we visit Soder's divorce lawyer. There had to be some justification for setting the bond. I'd like to know the details."

"You know Soder's divorce lawyer?"

I got in the car and looked over at Lula. "Dickie Orr."

Lula grinned. "Your ex? Every time we visit him he throws you out of the office. You think he's going to talk to you about a client?"

I had had the shortest marriage in the history of the Burg. I'd barely finished unpacking my wedding presents when I caught the jerk on the dining room table with my arch-enemy, Joyce Barnhardt. Looking at it in retrospect I can't imagine why I married Orr in the first place. I suppose I was in love with the idea of being in love.

There are certain expectations of girls from the Burg. You grow up, you get married, you have children, you spread out some in the beam, and you learn how to set a buffet for forty. My *dream* was that I would get irradiated like Spiderman and be able to fly like Superman. My *expectation* had been that I'd marry. I did the best I could to live up to the expectation, but it didn't work out. Guess I was stupid. Swayed by Dickie's good looks and education. My head turned by the fact that he was a lawyer.

I didn't see the flaws. The low opinion Dickie has of women. The way he can lie without remorse. I guess I shouldn't fault him so much for that since I'm pretty good at lying myself. Still, I don't lie about personal things . . . like love and fidelity.

"Maybe Dickie's having a good day," I said to Lula. "Maybe he'll be feeling chatty."

"Yeah, and it might help if you don't leap across the desk and try to choke him like you did last time."

Dickie's office was on the other side of town. He'd left a large firm and gone off on his own. From what I could tell he was having some success. He was now located in a two-room suite in the Carter Building. I'd been there, briefly, once before and had sort of lost control.

"I'll be better this time," I said to Lula.

Lula rolled her eyes and got into the CR-V.

I took State Street to Warren and turned onto Sommerset. I found a parking space directly across from Dickie's building and took it as a sign.

"Unh-uh," Lula said. "You just got good parking karma. It don't count for interpersonal relationships. You read your horoscope today?"

I looked over at her. "No. Was it bad?"

"It said your moons weren't in a good spot, and you need to be careful about making money decisions.

And not only that, you're going to have man trouble."

"I always have man trouble." I had two men in my life, and I didn't know what to do with either of them. Ranger scared the bejeezus out of me, and Morelli had pretty much decided that unless I changed my ways I was more trouble than I was worth. I hadn't heard from Morelli in *weeks*.

"Yeah, but this is going to be *big* trouble," Lula said.

"You're making that up."

"Am not."

"You *are*."

"Well, okay, maybe I made some of it up, but not the part about the man trouble."

I fed the meter a quarter and crossed the street. Lula and I entered the building and took the elevator to the third floor. Dickie's office was at the end of the hall. The sign beside the door read *Richard Orr, Attorney*. I resisted the urge to write *asshole* below the sign. I was, after all, a woman scorned, and that carried certain responsibilities. Still, best to write *asshole* on the way out.

The reception area of Dickie's office was tastefully done up in industrial chic. Blacks and grays and the occasional purple upholstered chair. If the Jetsons had hired Tim Burton to decorate, it would have turned out like this. Dickie's secretary was seated behind a large mahogany desk. Caroline Sawyer. I recognized her from my last visit. She looked up when Lula and I entered. Her eyes widened in alarm, and she reached for the phone.

"If you come any closer I'm calling the police," she said.

"I want to talk to Dickie."

"He isn't here."

"I bet she's fibbing," Lula said. "I got a knack for knowing when people are fibbing." Lula shook her finger at Sawyer. "The Lord don't like when people fib."

"Honest to God, he isn't here."

"Now you're blaspheming," Lula said. "You're in big trouble now."

The door to Dickie's inner office opened, and Dickie stuck his head out. "Oh shit," he said, spotting Lula and me. He pulled his head back and slammed his door shut.

"I need to talk to you," I yelled.

"No. Go away. Caroline, call the police."

Lula leaned on Caroline's desk. "You call the police and I'll break one of your fingernails. You'll need a new manicure."

Caroline looked down at her nails. "I just got them done yesterday."

"They did a good job," Lula said. "Where'd you go?"

"Kim's Nails on Second Street."

"They're the best. I go there, too," Lula said. "I got mine detailed this time. See, I got little-bitty stars painted on them."

Caroline looked over at Lula's nails. "Awesome," she said.

I scooted around Sawyer and knocked on Dickie's door. "Open up. I promise I won't try to choke you.

I need to talk to you about Annie Soder. She's missing."

The door opened a crack. "What do you mean . . . missing?"

"Evelyn apparently took off with her, and Les Sebring is enforcing the child custody bond."

The door opened all the way. "I was afraid this would happen."

"I'm trying to help find Annie. I was hoping you could give me some background information."

"I don't know how helpful I can be. I was Soder's attorney. Evelyn was represented by Albert Kloughn. There was so much acrimony during the divorce process, and so many threats were made on both sides, that the judge imposed the bonds."

"Soder had to post a bond, too?"

"Yes, although Soder's was relatively meaningless. Soder owns a local business and isn't likely to flee. Evelyn, on the other hand, had nothing holding her here."

"What do you think of Soder?"

"He was a decent client. Paid his bill on time. Got a little hot under the collar in court. There's no love lost between him and Evelyn."

"Do you think he's a good father?"

Dickie did a palms-up. "Don't know."

"What about Evelyn?"

"She never looked like she was totally with the program. A real space cadet. Probably in the kid's best interest to get found. Evelyn might misplace her and not realize it for days."

"Anything else?" I asked him.

"No, but it doesn't seem right that you haven't gone for my throat," Dickie said.

"Disappointed?"

"Yeah," he said. "I bought pepper spray."

It would have been funny if it had been casual banter, but I suspected Dickie was serious. "Maybe next time."

"You know where to find me."

Lula and I sashayed out of the office, down the hall, and into the elevator.

"That wasn't as much fun as last time," Lula said. "You didn't even threaten him. You didn't chase him around the desk, or anything."

"I don't think I hate him as much as I used to."

"Bummer."

We crossed the street and stared at my car. It had a parking ticket on the window.

"See this," Lula said. "It's your moons. You made a bad money decision when you picked this busted meter."

I stuffed the ticket into my bag and wrenched the door open.

"You better watch out," Lula said. "The man trouble's gonna come next."

I called Connie and asked for an address for Albert Kloughn. In minutes I had Kloughn's business address and Soder's home address. Both were in Hamilton Township.

We drove past Soder's home first. He lived in a complex of garden apartments. The buildings were two-story brick, decked out to be colonial style with white window shutters and white columns at the front doors. Soder's apartment was on the ground floor.

"Guess he hasn't got the little girl in his cellar," Lula said. "Since he hasn't got a cellar."

We sat and watched the apartment for a few minutes, but nothing happened, so we moved on to Kloughn.

Albert Kloughn had a two-room office, next to a Laundromat, in a strip mall. There was a desk for a secretary but no secretary was in residence. Instead, Kloughn was at the desk, typing at the computer. He was my height and looked like he was approaching puberty. He had sandy-colored hair, a face like a cherub, and the body of the Pillsbury Doughboy.

He looked up and smiled tentatively when we entered. Probably thought we were scrounging quarters to do our laundry. I could feel my feet vibrating from the drums tumbling next door, and there was a distant rumble from the large commercial washers.

"Albert Kloughn?" I asked.

He was wearing a white shirt, red-and-green striped tie, and khakis. He stood and self-consciously smoothed out his tie. "I'm Albert Kloughn," he said.

"Well, this is a big disappointment," Lula said. "Where's the red nose that goes *beep beep*? And where're your big clown feet?"

"I'm not that kind of clown. Yeesh. Everybody says that. Ever since kindergarten I've been hearing that. It's spelled 'K-l-o-u-g-h-n.' Kloughn!"

"Could be worse," Lula said. "You could be Albert Fuch."

I gave Kloughn my card. "I'm Stephanie Plum and this is my associate, Lula. I understand you represented Evelyn Soder in her divorce case."

"Wow," he said, "are you really a bounty hunter?"

"Bond enforcement," I told him.

"Yeah, that's a bounty hunter, right?"

"About Evelyn Soder . . ."

"Sure. What do you want to know? Is she in trouble?"

"Evelyn and Annie are missing. And it looks like Evelyn took Annie away so she wouldn't have to visit her father. She left a couple notes."

"She must have had a good reason to leave," Kloughn said. "She really didn't want to jeopardize her grandmother's house. She just didn't have any choice. She had no place to turn for the bond money."

"Any ideas where Evelyn and Annie might have gone?"

Kloughn shook his head. "No. Evelyn didn't talk much. From what I could tell, her entire family lived in the Burg. I don't want to be mean or anything, but she didn't impress me as being real bright. I'm not even sure she could drive. She always had someone bring her to the office."

"Where's your secretary?" Lula asked him.

"I don't have a secretary right now. I used to have someone who came in part-time, but she said the lint blowing around from the dryers bothered her sinuses. Probably I should put an ad in the paper, but I'm not real organized. I only opened this office a couple months ago. Evelyn was one of my first clients. That's why I remember her."

Probably Evelyn was his *only* client.

"Did she pay her bill?"

"She's paying it off monthly."

"If she mails in a check, I'd appreciate it if you'd let me know where it was postmarked."

"I was just gonna suggest that," Lula said. "I thought of that, too."

"Yeah, me, too," Kloughn said. "I was thinking the same thing."

A woman rapped on Kloughn's open door and stuck her head in. "The dryer at the far end don't work. It took all my quarters, and now it's just doing nothing. And on top of that, I can't get the door open."

"Hey," Lula said, "do we look like we care? This man's an attorney-at-law. He don't give a rat's ass about your quarters."

"This happens all the time," Kloughn said. He pulled a form from his top desk drawer. "Here," he said to the woman. "Fill this out and the management will refund your money."

"They gonna comp your rent for that?" Lula asked Kloughn.

"No. They'll probably evict me." He looked around the room. "This is my third office in six months. I had an accidental wastebasket fire in my first office that sort of spread throughout the building. And the office after that got condemned when there was a toilet incident above it and the roof caved in."

"Public restroom?" Lula asked.

"Yes. But I swear it wasn't me. I'm almost positive."

Lula looked at her watch. "It's my lunchtime."

"Hey, how about if I go to lunch with you guys,"

Kloughn said. "I have some ideas on this case. We could talk about it over lunch."

Lula cut her eyes to him. "Haven't got anybody to eat lunch with, hunh?"

"Sure, I've got lots of people to eat lunch with. Everybody wants to eat lunch with me. I didn't make any plans for today, though."

"You're an accident waiting to happen," Lula said. "We eat lunch with you we'll probably get food poisoning."

"If you were really sick I could get you some money," he said. "And if you died it would be *big* money."

"We're only getting fast food," I said.

His eyes lit up. "I *love* fast food. It's always the same. You can count on it. No surprises."

"And it's cheap," Lula said.

"Exactly!"

He put a small *out to lunch* sign in his office window and locked the door behind himself. He climbed into the backseat of the CR-V and leaned forward.

"What are you, part golden retriever?" Lula asked. "You're breathing on me. Sit back in your seat. Put your seat belt on. And if you start drooling, you're outta here."

"Boy, this is fun," he said. "What are we going to eat? Fried chicken? Fish sandwich? Cheeseburger?"

Ten minutes later, we pulled out of the McDonald's drive-thru, loaded with burgers and shakes and fries.

"Okay, here's what I think," Kloughn said. "I think Evelyn isn't far away. She's nice but she's a mouse, right? I mean, where's she gonna go? How do we know she's not at her grandma's?"

"Her grandmother is the one who hired me! She's going to lose her house."

"Oh yeah. I forgot."

Lula looked at him in the rearview mirror. "What'd you do, go to one of them offshore law schools?"

"Very funny." He did another tie-smoothing thing. "It was a correspondence course."

"Is that legal?"

"Sure, you take tests and everything."

I pulled into the Laundromat parking lot and stopped. "Here we are, back from lunch," I said.

"Already? But it's too short. I didn't even finish my fries," he said. "And after that I have a pie to eat."

"Sorry. We have work to do."

"Yeah? What kind of work? Are you going out after someone dangerous? I bet I could help."

"Don't you have lawyer things to do?"

"It's my lunch hour."

"You wouldn't want to tag along," I said. "We're not doing anything interesting. I was going back to Evelyn's house and maybe talk to some of her neighbors."

"I'm good at talking to people," he said. "That was one of my best courses . . . talking to people."

"Don't seem right to kick him out before he eats his pie," Lula said. She looked over the seatback at him. "You gonna eat that whole thing?"

"Alright, he can stay," I said. "But no talking to people. He has to stay in the car."

"Like I'm the wheel guy, right?" he said. "In case you have to make a fast getaway."

"*No.* There will be no fast getaways. And you're not the wheel guy. You don't drive. *I* drive."

"Sure. I know that," he said.

I rolled out of the lot, found Hamilton Avenue, and took it to the Burg, left-turning at St. Francis Hospital. I wound my way through the maze of streets and came to an idle in front of Evelyn's house. The neighborhood was quiet at midday. No kids on bikes. No porch sitters. No traffic to speak of.

I wanted to talk to Evelyn's neighbors, but I didn't want to do it with Lula and Kloughn tagging along. Lula scared the hell out of people. And Kloughn made us look like religious missionaries. I parked the car at the curb, Lula and I got out, and I pocketed the key. "Let's just take a look around," I said to Lula.

She cut her eyes to Kloughn, sitting in the backseat. "You think we should crack a window for him? Isn't there a law about that sort of thing?"

"I think the law applies to dogs."

"Seems like he fits in there, somehow," Lula said. "Actually, he's kind of cute, in a white bread kind of way."

I didn't want to go back to the car and open the door. I was afraid Kloughn would bound out. "He'll be okay," I said. "We won't be that long."

We walked to the porch, and I rang the bell. No answer. Still couldn't see in the front window.

Lula put her ear to the door. "I don't hear anything going on in there," she said.

We walked around the house and looked in the

kitchen window. The same two cereal bowls and glasses were on the counter next to the sink.

"We need to look around inside," Lula said. "I bet the house is lousy with clues."

"No one has a key."

Lula tried the window. "Locked." She gave the door the once-over. "Of course, we're bounty hunters and if we think there's some bad guy in there we have the right to bust the door apart."

I've been known to bend the law a little from time to time, but this was a multiple fracture. "I don't want to ruin Evelyn's door," I said.

I saw Lula eye the window.

"And I don't want to break her window. We're not acting as bond enforcement here, and we have no ground for forced entry."

"Yeah, but if the window broke by accident it would be neighborly of us to investigate it. Like, maybe we could fix it from the inside." Lula swung her big black leather shoulder bag in an arc and smashed the window. "Oops," she said.

I closed my eyes and rested my forehead against the door. I took a deep breath and told myself to stay calm. Sure, I'd like to yell at Lula and maybe choke her, but what would that accomplish? "You're going to pay to have that window fixed," I told her.

"The hell I am. This here's a rental. They got insurance on stuff like this." She knocked out a few remaining pieces of glass, stuck her arm through the open window, and unlocked the door.

I pulled some disposable rubber gloves out of my bag and we snapped them on. No point leaving prints

all over since this was sort of an illegal entry. With
the kind of luck I had, someone would come in and
burgle the place and the police would find my prints.

Lula and I slipped into the kitchen and closed the
door behind us. It was a small kitchen, and with Lula
next to me we were wall-to-wall people.

"Maybe you should do lookout in the front room,"
I said. "Make sure no one walks in on us."

"Lookout is my middle name," Lula said. "No one
will get by me."

I started with the countertop, going through the
usual kitchen clutter. There were no messages written
on the pad by the phone. I rifled through a pile of
junk mail. Aside from some nice towels on sale in the
Martha Stewart line, there wasn't anything of interest.
A drawing of a house done in red and green crayon
was taped to the refrigerator. Annie's, I thought. The
dishes were neatly stacked in over-the-counter cupboards. Glasses were spotless and lined by threes on
the shelves. The refrigerator was filled with condi-
ments but empty of food that might spoil. No milk or
orange juice. No fresh vegetables or fruit.

I drew some conclusions from the kitchen. Evelyn's cupboard was better stocked than mine. She left
quickly but still took the time to get rid of the milk.
If she was a drunk or on drugs or loony tunes, she
was a *responsible* drunk or druggie or loony.

I didn't find anything of help in the kitchen, so I
moved on to the dining room and living room. I
opened drawers and checked under cushions.

"You know where I'd go if I had to hide out?" Lula
said. "I'd go to Disney World. Have you ever been

to Disney World? I'd especially go there if I had a problem, because everybody's happy at Disney World."

"I've been to Disney World seven times," Kloughn said.

Lula and I both jumped at his voice.

"Hey," Lula said, "you're supposed to be in the car."

"I got tired of waiting."

I gave Lula the evil eye.

"I was watching," Lula said. "I don't know how he got past me." She turned to Kloughn. "How'd you get in here?"

"The back door was open. And the window was broken. You didn't break the window, did you? You could get into big trouble for something like that. That's breaking and entering."

"We found the window like that," Lula said. "That's how come we're wearing gloves. We don't want to screw up the evidence if anything's been stolen."

"Good thinking," Kloughn said, his eyes getting bright, his voice up an octave. "Do you really think stuff has been stolen? You think anybody got roughed up?"

Lula looked at him like she'd never seen anybody that dumb before.

"I'm checking upstairs," I said. "You two stay down here and don't touch anything."

"What are you looking for upstairs?" Kloughn wanted to know, following me up the stairs. "I bet you're looking for clues that'll lead you to Evelyn and

Annie. You know where I'd look? I'd look—"

I whirled around, almost knocking him off his feet. "*Down,*" I said, pointing stiff-armed, shouting at him nose to nose. "Go sit on the couch and don't get up until I tell you."

"Yeesh," he said. "You don't have to yell at me. Just tell me, okay? Boy, it must be one of those days for you, hunh?"

I narrowed my eyes. "One of *what* days?"

"You know."

"It is *not* one of those days," I said.

"Yeah, she's like this on a good day," Lula said. "You don't want to know what she's like on one of *those* days."

I left Lula and Kloughn downstairs, and I poked through the bedrooms on my own.

There were still clothes hanging in the closets and folded in dresser drawers. Evelyn must have only taken essentials. Either her disappearance was temporary or else she was in a rush to leave. Maybe both.

As far as I could tell there was no sign of Steven. Evelyn had sanitized the house of him. There were no leftover men's toiletries in the bathroom, no forgotten men's belts lurking in the closet, no family photo in a silver frame. I'd done a similar house cleaning when I'd divorced Dickie. Still, for months after our breakup I'd get bushwhacked by an overlooked item . . . a man's sock that had dropped behind the washing machine, a set of car keys that had gotten kicked under the couch and been given up for lost.

The medicine chest contained the usual . . . a bottle of Tylenol, a bottle of kids' cough syrup, dental floss, nail scissors, mouthwash, box of Band-Aids, talcum powder. No uppers or downers. No hallucinogens. No happy pills. Also, conspicuously missing was anything alcoholic. No wine or gin stashed in kitchen cupboards. No beer in the fridge. Could be Carol was mistaken about the booze and pills. Or could be Evelyn took it all with her.

Kloughn popped his head around the bathroom doorjamb. "You don't mind if I look, too, do you?"

"Yes! I mind. I told you to stay on the couch. And what's Lula doing? She was supposed to keep her eye on you."

"Lula's doing watch out. That doesn't take two people, so I decided to help you search. Did you already look in Annie's room? I just looked in there, and I didn't find any clues, but her drawings were real scary. Did you look at her drawings? I'm telling you, that's a messed-up kid. It's television. All that violence."

"The only picture I saw was of a red-and-green house."

"Did the red look like blood?"

"No. It looked like windows."

"Uh-oh," Lula said from the front room.

Damn. I hate *uh-oh.* "What?" I yelled down at her.

"There's a car pulled up behind your CR-V."

I peeked out Evelyn's bedroom window. It was a black Lincoln Towncar. Two guys got out and started walking toward Evelyn's front door. I grabbed Kloughn's hand and pulled him down the stairs after me. Don't panic, I thought. The door's locked. And they can't see in. I made a sign for everyone to be quiet, and we all stood still as statues, barely breathing, while one of the men rapped on the door.

"Nobody home," he said.

I carefully exhaled. They'd leave now, right? Wrong. There was the sound of a key being inserted in the lock. The lock clicked, and the door swung open.

Lula and Kloughn lined up behind me. The two men stood their ground on the front porch.

"Yes?" I asked, trying to look like I belonged to the house.

The men were late forties, early fifties. Medium height. Built solid. Dressed in business suits. Both Caucasian. Didn't look especially happy to see the Three Stooges in Evelyn's house.

"We're looking for Evelyn," one of the men said.

"Not here," I told him. "And you would be?"

"Eddie Abruzzi. And this is my associate, Melvin Darrow."

THREE

OH BOY. EDDIE ABRUZZI. TALK ABOUT A DAY GOING into the toilet.

"It's been brought to my attention that Evelyn moved out," Abruzzi said. "You wouldn't happen to know where she is, would you?"

"No," I said. "But as you can see, she hasn't moved out."

Abruzzi looked around. "Her furniture's here. That doesn't mean she hasn't moved out."

"Well, technically . . ." Kloughn said.

Abruzzi squinted at Kloughn. "Who are you?"

"I'm Albert Kloughn. I'm Evelyn's lawyer."

This got a smile out of Abruzzi. "Evelyn hired a clown for a lawyer. Perfect."

"K-l-o-u-g-h-n," Albert Kloughn said.

"And I'm Stephanie Plum," I said.

"I know who you are," Abruzzi said. His voice was eerily quiet, and his pupils were shrunk to the size of pinpricks. "You killed Benito Ramirez."

Benito Ramirez was a heavyweight boxer who tried to kill me on several occasions and finally was shot on my fire escape, poised to break through my window. He was criminally insane and flat-out evil, taking pleasure and finding strength through other people's pain.

"I owned Ramirez," Abruzzi said. "I had a lot of time and money invested in him. And I understood him. We enjoyed many of the same pursuits."

"I didn't kill him," I said. "You know that, don't you?"

"You didn't pull the trigger . . . but you killed him all the same." He turned his attention to Lula. "I know who you are, too. You're one of Benito's whores. How did it feel to spend time with Benito? Did you enjoy it? Did you feel privileged? Did you learn anything?"

"I don't feel so good," Lula said. And she fainted dead away, crashing into Kloughn, taking him down with her.

Lula had been brutalized by Ramirez. He'd tortured her and left her for dead. But Lula hadn't died. Turns out, it's not so easy to kill Lula.

Unlike Kloughn, who looked like he might be ready to cash in his chips any minute. Kloughn was squashed under Lula with only his feet showing, doing a good imitation of the Wicked Witch of the East when Dorothy's house fell on her. He made a sound that was half squeak, half death rattle. "Help," he whispered. "I can't breathe."

Darrow grabbed one of Lula's legs and I grabbed an arm, and we rolled Lula off Kloughn.

Kloughn lay there for a moment, eyes glazed, breath shallow. "Does anything look broken?" he asked. "Did I mess myself?"

"What are you doing here?" Abruzzi asked. "And how did you get in?"

"We came to visit Evelyn," I said. "The back door was open."

"You and your fat whore friend always wear rubber gloves?"

Lula opened an eye. "Who you calling fat?" She opened the other eye. "What happened? What am I doing on the floor?"

"You fainted," I told her.

"That's a lie," she said, getting to her feet. "I don't faint. I never fainted once in my life." She looked over at Kloughn, who was still on his back. "What's with him?"

"You landed on him."

"Squashed me like a bug," Kloughn said, struggling to stand. "I'm lucky I'm alive."

Abruzzi considered us all for a moment. "This is my property," he said. "Don't break in again. I don't care if you're friends of the family or lawyers, or murdering bitches. Got that?"

I pressed my lips tight together and said nothing.

Lula shifted her weight foot to foot. "Hunh," she said.

And Kloughn vigorously nodded his head. "Yessir," he said, "we understand. No problemo. We only came in this time on account of—"

Lula gave him a kick in the back of his calf.

"*Yow!*" Kloughn said, bending at the waist, grabbing his leg.

"Get out of this house," Abruzzi said to me. "And don't return."

"I've been employed by Evelyn's family to look after her interests. That includes stopping by here from time to time."

"You're not listening," Abruzzi said. "I'm telling you to stay out. Stay out of this house and stay out of Evelyn's affairs."

Bells and whistles were going off in my head. Why did Abruzzi care about Evelyn and her house? He was her landlord. My understanding of his business was that this wasn't even an important piece of real estate to him.

"And if I don't?"

"I'll make your life very unpleasant. I know how to make women uncomfortable. Benito and I had that in common. We knew how to make women pay attention. Tell me," Abruzzi said, "what were Benito's last moments like? Was he in pain? Was he afraid? Did he know he was going to die?"

"I don't know," I said. "He was on the other side of the glass. I don't know what he was feeling." Aside from insane rage.

Abruzzi stared at me for a moment. "Fate is a funny thing, isn't it? Here you are back in my life. And you're, once again, on the wrong side. It will be interesting to see how this campaign unfolds."

"Campaign?"

"I'm a student of military history. And, this is to some extent a war." He made a small hand gesture. "Maybe not a war. More of a skirmish, I think. Whatever we call it, it's a contest, of sorts. Because I'm feeling generous today, I'll give you an option. You can walk away from Evelyn and this house, and I'll let you go. You'll have bought amnesty. If you continue to participate, I'll consider you to be enemy troops. And the war game will begin."

Oh boy. This guy is a total fruitcake. I held my hand up in a stop gesture. "I'm not playing war games. I'm just a friend of the family, checking on things for Evelyn. We're going now. And I think you should do the same." And I think you should take a pill. A *big* pill.

I ushered Lula and Kloughn past Abruzzi and Darrow and through the door. I hustled them into the car, and we took off.

"Holy crap," Lula said. "What was that? I'm totally creeped out. Eddie Abruzzi has eyes like Ramirez. And Ramirez had no soul. I thought I put all that behind me, but I looked into those eyes just now and everything went black. It was like being with Ramirez all over again. I'm telling you, I'm freaked. I got the sweats. I'm hyperventilating is what I'm doing. I need a burger. No, wait a minute, I just had a burger. I need something else. I need . . . I need . . . I need to go shopping. I need shoes."

Kloughn's eyes brightened. "So Ramirez and Abruzzi are bad guys, right? And Ramirez is dead, right? What was he, a professional killer?"

"He was a professional boxer."

"Holy cow. *That* Ramirez. I remember reading about him in the paper. Holy cow, you're the one who killed Benito Ramirez."

"I didn't kill him," I said. "He was on my fire escape, trying to break in, and someone else shot him."

"Yeah, she almost never shoots anyone," Lula said. "And I don't care anyway. I'm getting out of here. I need mall air. I could breathe better if I had mall air."

I took Kloughn back to the Laundromat and dropped Lula at the office. Lula roared off in her red Trans Am, and I went in to visit with Connie.

"You know that guy you picked up yesterday," Connie said to me, "Martin Paulson? He's back on the street. There was something wrong with his original arrest, and the case has been dismissed."

"He should be locked up just for living."

"Apparently, when he was released his first words as a freed man were some unflattering references to you."

"Great." I slouched onto the couch. "Did you know Eddie Abruzzi owned Benito Ramirez? We ran into him at Evelyn's house. And speaking of Evelyn's house, she has a broken window that we need to repair. It's in the back."

"It was a kid with a baseball, right?" Connie said. "And after you saw him break the window, he ran away, and you don't know who he is. Wait, even better, you *never* saw him. You got there and the window was broken."

"On the nose. So, what do you know about Abruzzi?"

Connie punched the name into her computer. In less than a minute, information started coming in. Home address, previous address, work history, wives, children, arrest history. She printed it out and handed it over to me. "We can find out his toothpaste brand and the size of his right nut, but it'll take a little longer."

"Tempting, but I don't think I need to know his nut size just yet."

"I bet they're big."

I clapped my hands over my ears. "I'm not listening!" I looked sideways at Connie. "What else do you know about him?"

"I don't know much. Just that he owns a bunch of real estate in the Burg and downtown. I've heard he's not a nice guy, but I don't know any details. A while back he was arrested on a minor racketeering charge. The charge was dropped due to lack of *live* witnesses. Why do you want to know about Abruzzi?" Connie asked.

"Morbid curiosity."

"I got two skips in today. Laura Minello got picked up for shoplifting a couple weeks ago and was a no-show for her court appearance yesterday."

"What did she shoplift?"

"A brand-new BMW. Red. Took it right off the lot in broad daylight."

"Test drive?"

"Yeah, only she didn't tell anyone she was taking

it, and she tested it for four days before they caught her."

"You've got to respect a woman with that kind of initiative."

Connie passed me two files. "The second failure to appear is Andy Bender. He's a repeat for domestic violence. I think you might have picked him up on a previous charge. He's probably home, drunk as a skunk, without a clue if it's Monday or Friday."

I flipped through Bender's file. Connie was right. I'd tangled with him before. He was a scrawny waste-oid of a man. And he was a nasty drunk.

"This is the guy who came after me with a chain saw," I said.

"Yes, but look on the bright side," Connie said. "He didn't have a gun."

I tucked the two files into my bag. "Maybe you could run Evelyn Soder through the computer and see if you could pull out her innermost secrets."

"Innermost secrets is a forty-eight-hour search."

"Put it on my tab. I have to take off. I need to talk to the Wizard."

"The Wizard hasn't been answering his page," Connie said. "Tell him to call me."

The Wizard is Ranger. He's the Wizard because he's magic. He mysteriously passes through locked doors. He seems to read minds. He's able to refuse dessert. And he can give me a hot flash with the touch of a fingertip. I had mixed feelings about calling him. We were currently in a strange place, filled with dou-ble entendre and unresolved sexual tension. But we were also partners, of sorts, and he had contacts I'd never have. The Annie search would go much faster if I brought Ranger in.

I got into my car and dialed Ranger on my cell phone. I left a message on his machine and read through Bender's file. Didn't sound like much new had happened since I last saw Andy Bender. He was still unemployed. He was still beating on his wife. And he still lived in the projects on the other side of town. It wasn't going to be hard to find Bender. The hard part was going to be wrestling him into the CR-V.

Hey, I thought, no sense being negative right from the start. Look on the bright side, right? Be a cup-is-half-full person. Maybe Mr. Bender will be sorry he missed his court date. Maybe he'll be happy to see me. Maybe he won't have any gas in his chain saw.

I put the car in gear and headed across town. It was a pleasant afternoon, and the projects looked habitable. There was a hopefulness to the dirt front yards that suggested perhaps this year some grass might grow. Perhaps the junkers at the curb would stop leaking oil. Perhaps a Lotto ticket would pay out big. But then again, perhaps not.

I parked in front of Bender's unit and watched for a while. For lack of a better word, this part of the complex would be described as garden apartments. Bender lived on the ground floor. He had a battered wife and, thankfully, no kids.

An open-air bazaar, of sorts, was operating a short distance away. The bazaar consisted of two cars, an old Caddy and a new Oldsmobile. The owners had parked the cars at the curb and were selling handbags,

T-shirts, DVDs, and God knows what else from their trunks. A few people milled around the cars.

I rooted around in my bag and found a purse-size cylinder of pepper spray. I shook it to make sure it was active and stuffed it into my pants pocket for easy access. I took a pair of cuffs out of the glove compartment and slipped them into the back of my jeans, under the waistband. Okay, now I was all dressed up like a bounty hunter. I walked to Bender's door, took a deep breath, and knocked.

The door opened and Bender looked out at me. "What?"

"Andy Bender?"

He leaned forward and squinted. "Do I know you?"

Get right to it, I thought, reaching behind my back for the cuffs. Move fast and catch him by surprise. "Stephanie Plum," I said, whipping the cuffs out, clapping one on his left wrist. "Bond enforcement. We need to go to the station and reschedule your court date." I put my hand to his shoulder and spun him around, so I could cuff his right wrist.

"Hey, hold on here," he said, jerking away. "What the hell is this? I'm not going nowhere."

He took a swing at me, lost his balance, and listed sideways, knocking into an end table. A lamp and an ashtray crashed to the floor. Bender looked at them, dumbfounded. "You broke my lamp," he said. His face got red and his eyes narrowed. "I don't like that you broke my lamp."

"I didn't break your lamp!"

"I said you broke it. You hard of hearing?" He picked the lamp up from the floor and threw it at me.

I sidestepped, and the lamp sailed past me and hit the wall.

I rammed my hand into my pocket, but Bender tackled me before I could grab hold of the spray. He was a couple inches taller than me, thin and wiry. He wasn't especially strong, but he was mean as a snake. And he was motivated by hate and beer. We scrabbled around on the floor for a while, kicking and scratching. He was trying to do damage, and I was trying to get clear, and neither of us was having much luck.

The room was a mess of clutter with stacks of newspapers, dirty dishes, and empty beer cans. We were bumping into tables and chairs, dumping the dishes and cans on the floor, then rolling over it all. A floor lamp went down, followed by a pizza box.

I managed to slither from his grasp and get to my feet. He lunged after me and came up with a ten-inch chef's knife. I suppose it had been buried in the garbage heap in his living room. I yelped and bolted. No time for the pepper spray.

He was surprisingly fast, considering he was shit-faced drunk. I ran flat-out, up the street. And he ran close at my heels. I skidded to a stop when I got to the boosted goods market, putting the Cadillac between me and Bender while I caught my breath.

One of the vendors approached me. "I got some nice T-shirts," he said. "Exactly like what you'd see at the Gap. Got them in all sizes."

"Not interested," I said.

"Selling them for a good price."

Bender and I were doing a dance around the car. He'd move, then I'd move, then he'd move, then I'd move. Meanwhile, I was trying to get the pepper spray out of my pocket. Trouble was, my pants were tight, the spray was shoved to the bottom of my pocket, and my hands were sweating and shaking.

There was a guy sitting on the Oldsmobile's hood. "Andy," he called, "why're you going after this girl with a knife?"

"She ruined my lunch. I was just sitting down to eat my pizza, and she came and ruined it all."

"I can see that," the guy on the Oldsmobile said. "She got pizza all over her. Looks like she rolled in it."

There was a second guy sitting on the Olds. "Kinky," he said.

"How about one of you guys giving me a hand here," I said. "Get him to drop the knife. Call the police. Do something!"

"Hey, Andy," one of the men said, "she wants you to drop the knife."

"I'm gonna gut her like a fish," Bender said. "I'm gonna filet her like a trout. No bitch just walks in and ruins *my* lunch."

The two guys on the Olds were smiling. "Andy needs some anger management courses," one of them said.

The T-shirt salesman was next to me. "Yeah, and he don't know much about fishing, either. That ain't no filet knife."

I finally pried the pepper spray loose from my pocket. I shook it and aimed it at Bender.

The three men mobilized into action, slamming the trunks shut, putting some distance between us.

"Hey, you want to watch which way the wind is blowing," one of them said. "I don't need my sinuses cleaned. And I don't want my merchandise ruined, either. I'm a businessman, you see what I'm saying? We got inventory here."

"That stuff doesn't scare me," Bender said, inching his way around the Caddy, waving the knife at me. "I love it. Bring it on. I've had so much pepper spray I got an addiction."

"What you got on your wrist?" one of the men asked Bender. "Looks like you got a bracelet on. You and the old lady doing S and M shit now?"

"Those are my cuffs," I said. "He's in violation of his bail bond agreement."

"Hey, I know you," one of the men said. "I remember seeing your picture in the paper. You burned down a funeral home and set your eyebrows on fire."

"It wasn't my fault!"

They were all smiling again. "Didn't Andy go after you with a chain saw last year? And all you got now is this puny girlie-size pepper spray? Where's your gun? You're probably the only one in the whole project not got a gun."

"Gimme the keys," Bender said to the T-shirt guy. "I'm getting out of here. This is turning into a real downer."

"I'm not done selling."

"Sell some other time."

"Shit," the guy said, and flipped him the keys.

Bender got into the Cadillac and roared away.

"What was that?" I asked. "Why did you give him the keys?"

The T-shirt guy shrugged. "It's his car."

"He doesn't have a car listed on his bond agreement," I said.

"Guess ol' Andy don't tell everything. Anyways, it's a recent acquisition."

Recent acquisition. Probably stole it last night along with the T-shirts.

"You sure you don't want a T-shirt? We got more in the Oldsmobile," the guy said. He opened the trunk and took a couple shirts out. "Look at this. This here's the V-neck model. Even got some spandex in it. You'd look fine in this shirt. Show off your boobies."

"How much?" I asked.

"How much you got?"

I shoved my hand back into my pocket and pulled out two dollars.

"This here's your lucky day," the guy said, "on account of this shirt is on sale for two bucks."

I gave him the two dollars, took the shirt, and trudged back to my CR-V.

There was a sleek black car parked just in front of mine. A man leaned against the car, watching me, smiling. Ranger. His black hair was pulled back from his face, tied into a ponytail. He was dressed in black cargo pants, black Bates boots, and a black T-shirt that stretched taut over muscles he'd acquired when he was in Special Forces.

"Looks like you've been shopping," he said.

I tossed the shirt into the CR-V. "I need some help."

"Again?"

A while ago I'd asked Ranger to help me capture

a guy named Eddie DeChooch. DeChooch had been accused of trafficking contraband cigarettes and had been causing all kinds of problems for me. Ranger, being of mercenary mentality, had quoted his price for assistance as a night of his choosing, spent together. The *whole* night. And he got to pick the night's *activities*. Not exactly a hardship, since I'm attracted to Ranger in a moth-to-the-flame sort of way. Still, the idea was scary. I mean, he's the Wizard, right? I practically have an orgasm standing next to him. What would happen with actual penetration? My God, my entire vagina might go up in flames. Not to mention, I can't figure out if I'm still attached to Morelli.

As it turns out, I'd needed Ranger for the takedown. And it had been an okay takedown except for a couple small hitches . . . like DeChooch getting his ear shot off. Ranger had hauled DeChooch off to the lockdown prison ward of St. Francis Hospital, and I had retreated to my apartment and crawled into bed, not wanting to think too hard about the day's events.

What happened after that is still vivid in my mind. At one o'clock the lock tumbled on my front door, and I heard the security chain swing free. I knew a lot of people who could pick a lock. I only knew one man who could release a security chain from the outside.

Ranger stepped into the doorway to my bedroom and knocked softly on the jamb. "Are you awake?"

"I am now. You scared the hell out of me. You ever think about ringing a doorbell?"

"Didn't want to get you out of bed."

"So what's going on?" I asked. "Is DeChooch okay?"

Ranger removed his gun belt and dropped it on the floor. "DeChooch is fine, but *we* have unfinished business."

Unfinished business? Omigod, was he talking about his price for the takedown? The room whirled in front of my eyes, and I involuntarily clutched the sheet to my breast.

"This is sort of sudden," I said. "I mean, I didn't think it would be tonight. I didn't even know if it would be *any* night. I wasn't sure you were serious. Not that I'd go back on a deal, but, um, what I'm trying to say is . . ."

Ranger raised an eyebrow. "I make you nervous?"

"Yes." Damn.

He sat in the rocker in the corner. He slouched slightly, elbows on the arms of the chair, fingers steepled against each other.

"Well?" I asked.

"You can relax. I'm not here to collect on the deal."

I blinked. "You're not? Then why did you drop your gun belt?"

"I'm tired. I wanted to sit and the belt is uncomfortable."

"Oh."

He smiled. "Disappointed?"

"No." Liar, liar, pants on fire.

The smile widened.

"So what's the unfinished business?"

"The hospital is holding DeChooch overnight. He'll be transferred out first thing tomorrow morning.

Someone should be present during the transfer to make sure the paperwork is handled correctly."

"And that would be me?"

Ranger looked at me over his steepled fingers. "That would be you."

"You could have called with this information."

He picked the gun belt off the floor and stood. "I could have, but it wouldn't have been as interesting." He kissed me lightly on the lips and walked to the doorway.

"Hey," I said, ". . . about the deal. You were kidding, right?"

It was the second time I'd asked, and I got the same answer. A smile.

And now, here we were weeks later. Ranger still hadn't collected his fee, and I was in the undesirable position of negotiating more assistance. "Do you know about child custody bonds?" I asked him.

He inclined his head a fraction of an inch. This was the equivalent to intense nodding for Ranger. "Yes."

"I'm looking for a mother and a little girl."

"How old is the little girl?"

"Seven."

"From the Burg?"

"Yes."

"It's difficult to hide a seven-year-old," Ranger said. "They peek out windows and stand in open doorways. If the child is in the Burg, word will get around. The Burg isn't good at keeping a secret."

"I haven't heard anything. I have no leads. I have Connie running a computer check, but I won't get that back for a day or two."

"Give me whatever information you have, and I'll ask around."

I looked past Ranger and saw the Cadillac in the distance, cruising toward us. Bender was still behind the wheel. He slowed when he reached us, gave me the finger, and rolled away around the corner, out of sight.

"A friend of yours?" Ranger asked.

I opened the driver's side door to the CR-V. "I'm supposed to be capturing him."

"And?"

"Tomorrow."

"I could help you with that, too. We could run a tab for you."

I sent him a grimace. "Do you know Eddie Abruzzi?"

Ranger removed a slice of pepperoni from my hair and picked some crushed potato chip crumbs off my T-shirt. "Abruzzi's not a nice guy. You want to stay away from Abruzzi."

I was trying to ignore Ranger's hands on my chest. On the surface it seemed like innocent grooming. In the pit of my stomach it felt like sex. "Stop fondling me," I said.

"Maybe you should get used to it, considering what you owe me."

"I'm trying to have a conversation here! The missing mother is renting a house owned by Abruzzi. I sort of ran into him this morning."

"Let me guess—you rolled on his lunch?"

I looked down at my shirt. "No. Lunch belongs to the guy who gave me the finger."

"Where did you meet up with Abruzzi?"

"At the rental house. This is the weird thing . . . Abruzzi didn't want me in the house, and he didn't want me involved with Evelyn. I mean, what's it to him? This isn't even a significant property for him. And then he got really freaky about this being a military campaign and a war game."

"Abruzzi makes his money primarily through loan sharking," Ranger said. "Then he invests it in legitimate ventures like real estate. His hobby is war gaming. Do you know what that is?"

"No."

"A war gamer studies military strategy. When it first started it was a bunch of guys in a room, pushing toy soldiers around on a map on the table. Like the board game Risk, or Axis and Allies. Imaginary battles are constructed and fought. A lot of war gamers play by computer now. It's Dungeons and Dragons for adults. I'm told Abruzzi takes it seriously."

"He's crazy."

"That's the general consensus. Anything else?" Ranger asked.

"Nope. That's about it."

Ranger angled into his car and drove away.

So much for the part of my day where I actually tried to earn some money. I still had Laura Minello, grand theft auto, but I was feeling discouraged and I didn't have any handcuffs. Probably I needed to get back to the kid search, anyway. If I went back to the house now chances were good that Abruzzi wouldn't be there. He probably left in a huff after threatening me and went home to shove some toy soldiers around.

I drove back to Key Street and parked in front of Carol Nadich's half of the house. I rang her bell and scraped some pizza cheese off my breast while I waited.

"Hey," Carol said, opening the door. "Now what?"

"Did Annie play with any kids in the neighborhood? Did she seem to have a best friend?"

"Most of the kids on this street are older, and Annie stayed inside a lot. Is that pizza in your hair?"

I put my hand to my head and felt around. "Any pepperoni?"

"No. Just cheese and tomato sauce."

"Well," I said, "as long as there aren't any pepperonis."

"Hold on," Carol said. "I remember Evelyn telling me that Annie had a new friend at school. Evelyn was worried about it because the little girl thought she was a horse."

Mental head slap. My niece, Mary Alice.

"Sorry, I don't know the horse kid's name," Carol said.

I left Carol and drove two blocks to my parents' house. It was midafternoon. School would be out, and Mary Alice and Angie would be in the kitchen, eating cookies, getting grilled by my mother. One of my early lessons was that everything has a price. If you want an after-school cookie, you have to tell my mother about your day.

When we were kids, Valerie always had lots to report. She made glee club. She won the spelling contest. She was chosen for the Christmas pageant. Susan

Marrone told her Jimmy Wizneski thought she was pretty.

I had lots to report, too. I didn't make glee club. I didn't win the spelling contest. I wasn't chosen for the Christmas pageant. And I accidentally knocked Billy Bartolucci down the stairs, and he ripped the knee out of his pants.

Grandma met me at the door. "Just in time to have a cookie and tell us about your day," she said. "I bet it was a pip. You've got food all over you. Were you after a killer?"

"I was after a guy wanted for domestic violence."

"I hope you kicked him where it hurt."

"I didn't actually get to kick him, but I ruined his pizza." I sat down at the table with Angie and Mary Alice. "How's it going?" I asked.

"I made the glee club," Angie said.

I stifled the urge to scream and took a cookie. "How about you?" I asked Mary Alice.

Mary Alice took a drink of milk and wiped her mouth with the back of her hand. "I'm not a reindeer anymore on account of I lost my antlers."

"They fell off on the way home from school, and a dog went to the bathroom on them," Angie said.

"I didn't want to be a reindeer anyway," Mary Alice said. "Reindeers don't got nice tails like horses."

"Do you know Annie Soder?"

"Sure," Mary Alice said, "she's in my class. She's my best friend, except she's never in school lately."

"I went to see her today, but she wasn't home. Do you know where she is?"

"Nope," Mary Alice said. "I guess she's gone. That happens when you get divorced."

"If Annie could go anywhere she wanted . . . where would she go?"

"Disney World."

"Where else?"

"Her grandma's."

"Where else?"

Mary Alice shrugged.

"How about her mom? Where would her mom want to go?"

Another shrug.

"Help me out here," I said. "I'm trying to find Annie."

"Annie is a horse, too," Mary Alice said. "Annie is a brown horse, only thing, she can't gallop as fast as me."

Grandma moved to the front door, driven there by Burg radar. A good Burg housewife never missed anything happening on the street. A good Burg housewife could pick up street sounds not ordinarily heard by the human ear.

"Look at this," Grandma said, "Mabel's got company. Somebody I never saw before."

My mother and I joined Grandma at the door.

"Fancy car," my mother said.

It was a black Jaguar. Brand new. Not a splatter of mud or a speck of dust on it. A woman emerged from behind the wheel. She was dressed in black leather pants, high-heeled black leather boots, and a short form-fitting black leather jacket. I knew who she was. I'd run into her once before. She was the female equivalent of Ranger. My understanding was that, like Ranger, she did a variety of things including but not limited to bodyguarding, bounty hunting, and private investigating. Her name was Jeanne Ellen Burrows.

FOUR

"MABEL'S VISITOR LOOKS LIKE CATWOMAN,"
Grandma said. "Except she hasn't got pointy cat ears
and whiskers."

And the cat suit was by Donna Karan.

"I know her," I said. "Her name is Jeanne Ellen
Burrows, and she's probably connected to the child
custody bond, somehow. I need to talk to her."

"Me, too," Grandma said.

"*No.* Not a good idea. Stay here. I'll be right back."

Jeanne Ellen saw me approach and paused on the
sidewalk. I extended my hand to her. "Stephanie
Plum," I said.

She had a firm handshake. "I remember."

"I assume you've been hired by someone connected to the bond."

"Steven Soder."

"I've been hired by Mabel."

"I hope we won't have an adversarial relationship."

"That would be my hope, too," I said.

"Would you like to share any information with me?"

I took a beat to think about it and decided I didn't have any information to share. "No."

Her mouth curved into a small, polite smile. "Well, then."

Mabel opened her door and peered out at us.

"This is Jeanne Ellen Burrows," I told Mabel. "She's working for Steven Soder. She'd like to ask you some questions. I'd prefer you didn't answer them." I was getting strange vibes on Evelyn and Annie's disappearance, and I didn't want Annie given up to Steven until I heard Evelyn's reason for leaving.

"It would be in your best interest to talk to me," Jeanne Ellen said to Mabel. "Your great-granddaughter could be in danger. I could help find her. I'm very good at finding people."

"Stephanie's good at finding people, too," Mabel said.

Again, the small smile returned to Jeanne Ellen's mouth. "I'm better," she said.

It was true. Jeanne Ellen was better at finding people. I relied more on dumb luck and blind persistence.

"I don't know," Mabel said. "I don't feel comfortable going against Stephanie. You look like a per-

fectly nice young woman, but I'd rather not talk to
you about this."

Jeanne Ellen gave Mabel her card. "If you change
you mind, you can reach me at one of these numbers."

Mabel and I watched Jeanne Ellen get into her car
and drive off.

"She reminds me of someone," Mabel said. "I can't
put my finger on it."

"Catwoman," I said.

"*Yes!* That's it, except for the ears."

I left Mabel, filled my mother and grandmother in
on Jeanne Ellen, took a cookie for the road, and
headed for home, making a fast stop at the office first.

Lula pulled in behind me. "Wait until you see the
boots I got. I got myself a pair of biker boots." She
tossed her bag and her jacket on the couch and opened
the shoe box. "Look at this. Are these hot, or what?"

They were black with a high stacked heel with an
eagle stitched onto the side. Connie and I agreed. The
boots were hot.

"So what have you been up to?" Lula asked me. "I
miss anything interesting?"

"I ran into Jeanne Ellen Burrows," I said.

Connie and Lula did a double mouth drop. Jeanne
Ellen wasn't seen a lot. She mostly worked at night
and was as elusive as smoke.

"Tell me," Lula said. "I gotta know everything."

"Steven Soder hired her to find Evelyn and Annie."

Connie and Lula exchanged glances. "Does Ranger
know about this?" Connie asked.

There were a lot of rumors about Ranger and
Jeanne Ellen. One rumor had them secretly living to-

gether. One rumor had them as mentor and mentee. Clearly there'd been some sort of relationship at some point. And I was pretty sure it no longer existed, although it was hard to know anything for sure with Ranger.

"This is going to be good," Lula said. "You and Ranger and Jeanne Ellen Burrows. If I was you, I'd go home and do my hair and put some mascara on. And I'd stop at the Harley store and get a pair of these cool boots. You need a pair of these boots just in case you need to walk over Jeanne Ellen."

My cousin Vinnie stuck his head out of his office. "Are you talking about Jeanne Ellen Burrows?"

"Stephanie ran into her today," Connie said. "They're working a case together, from opposite sides."

Vinnie grinned at me. "You're going up against Jeanne Ellen? Are you nuts? This isn't one of *my* FTAs, is it?"

"Child custody bond," I said. "Mabel's great-granddaughter."

"The Mabel next door to your parents? The old-as-dirt Mabel?"

"That's the one. Evelyn and Steven got a divorce and Evelyn took off with Annie."

"So Jeanne Ellen is working for Soder. That makes sense. Sebring probably wrote the bond, right? Jeanne Ellen works for Sebring. Sebring can't go after Evelyn, but he can recommend that Soder hires Jeanne Ellen. Just the sort of case Jeanne Ellen would take, too. A missing kid. Jeanne Ellen loves to have a cause."

"How do you know so much about Jeanne Ellen?"

"Everybody knows about Jeanne Ellen," Vinnie said. "She's a legend. Cripes, you're gonna get your ass kicked."

This Jeanne Ellen thing was starting to annoy me.

"Gotta go," I said. "Things to do. I just stopped in to borrow a pair of cuffs."

Everyone's eyebrows rose a couple inches.

"You need another pair of cuffs?" Vinnie asked.

I gave him my PMS look. "You got a problem with that?"

"Hell no," Vinnie said. "I'm gonna go with S and M. I'm gonna pretend you got a man chained up naked somewhere. It's more comforting than thinking one of my FTAs is running around with your bracelet attached."

I PARKED IN THE BACK OF THE LOT, NEXT TO THE Dumpster, and walked the short distance to my apartment building's rear entrance. Mr. Spiga had just docked his twenty-year-old Oldsmobile in one of the coveted handicapped slots, close to the door, his handicapped sign proudly affixed to his windshield. He was in his seventies, retired from his job at the button factory and, with the exception of his addiction to Metamucil, was in perfect health. Lucky for him, his wife is legally blind and lame from a hip replacement gone bad. Not that it cuts a lot of slack in this lot. Half the people in the building have poked out an eye and run over their foot to get handicapped status. In Jersey, parking is often more important than sight.

"Nice day," I said to Mr. Spiga.

He grabbed a grocery bag from the backseat. "Have you bought ground chuck lately? Who decides these prices? How can people afford to eat? And why is the meat so red? You ever notice it's only red on the outside? They spray it with something, so you think it's fresh. The food industry's going to hell."

I opened the door for him.

"Another thing," he said, "half the men in this country have breasts. I'm telling you, it's from those hormones they feed the cows. You drink the milk from the cows and you grow breasts."

Ah, I thought, if only it was that easy.

The elevator doors opened and Mrs. Bestler peeked out. "Going up," she said.

Mrs. Bestler was about two hundred years old and liked to play elevator operator.

"Second floor," I told her.

"Second floor, ladies handbags and better dresses," she sang out, punching the button.

"Cripes," Mr. Spiga said. "This place is filled with loonies."

First thing I did when I entered my apartment was check my messages. I work with a mysterious bounty hunter guy who turns me to jelly and makes sexual innuendoes and never follows through. And I'm in the off-again phase of an off-again-on-again relationship with a cop guy I think I might want to marry . . . someday, but not now. That's my love life. In other words, my love life is a big zero. I can't remember the last time I had a date. An orgasm is nothing more than a distant memory. And there were no messages on my machine.

I flopped onto my couch and closed my eyes. My life was in the toilet. I did about a half hour of self-pity and was about to get up and take a shower when my doorbell rang. I went to the door and looked out my security peephole. Nobody there. I turned to walk away and heard rustling on the other side of the door. I looked out again. Still no one there.

I called my neighbor across the hall and asked him to look out his door and tell me if anyone was there. Okay, so this is a little despicable on my part, but no one ever wants to kill Mr. Wolesky and from time to time people want to kill me. Doesn't hurt to be careful, right?

"What are you crazy?" Mr. Wolesky said. "I'm watching *The Brady Bunch.* You called right in the middle of *The Brady Bunch.*"

And he hung up.

I was still hearing the rustling sounds, so I got my gun out of the cookie jar, found a bullet in the bottom of my purse, put the bullet in the gun, and opened the door. There was a dark green canvas bag hanging from my doorknob. The bag had a drawstring pulled tight at the top and something was moving in the bag. My first thought was an abandoned kitten. I removed the bag from the doorknob, opened the drawstring, and looked inside.

Snakes. The bag was filled with big black snakes.

I shrieked and dropped the bag on the floor, and the snakes slid out. I jumped back into my apartment and slammed my door shut. I looked out my peephole. The snakes were scattering. Shit. I opened the door and shot a snake. Now I was out of bullets. Shit again.

Mr. Wolesky opened his door and looked out. "What the . . . ?" he said, and slammed his door shut.

I ran into my kitchen to look for more bullets, and a snake followed me in. Another shriek and I climbed onto my kitchen counter.

I was still on the counter when the police arrived. Carl Costanza and his partner, Big Dog. I'd gone to school with Carl, and we were friends, in a strange, distant sort of way.

"We got a weird call from your neighbor about snakes," Carl said. "Since there's one shot to shit on your doorstep, and you're up there on the counter, I suppose the call isn't a hoax."

"I ran out of bullets," I said.

"So by a rough estimate, how many snakes do you think we got here?"

"I'm pretty sure there were four in the bag. I shot one. I saw one go down the hall. I saw one head for my bedroom. And one is God knows where."

Carl and Big Dog grinned up at me. "Is the big, bad bounty hunter afraid of snakes?"

"Just *find* them, okay?" *Yeesh.*

Carl adjusted his gun belt and swaggered off with Big Dog a step behind him.

"Here, snakey, snakey, snakey," Carl crooned.

"I think we should look in her panties drawer," Big Dog said. "That's where I'd go if I was a snake."

"Pervert!" I yelled.

"I don't see any snakes here," Carl said.

"They go under things, and they hide in corners," I told him. "Did you check under the couch? Did you look in my closet? Under my bed?"

"I'm not looking under your bed," Carl said. "I'm afraid I'll find some knuckle dragger hiding there."

This got a laugh out of Big Dog. I didn't think it was funny since it was one of my constant fears.

"Listen, Steph," Carl called from the bedroom, "we really have searched everywhere, but we're not seeing any snakes. Are you sure there's one in here?"

"Yes!"

"How about her closet?" Big Dog said. "Did you look in the closet?"

"The door's closed. A snake couldn't get in there."

I heard one of them pull the closet door open, and then they both started shouting.

"Jesus *Christ*."

"Holy *shit*!"

"Shoot it. *Shoot it!*" Carl yelled. "Kill the motherfucker!"

There was a lot of gunshot and more shouting.

"We didn't get it. It's coming out," Carl said. "Goddamn, there are two of them."

I heard the door to my bedroom slam shut.

"Stay here and watch the door," Carl told Big Dog. "Make sure they don't come out."

Carl stormed into my kitchen and started going through my cupboards. He found a half-empty bottle of gin and drank two fingers from the bottle.

"Jesus," he said, capping the bottle, returning it to the cupboard shelf.

"I thought you weren't supposed to drink on duty."

"Yeah, except when you find snakes in closets. I'm calling Animal Control."

I was still on the counter when two Animal Control

guys arrived. Carl and Big Dog were in my living room, guns drawn, eyes trained on my bedroom door.

"They're in the bedroom," Carl told the Animal Control officers. "Two of them."

Joe Morelli showed up a couple minutes later. Morelli wears his hair short but always needs a cut. Today was no exception. His dark hair curled over his ears and his collar and fell onto his forehead. His eyes were melted-chocolate brown. He wore jeans and running shoes and a gray-green thermal Henley. Under the shirt his body was hard and perfect. Fortunately, at this particular moment, under the jeans he was *just perfect*. Although I'd seen that part of him hard, and it was pretty damn fantastic. His gun and his badge were also under the Henley.

Morelli grinned when he saw me on the counter. "What's going on?"

"Someone left a bag of snakes on my doorknob."

"And you let them loose?"

"They took me by surprise."

He looked back at the one I'd shot, still untouched on the hall floor. "Is that the one *you* shot?"

"I ran out of bullets."

"How many bullets did you start with?"

"One."

The grin widened.

The Animal Control officers came out of the bedroom with the two snakes in a bag. "Racers," they said. "Harmless." One of them toed the dead snake in the hall. "You want us to take this one, too?"

"Yes!" I said. "And there's another snake somewhere."

Someone screamed at the far end of the hall.

"Guess we know where to look for snake number four," Joe said.

The Animal Control guys took off with the snakes, and Carl and Big Dog shuffled out of my living room, into my foyer.

"Guess we're done here," Carl said. "You might want to check out your closet. I think Big Dog killed a pair of shoes."

Joe closed the door behind them. "You can get off the counter now."

"It was scary."

"Cupcake, your *life* is scary."

"What's that supposed to mean?"

"Your job sucks."

"It's no suckier than yours."

"I don't have people leaving snakes on my door-knob."

"Animal Control said they were harmless."

He threw his hands into the air. "You're impossible."

"What are you doing here, anyway? I haven't heard from you in weeks."

"I heard the call go out on the radio and had a misguided urge to make sure you were okay. You haven't heard from me because we broke up, remember?"

"Yes, but there's all kinds of broken up."

"Oh yeah? What kind is this? First you decide you don't want to marry me . . ."

"That was a mutual agreement."

"Then you go off with Ranger . . ."

"That was work-related."

He had his hands planted on his hips. "Let's get back to the snakes, okay? You have any idea who left them?"

"I guess I could make a list."

"Jesus," he said, "you've got a list. Not one or two people. A whole list. You have a whole list of people who might want to leave snakes on your doorknob."

"The last couple days have been sort of busy."

"Is that pizza in your hair?"

"I accidentally rolled on Andy Bender's lunch. He would be on the list. A guy named Martin Paulson isn't too happy with me. There's my ex-husband. Then I had an unfortunate encounter with Eddie Abruzzi."

That caught Morelli's attention. "Eddie Abruzzi?"

I told him about Evelyn and Annie and the Abruzzi connection.

"I don't suppose you'd listen to me if I told you to stay away from Abruzzi," Morelli said.

"I'm *trying* to stay away from Abruzzi."

Morelli grabbed me by the front of my shirt, pulled me to him, and kissed me. His tongue touched mine, and I felt liquid fire slide through my stomach and head south. He released me and turned to go.

"Hey!" I said. "What was that?"

"Temporary insanity. You drive me nuts."

And he stalked off down the hall and disappeared into the elevator.

I TOOK A SHOWER AND DRESSED IN CLEAN JEANS AND T-shirt. I did the makeup thing this time and put some gel in my hair. Sort of like locking the barn after the horses have escaped.

I went into the kitchen and stared into the refrigerator for a while, but nothing materialized. No cake. No hot sausage sandwich. No macaroni and cheese magically appeared. I took a bag of chocolate chip cookies out of the freezer and ate one. You were supposed to bake them first, but that seemed like unnecessary effort.

I'd talked to Annie's best friend and that hadn't given me a lot. Okay, so what would I do if I needed to protect my daughter from her father? Where would I go?

I wouldn't have a lot of money, so I'd need to rely on a friend or relative. I'd need to go far enough that my car wouldn't be recognized, and I wouldn't run the risk of bumping into Soder or one of his friends. This narrowed the search down to the entire world, except for the Burg.

I was contemplating the world when my doorbell rang. I wasn't expecting anyone, and I'd just received a bag of snakes, so I wasn't all that crazy about answering the door. I looked out my peephole and grimaced. It was Albert Kloughn. But wait a minute, he was holding a pizza box. *Hello.*

I opened the door and gave a quick look up and down the hall. I was pretty sure there'd been four snakes in the bag . . . still, doesn't hurt to keep your eyes open for renegade reptiles.

"Hope I'm not disturbing anything," Kloughn said, stretching his neck out to look around me into my apartment. "You aren't entertaining or anything, are you? I didn't know if you were living with anyone."

"What's up?"

"I've been thinking about the Soder case, and I have some ideas. I thought we could, like, brainstorm."

I looked down at the box he was holding.

"I brought a pizza," he said. "I didn't know if you'd eaten yet. Do you like pizza? If you don't like pizza I could get something else. I could get Mexican or Chinese or Thai . . ."

Please, Lord, tell me this isn't a date. "I'm sort of engaged."

He vigorously nodded his head. Up and down, up and down, like one of those dogs people put in their back car windows. "Absolutely. I knew you would be. Understood. I'm almost engaged, too. I have a girlfriend."

"Really?"

He took a deep breath. "No. I just made that up."

I took the pizza box from him and dragged him into my apartment. I got some napkins and a couple beers, and we sat at my small dining room table and ate pizza.

"What are these ideas you have about Evelyn Soder?"

"I figure she's with a friend, right? So she had to get in touch with the friend somehow. She had to tell her she was coming to stay. I figure she did this on the phone. So what we need is a phone bill."

"And?"

"That's it."

"Good thing you brought a pizza."

"Actually, it's a tomato pie. In the Burg they call it a tomato pie."

"Sometimes. You know anyone at the phone company? Anyone in the billing department?"

"I figured *you'd* have the contacts. See, that's why we're such a good team. I have the ideas. And you have the contacts. Bounty hunters have contacts, right?"

"Right." Unfortunately, not in the phone company.

We finished the pizza, and I brought out the bag of frozen cookies for dessert.

"I heard you get cancer from eating raw cookie dough," Kloughn said. "Don't you think you should bake this?"

I ate a bag of raw dough a week. I considered it to be one of the four major food groups. "I always eat raw cookie dough," I said.

"Me, too," Kloughn said. "I eat raw cookie dough all the time. I don't believe that stuff about the cancer." He looked into the bag and tentatively took out a frozen lump of dough. "So what do you do here? Do you, like, nibble on it? Or do you put it all in your mouth at once?"

"You've never had raw cookie dough, have you?"

"No." He took a bite and chewed. "I like it," he said. "Very good."

I glanced down at my watch. "You're going to have to go now. I have some unfinished business to take care of."

"Is it bounty hunter business? You can tell me. I won't tell anybody, I swear. What are you doing? I bet you're going after someone. You were waiting for nighttime, right?"

"Right."

"So who are you going after? Is it anyone I know? Is it, like, a high-profile case? A killer?"

"It's no one you know. It's domestic abuse. A repeat offender. I'm waiting until he passes out in a drunken stupor, and then I'm going to capture him when he's unconscious."

"I could help you—"

"No!"

"You didn't let me finish. I could help you drag him to the car. How are you going to get him to the car? You're going to need help, right?"

"Lula will help me."

"Lula has class tonight. Remember she said she had to go to school tonight. Do you have anyone else who helps you? I bet you don't have anyone else, right?"

I was getting an eye twitch. Tiny, annoying muscle contractions below my right lower lid. "Okay," I said, "you can come with me, but you can't talk. *No talking.*"

"Sure. No talking. My lips are sealed. Look at me, I'm locking my lips and throwing the key away."

I PARKED HALF A BLOCK FROM ANDY BENDER'S apartment, positioning my car between pools of light thrown by overhead halogens. Traffic was minimal. Vendors had closed up shop for the day, switching to nighttime pursuits of hijacking and shoplifting. Residents were locked behind closed doors, beer can in hand, watching reality television. A nice break from their own reality, which wasn't all that terrific.

Kloughn gave me a look that said *now what?*

"Now we wait," I told him. "We make sure nothing unusual is going on."

Kloughn nodded and made the zippered mouth sign again. If he made the zippered mouth sign one more time I was going to smack him in the head.

After a half hour of sitting and waiting I was convinced that I didn't want to sit and wait anymore. "Let's take a closer look," I said to Kloughn. "Follow me."

"Shouldn't I have a gun or something? What if there's a shoot-out? Do you have a gun? Where's your gun?"

"I left my gun home. We don't need guns. Andy Bender has never been known to carry a gun." Best not to mention he prefers chain saws and kitchen knives.

I approached Bender's unit as if I owned it. Bounty hunter rule number seventeen—don't look sneaky. Lights were on inside. The windows were curtained, but the curtains were a skimpy fit, and it was possible to look around the fabric. I put my nose to the window and stared in at the Benders. Andy was in a big, overstuffed recliner, feet up, open bag of chips on his chest, dead to the world. His wife sat on the tattered couch, eyes glued to the television.

"I'm pretty sure we're doing something illegal," Kloughn whispered.

"There's all kinds of illegal. This is one of those things that's only a little illegal."

"I guess it's okay if you're a bounty hunter. There

are special rules for bounty hunters, right?"

Right. And there really *is* an Easter bunny.

I wanted to get into the apartment, but I didn't want to wake Bender. I walked around the building and carefully tried Bender's back door. Locked. I returned to the front and found that door locked, too. I gave a couple light raps on the door with my knuckles, hoping to get the wife's attention without waking Bender.

Kloughn was looking in the window. He shook his head. No one was getting up to answer the door. I rapped louder. Nothing. Bender's wife was concentrating on the television show. Damn. I rang the bell.

Kloughn jumped away from the window and rushed to my side. "She's coming!"

The door opened, and Bender's wife stood flat-footed in front of us. She was a large woman with pale skin, and a dagger tattooed on her arm. Her eyes were red-rimmed and dull. Her face expressionless. She wasn't as wasted as her husband, but she was well on the way. She took a step back when I introduced myself.

"Andy don't like to be disturbed," she said. "He gets in a real bad mood when he's disturbed."

"Maybe you should go to a friend's house, so you're not here if Andy gets disturbed." Last thing I wanted was for Andy to beat on his wife because she let us *disturb* him.

She looked at her husband, still asleep in his chair. Then she looked at us. And then she took off, out the door, disappearing into the darkness.

Kloughn and I tiptoed up to Bender and took a closer look.

"Maybe he's dead," Kloughn said.

"I don't think so."

"He smells dead."

"He always smells like that." I was prepared this time. I had my stun gun with me. I leaned forward, pressed my stun gun to Bender, and hit the juice button. Nothing happened. I examined the stun gun. It looked okay. I put it to Bender again. Nothing. Goddamn electronic piece of shit. Okay, go to backup plan. I grabbed the cuffs I had tucked into my back pocket and quietly clicked a bracelet on Bender's right wrist.

Bender's eyes flew open. "What the hell?"

I pulled his cuffed hand across his body and secured the second bracelet onto his left wrist.

"Goddamn," he yelled. "I hate being disturbed when I'm watching television! What the fuck are you doing in my house?"

"The same thing I was doing in your house yesterday. Bond enforcement," I said. "You're in violation of your bond. You need to reschedule."

He glared at Kloughn. "What's with the dough boy?"

Kloughn handed Bender his business card. "Albert Kloughn, attorney at law."

"I hate clowns. They creep me out."

Kloughn pointed to his name on the card. "K-l-o-u-g-h-n," he said. "If you ever need a lawyer, I'm real good."

"Oh yeah?" Bender said. "Well, I hate lawyers even more than clowns." He jumped forward and knocked Kloughn on his ass with a head butt to

Kloughn's face. "And I hate *you*," he said, lunging at me, head down.

I sidestepped and tried the stun gun on him again. No effect. I ran after him and made another stab. He never broke stride. He was across the room, through the open front door. I threw the stun gun at him. It bounced off his head, he yelled *ouch*, and he was gone, into the darkness.

I was torn between following after him and helping Kloughn. Kloughn was on his back, blood trickling from his nose, mouth open, eyes glazed. Hard to tell if he was just stunned or in a genuine coma.

"Are you okay?" I yelled at Kloughn.

Kloughn didn't say anything. His arms were in motion, but he wasn't making any progress at getting up. I went to his side and dropped to one knee.

"Are you okay?" I asked again.

His eyes focused, and he reached for me, grabbing a handful of shirt. "Did I hit him?"

"Yeah. You hit him with your face."

"I knew it. I knew I'd be good under pressure. I'm pretty tough, right?"

"Right." God help me, I was starting to like him.

I dragged him up and got him some paper towels from the kitchen. Bender was long gone, along with my cuffs. Again.

I retrieved the useless stun gun, packed Kloughn into the CR-V, and took off. It was a cloudy, moonless night. The projects were dark. Lights burned behind drawn shades but did nothing to illuminate lawns. I drove along the streets surrounding the projects, searching the shadows for movement, staring into the occasional uncurtained window.

Kloughn had his head tipped back with the towels stuffed up his nose. "Does this happen a lot?" he asked. "I thought it would be different. I mean, this was pretty fun, but he got away. And he didn't smell good. I didn't expect him to smell that bad."

I looked over at Kloughn. He seemed different. Crooked, somehow. "Has your nose always curved to the left?" I asked him.

He gingerly touched his nose. "It feels funny. You don't think it's broken, do you? I've never had anything broken before."

It was just about the most broken nose I'd ever seen. "It doesn't look broken to me," I said. "Still, it wouldn't hurt to have a doctor look at it. Maybe we should make a quick stop-off at the emergency room."

FIVE

I OPENED MY EYES AND LOOKED AT THE CLOCK: 8:30. Not exactly an early start to the day. I could hear rain spattering on my fire escape and on my windowpane. My feeling on rain is that it should only occur at night when people are sleeping. At night, rain is cozy. During the day, rain is a pain in the gumpy. Another screwup on the part of creation. Like waste management. When you're planning a universe you have to think ahead.

I rolled out of bed and sleepwalked to the kitchen. Rex was done running for the night, sound asleep in his soup can. I got coffee going and shuffled to the bathroom. An hour later I was in my car, ready to start the day, not sure what to do first. Probably I should pay a condolence visit on Kloughn. I'd gotten his nose broken. By the time I'd dropped him at his car, his eyes were black and his nose was being held straight by a Band-Aid. Problem is, if I go see him now, I run the risk of having him latch onto me for the day. And I really didn't want Kloughn tagging along. I was fairly inept when left to my own devices. With Kloughn tagging along, I was a disaster waiting to happen.

I was sitting in my lot, staring out the rain-smeared window, and I realized there was a plastic sandwich bag attached to my windshield wiper. I opened the door and snatched the bag off the wiper. There was a note-size piece of white paper folded four times inside the bag. The message on the paper was written in black marker.

Did you like the snakes?

Wonderful. Just the way I wanted to start my day. I returned the note to the bag and put the bag in the glove compartment. On the seat beside me were the two FTA folders Connie had given me. Andrew Bender, still at large. And Laura Minello. I'd go out and capture one of them this morning, but I didn't have any handcuffs. And I'd rather poke myself in the eye with a fork than get another pair of cuffs from the office. That left Annie Soder.

I put the CR-V in gear and drove to the Burg. I parked in front of my parents' house, but I knocked on Mabel's door.

"Who did Evelyn hang out with when she was a kid?" I asked Mabel. "Did she have a best friend?"

"Dotty Palowski. They went all through grade

school together. High school, too. Then Evelyn got married and Dotty moved away."

"Did they stay friends?"

"I think they lost touch. Evelyn kept more and more to herself after she married."

"Do you know where Dotty is now?"

"I don't know where Dotty's living but her folks are still here in the Burg."

I knew the family. Dotty's parents lived on Roebling. There were some aunts and uncles and cousins in the Burg, too. "I need one more thing," I said to Mabel. "I need a list of Evelyn's relatives. All of them."

I had the list in my hand when I left. It wasn't a long list. An aunt and an uncle in the Burg. Three cousins, all in the Trenton area. A cousin in Delaware.

I jumped the railing that divided the porches and went next door to see Grandma Mazur.

"I went to the Shleckner viewing," Grandma said. "I'm telling you, that Stiva is a genius. When it comes to morticians, you can't beat Stiva. You know how old Shleckner had all those big scabby things on his face? Well, Stiva covered them all somehow. And you couldn't even tell Shleckner had a glass eye. They both look just the same. It was a miracle."

"How do you know about the glass eye? Didn't they have his eyes closed?"

"Yeah, but they might have come open for a second while I was standing there. It might have happened when I accidentally dropped my reading glasses into the casket."

"Hmmm," I said to Grandma.

"Well, you can't blame a person for wondering about those things. Wasn't my fault, either. If they'd left his eyes open I wouldn't have had to wonder."

"Did anyone see you prying Shleckner's eyes open?"

"No. I was real sneaky."

"Did you hear anything useful about Evelyn or Annie?"

"No, but I got an earful about Steven Soder. He likes to drink. And he likes to gamble. The rumor is that he's lost a lot of money, and that he lost the bar. The story goes that he lost the bar in a card game a while back, and now he's got *partners.*"

"I've heard some of those same rumors. Anyone give names to the partners?"

"Eddie Abruzzi is what I heard."

Oh boy. Why am I not surprised at this?

I was in my car, ready to roll, when my cell phone rang. It was Kloughn.

"Boy, you should see me," he said. "I've got two black eyes. And my nose is swollen. At least it's straight now. I was real careful how I slept on it."

"I'm sorry. Really, really sorry."

"Hey, no biggie. I guess you have to expect stuff like this when you're a crime fighter. So what are we doing today? Are we going after Bender again? I have some ideas. Maybe I could meet you for lunch."

"See, here's the thing . . . I usually work alone."

"Sure, but once in a while you work with a partner, right? And I could be that partner sometimes, right? I got myself all prepared. I got a black hat with BOND ENFORCEMENT printed on it this morning.

And I got pepper spray and handcuffs . . ."

Handcuffs? Be still, my fast-beating heart. "Are these regulation handcuffs with a key and everything?"

"Yeah. I got them at that gun store on Rider Street. I would have gotten a gun, too, but I didn't have enough money."

"I'll pick you up at twelve."

"Oh boy, this is going to be great. I'll be all ready. I'll be at my office. Maybe we can get fried chicken this time. Unless you don't want fried chicken. If you don't want fried chicken, we could get a burrito, or we could get a burger, or we could—"

I made crackling sounds into the phone. "Can't hear you," I yelled. "You're breaking up. See you at twelve." And I disconnected.

I cruised out of the Burg and turned onto Hamilton. In a few minutes I was at the office. I parked at the curb behind a new black Porsche, which I suspected belonged to Ranger.

Everyone looked over when I swung through the door. Ranger was at Connie's desk. He was dressed in SWAT black, again. He caught my eye, and I felt my stomach do a nervous roll.

"I had a friend working the emergency room last night, and she told me you came in with a little guy who was all busted up," Lula said.

"Kloughn. And he wasn't *all* busted up. He just had a broken nose. Don't ask."

Vinnie was lounging in the doorway to his inner office. "Who's this clown?" Vinnie asked.

"Albert Kloughn," Ranger said. "He's an attorney."

I stopped short of asking how Ranger knew
Kloughn. The answer was obvious. Ranger knew
everything.

"Let me guess," Vinnie said to me. "You need another pair of cuffs."

"Wrong. I need an address. I need to talk to Dotty
Palowski."

Connie fed the name to the search system. A minute later the information started coming in. "She's
Dotty Rheinhold now. And she's living in South
River." Connie printed the page and handed it over to
me. "She's divorced with two kids, and she works for
the Turnpike Authority in East Brunswick."

Ordinarily I'd stay to chat, but I was afraid someone would ask about Kloughn's nose.

"Gotta run," I said. "Things to do."

I paused just outside the office door. I was sheltered
by a small overhead awning. Beyond the awning, the
rain fell in a relentless drizzle that didn't measure up
to downpour status but was enough to ruin my hair
and soak into my jeans.

Ranger followed me out. "It might be good to keep
more than one bullet in your gun, babe."

"You heard about the snakes?"

"I ran into Costanza. He was looking at life through
the bottom of a beer glass."

"I'm not having much luck finding Annie Soder."

"You're not the only one."

"Jeanne Ellen can't find her, either?"

"Not yet."

Our eyes held for a moment. "Which team are you
on?" I asked.

He tucked my hair behind my ear, his fingertips brushing feather light across my temple, his thumb at the line of my jaw. "I have my own team."

"Tell me about Jeanne Ellen."

Ranger smiled. "The information would have a price."

"And the price would be what?"

The smile widened. "Try not to get too wet today," he said. And he was gone.

Damn. What's with the men in my life? Why do they always leave first? Why don't *I* ever walk away and leave first? Because I'm a dope, that's why. I'm a big dope.

I PICKED KLOUGHN UP AT THE LAUNDROMAT. He was dressed in a black T-shirt and black jeans, wearing his new bond enforcement hat. And he had brown tassel loafers on his feet. The pepper spray was clipped to his belt. The cuffs had been shoved into his back pocket. His eyes and nose were an alarming shade of black, blue, and green.

"Wow," I said. "You look awful."

"It's the tassels, right? I wasn't sure if the tassels went with the outfit. I could go home and change. I could have worn black shoes, but I thought they were too dressy."

"It's not the tassels, it's your eyes and nose." Okay, and it's the tassels.

Kloughn got in and buckled his seat belt. "I guess that's all part of the job. Gotta get physical sometimes, right? Goes with the territory, you know what I mean?"

"Your territory is law."

"Yeah, but I'm an assistant bond enforcer, too, right? I'm walking the mean streets with you, right?"

You see, Stephanie, I told myself, this is what happens when you run your credit card up buying non-essentials like shoes and underwear and then can't afford to buy handcuffs.

"I was going to get a stun gun," Kloughn said, "but yours didn't work last night. What's with that? You pay good money for these things and then they don't work. That's always the way, isn't it? You know what you need? You need a lawyer. You were mislead by product promises."

I stopped for a light and pulled the stun gun out of my bag and checked it over. "I don't understand this," I said to Kloughn. "It's always worked just fine."

He took the stun gun from me and turned it around in his hand. "Maybe it needs batteries."

"No. They're new. They test out okay."

"Maybe you were doing it wrong?"

"Hardly. It's not that complicated. You press the prongs against someone's skin and push the button."

"Like this?" Kloughn said, pressing the prongs against his arm, pushing the button. He gave a tiny squeak and slumped in his seat.

I took the stun gun from his inert hand and studied it. It seemed to work okay now.

I dropped the stun gun back into my bag, drove back to the Burg, and stopped at Corner Hardware. Corner Hardware was a ramshackle affair that had been in existence for as long as I could remember. The store itself occupied two adjoining buildings with a door carved into the common wall. The floor was unvarnished wood and cracked linoleum. The shelves were dusty, and the air smelled of fertilizer and socket wrenches. Everything you might need could be found in the store at a price higher than could be found elsewhere. The advantage to Corner Hardware was the location. It was in the Burg. No need to drive down Route 1 or go to Hamilton Township. The additional advantage for me today was the fact that no one at Corner Hardware would think it odd that I was schlepping around with a guy with two black eyes. Everyone in the Burg would have heard about Kloughn.

By the time I got to the hardware store, Kloughn was starting to come around. His fingers were twitching, and he had one eye open. I left Kloughn in the car while I ran into the store and bought twenty feet of medium-weight chain and a padlock. I had a plan for capturing Bender.

I dumped the twenty feet of chain onto the street behind the CR-V. I got the cuffs from Kloughn's back pocket, and I attached one end of the chain to one of the bracelets. Then I padlocked the other end of the chain to the tow hitch on my car. I tossed the remaining chain and cuffs into the back window and got behind the wheel. I was soaked, but it was worth it. No way was Bender going to run off with my cuffs this time. The instant I cuffed Bender, he'd be attached to my car.

I drove across town, idled one block over from Bender's apartment, and dialed his number. When he answered I hung up.

"He's home," I told Kloughn. "Let's roll."

Kloughn was examining his hand, wiggling his fingers. "I feel kind of tingly."

"That's because you zapped yourself with my stun gun."

"I thought it didn't work."

"I guess you fixed it."

"I'm real handy," Kloughn said. "I'm good at all kinds of things like that."

I jumped the curb in front of Bender's apartment, drove across the mud yard, and parked with my rear bumper pressed to Bender's front stoop. I leaped out of the car, ran to Bender's door, and barged into his living room.

Bender was in his chair, watching television. He saw me enter and went bug-eyed and slack-jawed. "You!" he said. "What the fuck?" A second later he was out of his chair, bolting for the back door.

"Grab him," I yelled to Kloughn. "Gas him. Trip him. *Do something!*"

Kloughn took a flying leap and caught Bender by the pants leg. Both men went down to the floor. I threw myself on Bender and cuffed him. I rolled off, elated.

Bender scrambled to his feet and ran for the door, dragging the chain behind him.

Kloughn and I did a high five.

"Boy, you're smart," Kloughn said. "I would never have thought of hooking him up to the bumper. I gotta hand it to you. You're good. You're really good."

"Make sure the back door is locked," I said to Kloughn. "I don't want the apartment burgled." I clicked the television off, and Kloughn and I walked to the door just in time to see Bender drive off in my CR-V.

Shit.

"Hey," Kloughn yelled to Bender, "you've got my handcuffs!"

Bender had his arm out the window, holding the door on the driver's side closed. The chain snaked from the door to the back bumper, a loop of chain dragging on the ground, sending up sparks. Bender raised his arm and gave us the finger just before turning the corner and disappearing from view.

"I bet you left the key in the ignition," Kloughn said. "I think that might be illegal. I bet you didn't lock your door, either. You should always take the key and lock the door."

I gave Kloughn my bitch look.

"Of course, these were special circumstances," he added.

KLOUGHN HUDDLED UNDER THE SMALL OVERHANG that protected the front stoop to Bender's apartment. I was at curbside, in the rain, sopping wet, waiting for the blue-and-white. You reach a point with rain where it just doesn't matter anymore.

I'd hoped to get Costanza or my pal Eddie Gazarra when I'd put the call in for a stolen vehicle. The car that responded wasn't either.

"So you're the famous Stephanie Plum?" the cop said.

"I almost never shoot people," I said, sliding onto the backseat of the cruiser. "And the fire in the funeral parlor wasn't my fault." I leaned forward and water dripped from the tip of my nose onto the floor of the car. "Usually Costanza answers my calls," I said.

"He didn't win the pool."

"There's a pool?"

"Yeah. Participation really dropped after that thing with the snakes."

Fifteen minutes later the blue-and-white left, and Morelli showed up.

"Listening to your radio again?" I asked.

"I don't have to listen to my radio anymore. As soon as your name pops up somewhere in the system, I get forty-five phone calls."

I did a small grimace, which I hoped was endearing. "Sorry."

"Let me get this straight," Morelli said. "Bender drove away chained to the car."

"It seemed like a good idea at the time."

"And your handbag was in the car?"

"Yep."

Morelli looked over at Kloughn. "Who's the little guy in the tassel loafers and black eyes?"

"Albert Kloughn."

"And you brought him along because . . . ?"

"He had the handcuffs."

Morelli struggled not to smile and lost. "Get in the truck. I'll take you home."

We dropped Kloughn off first.

"Hey, you know what?" Kloughn said. "We never had lunch. Do you think we should all go to lunch? There's Mexican just down the street. Or we could catch a burger, or an egg roll. I know a place that makes good egg rolls."

"I'll call you," I said.

He waved us out of sight. "That'll be great. Call me. Do you have my number? You can call anytime. I hardly ever sleep, even."

Morelli stopped for a light, looked at me, and shook his head.

"Okay, so I'm wet," I said.

"Albert thinks you're cute."

"He just wants to be part of the gang." I brushed a clump of hair from my face. "How about you? Do you think I'm cute?"

"I think you're crazy."

"Yes. But besides that, you think I'm cute, right?" I gave him my Miss America smile and fluttered my lashes.

He glanced over at me, stone-faced.

I was feeling a little like Scarlett O'Hara at the end of *Gone with the Wind* when she's determined to get Rhett Butler back. Problem was, if I got Morelli back, I wasn't sure what I'd do with him.

"Life is complicated," I said to Morelli.

"No shit, cupcake."

I WAVED GOOD-BYE TO MORELLI AND DRIPPED through the lobby to my building. I dripped in the elevator, and I dripped down the hall to my next-door neighbor, Mrs. Karwatt. I got my spare key from Mrs. Karwatt and then I dripped into my apartment. I stood in the middle of my kitchen floor and peeled my clothes off. I toweled my hair until it stopped dripping. I checked my messages. None. Rex popped out of his soup can, gave me a startled look, and rushed back into the can. Not the sort of reaction that makes a naked woman feel great . . . even from a hamster.

An hour later I was dressed in dry clothes, and I was downstairs waiting for Lula.

"Okay, let me get this straight," Lula said when I settled into her Trans Am. "You need to do surveillance and you don't got a car."

I held my hand up to ward off the next question. "Don't ask."

"I'm hearing 'don't ask' a lot lately."

"It was stolen. My car was stolen."

"Get out!"

"I'm sure the police will find it. In the meantime, I want to take a look at Dotty Palowski Rheinhold. She's living in South River."

"And South River is *where*?"

"I've got a map. Turn left out of the lot."

South River jug-handles off Route 18. It's a small town squashed between strip malls and clay pits and has more bars per square mile than any other town in the state. The entrance provides a scenic overlook of the landfill. The exit crosses the river into Sayreville, famous for the great dirt swindle of 1957 and Jon Bon Jovi.

Dotty Rheinhold lived in a neighborhood of tract houses built in the sixties. Yards were small. Houses were smaller. Cars were large and plentiful.

"You ever see so many cars?" Lula said. "Every house has at least three cars. They're everywhere."

It was an easy neighborhood for surveillance. It had reached an age where houses were filled with teen-agers. The teenagers had cars of their own, and the teenagers had friends who had cars. One more car on the street would never be noticed. Even better, this was suburbia. There were no front-porch-stoop sitters. Everyone migrated to the postage stamp–size back-yards, which were crammed full of outdoor grills, above-ground pools, and herds of lawn chairs.

Lula parked the Trans Am one house down and across the street from Dotty. "Do you think Annie and her mom are living with Dotty?"

"If they are, we'll know right away. You can't hide two people in your cellar with kids underfoot. It's too weird. And kids talk. If Annie and Evelyn are here, they're coming and going like normal house guests."

"And we're going to sit here until we figure this out? This sounds like it could take a long time. I don't know if I'm prepared to sit here for a long time. I mean, what about food? And I have to go to the bath-room. I had a super-size soda before I picked you up. You didn't say anything about a long time."

I gave Lula the squinty eye.

"Well, I gotta go," Lula said. "I can't help it. I gotta wee."

"Okay, how about this. We passed a mall on the way in. How about if I drop you at the mall, and then I take the car and do the surveillance."

Half an hour later, I was back at the curb, alone, snooping on Dotty. The drizzle had turned to rain and lights were on in some of the houses. Dotty's house was dark. A blue Honda Civic rolled past me and pulled into Dotty's driveway. A woman got out and unbuckled two kids from kiddie seats in the back. The woman was shrouded in a hooded raincoat, but I caught a look at her face in the gloom, and I was certain it was Dotty. Or, to be more precise, I was certain it wasn't Evelyn. The kids were young. Maybe two and seven. Not that I'm an expert on kids. My entire kid knowledge is based on my two nieces.

The little family entered the house and lights went on. I put the Trans Am into gear and inched my way up until I was directly across from the Rheinholds'. I could clearly see Dotty now. She had the raincoat off, and she was moving around. The living room was in the front of the house. A television was switched on in the living room. A door opened off the living room, and the room beyond was obviously the kitchen. Dotty was traveling back and forth across the doorway, from refrigerator to table. No other adult appeared. Dotty made no move to draw the living room curtains.

The kids were in bed and their bedroom lights were out by 9:00. At 9:15 Dotty got a phone call. At 9:30 Dotty was still on the phone, and I left to pick Lula up at the mall. A block and a half from Dotty's house, a sleek black car slid by me, traveling in the opposite direction. I caught a glimpse of the driver. Jeanne Ellen Burrows. I almost took the curb and ran across a lawn.

Lula was waiting at the mall entrance when I got there.

"Get in!" I yelled. "I have to get back to Dotty's house. I passed Jeanne Ellen Burrows when I was leaving the neighborhood."

"What about Evelyn and Annie?"

"No sign of them."

The house was dark when we returned. The car was in the driveway. Jeanne Ellen was nowhere to be found.

"You sure it was Jeanne Ellen?" Lula asked.

"Positive. All the hair stood up on my arm, and I got an ice-cream headache."

"Yep. That would be Jeanne Ellen."

LULA DROPPED ME AT THE DOOR TO MY APARTMENT building. "Anytime you want to do surveillance, you just let me know," Lula said. "Surveillance is one of my favorite things."

Rex was in his wheel when I came into the kitchen. He stopped running and looked at me, eyes bright.

"Good news, big guy," I said. "I stopped at the store on the way home and got supper."

I dumped the contents of the bag on the counter. Seven Tastykakes. Two Butterscotch Krimpets, a Coconut Junior, two Peanut Butter KandyKakes, Creme-filled Cupcakes, and a Chocolate Junior. Life doesn't get much better than this. Tastykakes are just another of the many advantages of living in Jersey. They're made in Philly and shipped to Trenton in all their fresh squishiness. I read once that 439,000 Butterscotch Krimpets are baked every day. And not a heck of a lot of them find their way to New Hampshire. All that snow and scenery and what good does it do you without Tastykakes?

I ate the Coconut Junior, a Butterscotch Krimpet, and a KandyKake. Rex had part of the Butterscotch Krimpet.

Things haven't been going too great for me lately.

In the past week I've lost three pairs of handcuffs, a car, and I've had a bag of snakes delivered to my door. On the other hand, things aren't *all* bad. In fact, things could be a lot worse. I could be living in New Hampshire, where I would be forced to mail order Tastykakes.

It was close to twelve when I crawled into bed. The rain had stopped and the moon was shining between the broken cloud cover. My curtains were drawn, and my room was dark.

An old-fashioned fire escape attached to my bedroom window. The fire escape was good for catching a cool breeze on a hot night. It could be used to dry clothes, quarantine house plants with aphids, and chill beer when the weather turned cold. Unfortunately, it was also a place where bad things happened. Benito Ramirez had been shot to death on my fire escape. As it happens, it isn't easy to climb up my fire escape, but it isn't impossible, either.

I was laying in the dark, debating the merits of the Coconut Junior over the Butterscotch Krimpet, when I heard scraping sounds beyond the closed bedroom curtains. Someone was on my fire escape. I felt a shot of adrenaline burn into my heart and flash into my gut. I jumped out of bed, ran into the kitchen, and called the police. Then I took the gun out of the cookie jar. No bullets. *Damn.* Think, Stephanie—where did you put the bullets? There used to be some in the sugar bowl. Not anymore. The sugar bowl was empty. I rummaged through the junk drawer and came up with four bullets. I shoved them into my Smith & Wesson five-shot .38 and ran back into my bedroom.

I stood in the dark and listened. No more scraping sounds. My heart was pounding, and the gun was shaking in my hand. Get a grip, I told myself. It was probably a bird. An owl. They fly at night, right? Silly Stephanie, freaked out by an owl.

I crept to the window and listened again. Silence. I opened the curtain a fraction of an inch and peeked out.

Yikes!

There was a huge guy on my fire escape. I only saw him for an instant, but he looked like Benito Ramirez. How could that be? Ramirez was dead.

There was a lot of noise, and I realized I'd fired all four rounds through my window, into the guy on my fire escape.

Rats! This isn't a good thing. First off, I might have killed someone. I *hate* when that happens. Second, I haven't a clue if the guy had a gun, and the law frowns on shooting unarmed people. The law isn't even all that fond of citizens shooting *armed* people. Even worse, my window was trashed.

I ripped the curtain aside, and pressed my nose to the window pane. No one out there. I looked more closely and saw that I'd blasted a life-size cardboard cutout. It was laying flat on the fire escape and there were a bunch of holes in it.

I was standing there dumbfounded, breathing heavy with the gun still in my hand, when I heard the police siren whining in the distance. Good going, Stephanie. The one time I call the police, and it turns out to be an embarrassing false alarm. An evil prank. Like the snakes.

So who would do something like this? Someone who knew about Ramirez getting killed on my fire escape. I gave up a sigh. The entire state knew about Ramirez. It was in all the papers. Okay, someone who had access to a life-size cutout. There had been a lot of the cutouts floating around when Ramirez was fighting. Not many of them floating around now. One person came to mind. Eddie Abruzzi.

A blue-and-white pulled into my parking lot, lights flashing, and a uniform got out.

I opened my window and leaned out. "False alarm," I yelled down. "Nobody here. It must have been a bird."

He looked up at me. "A bird?"

"I think it was an owl. A real big owl. Sorry you got called out."

He waved, got back into the car, and drove off.

I closed and locked the window, but it was an empty gesture since a lot of the glass was missing. I ran into the kitchen and ate the Chocolate Junior.

I WAS HALF-ASLEEP, CONTEMPLATING THE NUTRI-tional value of a Creme-filled Cupcake for breakfast, when there was a knock at my door.

It was Tank, Ranger's right-hand man. "Your car turned up at a chop shop," he said. He handed my bag over to me. "This was on the floor in the back."

"And my car?"

"In your parking lot." He gave me my keys. "The car's fine except for a chain attached to the tow. We didn't know what the chain was all about."

I closed and locked the door after Tank, stumbled

into the kitchen, and ate the package of cupcakes. I told myself it was okay to eat the cupcakes because it was a celebration. I had my car back. Calories don't count if they're connected to a celebration. Everyone knows this.

Coffee would taste good, but it seemed like a lot of work this morning. I had to change the filter, add the coffee and water, and push the button. Not to mention, if I had coffee I might wake up, and I didn't think I was ready to face the day. Better to go back to bed.

I'd just crawled into bed when the doorbell rang again. I put the pillow over my head and closed my eyes. The doorbell kept ringing. "Go away," I yelled. "Nobody's home!" Now there was knocking. And more ringing. I threw the pillow off and heaved myself out of bed. I stomped to the door, wrenched it open, and glared out. "What?"

It was Kloughn. "It's Saturday," he said. "I brought doughnuts. I always have doughnuts on Saturday morning." He looked more closely. "Did I wake you up? Boy, you don't look all that good when you wake up, do you? No wonder you're not married. Do you always sleep in sweats? How'd you get your hair to stick out like that?"

"How'd you like to have your nose broken a second time?" I asked.

Kloughn pushed past me, into my apartment. "I saw the car in the parking lot. Did the police find it? Do you have my handcuffs?"

"I don't have your handcuffs. And get out of my apartment. Go away."

"You just need some coffee," Kloughn said. "Where do you keep the filters? I'm always a cranky pants in the morning, too. And then I have my coffee, and I'm a new person."

Why me? I thought.

Kloughn got the coffee out of the refrigerator and started the machine. "I didn't know if bounty hunters worked on Saturday," he said. "But I thought better safe than sorry. So here I am."

I was speechless.

The front door was still open, and there was a rap on the doorjamb behind me.

It was Morelli. "Am I interrupting something?" he asked.

"It's not what it looks like," Kloughn said. "I just brought jelly doughnuts."

Morelli gave me the once-over. "Frightening," he said.

I narrowed my eyes at him. "I had a bad night."

"That's what they tell me. I understand you were visited by a large bird. An owl?"

"So?"

"The owl do any damage?"

"Nothing worth mentioning."

"I'm seeing more of you now than I did when we were living together," Morelli said. "You aren't doing all this stuff just to have me stop around, are you?"

SIX

"OH JEEZ, I DIDN'T KNOW YOU TWO USED TO LIVE together," Kloughn said. "Hey, I'm not trying to cut in on anything. We just work together, right?"

"Right," I said.

"So, is this the guy you're engaged to?" Kloughn asked.

A smile twitched at the corner of Morelli's mouth. "You're engaged?"

"Sort of," I said. "I don't want to talk about it."

Morelli reached into the bag and selected a doughnut. "I don't see a ring on your finger."

"I *don't* want to *talk* about it."

Kloughn's voice was apologetic. "She hasn't had any coffee yet."

Morelli took a bite of doughnut. "You think coffee will help?"

They both looked at me.

I pointed stiff-armed to the door. *"Out."*

I slammed the door after them and slid the security bolt. I leaned against the door and closed my eyes. Morelli had looked great. T-shirt and jeans and a red flannel shirt worn open like a jacket. And he'd smelled good, too. The scent still lingered in my foyer, mingling with jelly doughnuts. I took a deep breath and had a lust attack. The lust attack was followed by a mental head slap. I sent him away! What was I thinking? Oh yeah, now I remember. I was thinking he'd just said I was frightening. *Frightening!* I'm having a hot flash over a guy who thinks I'm frightening. On the other hand, he did stop by to see if I was okay.

I was running this through while I walked to the bathroom. I was up and awake now. Might as well get on with the day. I switched the light on and caught a glimpse of myself in the mirror. *Eeeek!* Frightening.

I THOUGHT SATURDAY WOULD BE A GOOD DAY TO follow Dotty around. I had no real reason to think she was helping Evelyn. Only instinct. But sometimes instinct is all you need. There's something special about childhood friendships. They might be set aside for reasons of convenience, but they're seldom forgotten.

Mary Lou Molnar has been my best friend for as long as I can remember. Truth is, we haven't got a whole lot in common anymore. She's Mary Lou Stankovik now. She's married and has a couple kids. And

I'm living with a hamster. Still, if I had to tell someone a secret, it would be Mary Lou. And if I was
Evelyn, I'd turn to Dotty Palowski.

It was close to ten by the time I reached South
River. I cruised past Dotty's house and parked a short
distance down the street. Dotty's car was in the driveway. A red Jeep was parked curbside. Not Evelyn's
car. Evelyn drove a nine-year-old gray Sentra. I
pushed my seat back and stretched my legs. If I was
a man lurking in front of a house, I'd be suspect.
Fortunately, no one paid much attention to a woman.

Dotty's front door opened, and a man stepped out.
Dotty's two kids jumped out after him and ran around
him in circles. He took them by the hand, and they
all walked to the Jeep and got in.

The ex-husband on visitation day.

The Jeep pulled away and five minutes later Dotty
locked the house up and got into her Honda. I followed her easily, out of the neighborhood, onto the
highway. She wasn't looking for a tail. Never picked
me up in her rearview mirror.

We went straight to one of the strip malls on Route
18 and parked in front of a chain bookstore. I watched
Dotty get out of her car and cross the lot to the store.
She was barelegged, wearing a sundress with a
sweater. I would have been cold in the outfit. The sun
was shining but the air was cool. I guess Dotty had
run out of patience for warm weather. She pushed
through the doors and went straight for the coffee bar.
I could see her through the plate glass window. She
ordered a coffee and took it to a table. She sat with
her back to the window and looked around. She

checked her watch and sipped her coffee. She was waiting for someone.

Please let it be Evelyn. It would make everything so easy.

I left my car and walked the short distance to the store. I browsed the section to the rear of the coffee bar, staying hidden behind racks of books. I didn't know Dotty personally, but I worried that she might recognize me, all the same. I scanned the store for Evelyn and Annie. I didn't want them to see me, either.

Dotty looked up from her coffee and focused. I followed her line of sight, but I didn't see Annie or Evelyn. I was looking so intently for Annie and Evelyn that I almost missed the red-haired guy making his way toward Dotty. It was Steven Soder. My first reaction was to intercept him. I didn't know what he was doing here, but he was going to ruin everything. Evelyn would run when she saw him. And then it hit me, brain surgeon that I am. Dotty was waiting for Soder.

Soder got a coffee and took it to Dotty's table. He sat across from her and slouched in his chair. An arrogant posture. I could see his face, and he didn't look friendly.

Dotty leaned forward and said something to Soder. He made a crooked smile that was close to a snarl and nodded his head. They had a brief conversation. Soder stuck his finger in Dotty's face and said something that turned Dotty white. He stood, made one last parting remark, and left. His coffee remained, untouched, on the table. Dotty collected herself, made certain Soder was out of sight, and then she left, too.

I followed Dotty to the parking lot. She got into her car, and I ran for mine. Hold the phone. No car. Okay, I know I'm a little dingy sometimes, but I usually remember where I've parked the car. I trotted up and down the aisle. I tried one aisle over. No car.

Dotty pulled out of her space and headed for the exit. A sleek black car followed a short distance behind Dotty. Jeanne Ellen.

"Damn!"

I rammed my hand into my bag, found my cell phone, and pounded out Ranger's number.

"Call Jeanne Ellen and find out what she did with my car," I said to Ranger. *"Now!"*

A minute later Jeanne Ellen called me. "I might have seen a black CR-V in front of the deli," she said.

I punched the end button so hard I broke a nail. I dropped the phone back into my bag and stomped off, down the strip mall to the deli. I found my car and checked it over. There were no scratch marks from where Jeanne Ellen had popped the lock. No loose wires from hot-wiring. Somehow she'd gotten into the car and moved it without leaving a trace of herself. This was a trick Ranger could easily accomplish, and I couldn't hope to pull off. The fact that Jeanne Ellen could do it really grated on me.

I left the strip mall and returned to Dotty's house. No one was home. No car in the driveway. Probably Dotty had taken Jeanne Ellen straight to Evelyn. Fine. Who cares. I'm not even making any money on this. I did an eye roll. It wasn't fine. If I go back to Mabel with nothing, she'll start bawling again. I'd walk on molten lava and shards of glass before I'd face more of Mabel crying.

I hung around until early afternoon. I read the paper, filed my nails, organized my shoulder bag, and talked on my cell phone with Mary Lou Stankovik for a half hour. My legs were twitchy from the confinement, and my butt was asleep. I'd had a lot of time to think about Jeanne Ellen Burrows, and none of the thoughts were friendly. In fact, after about an hour of Jeanne Ellen Burrows thinking I was darn cranky, and I'm not sure, but I think steam might have started escaping from the top of my head. Jeanne Ellen had bigger boobs and a smaller ass than me. She was a better bounty hunter. She had a nicer car. And she had leather pants. I could deal with this. What I couldn't deal with was her involvement with Ranger. I'd thought their relationship had ended, but clearly I was wrong. He knew where she was every minute of the day.

While *she* had a relationship, *I* had the threat of a single night of gorilla sex hanging over my head. Okay, so I'd made the deal during a moment of professional desperation. His aid in exchange for my body. And yes, maybe it had been flirty and fun, in a scary sort of way. And true, I'm attracted to him. I mean, I'm only human, for crying out loud. A woman would have to be *dead* not to be attracted to Ranger. And it's not like I'm having any luck getting Morelli into my bed these days.

So here I am with my one night. And there's Jeanne Ellen with some sort of relationship. Well, forget it. I'm not fooling around with a man who's possibly in a relationship.

I dialed Ranger and drummed my fingers on the steering wheel while I waited for the connection.

"Yo," Ranger said.

"I owe you *nothing*," I said. "The deal is off."

Ranger was silent for a couple beats. Probably wondering why he ever made the deal in the first place. "Having a bad day?" he finally asked.

"My bad day has nothing to do with this," I said. And I hung up.

My cell phone chirped, and I debated answering. Curiosity ultimately won out over cowardice. Pretty much the story of my life.

"I've been under a lot of stress," I said. "I might even be sick with a fever."

"And?"

"And what?"

"I thought you might want to retract the part where you tell me the deal is off," Ranger said.

There was a long silence on the phone.

"Well?" Ranger asked.

"I'm thinking."

"That's always dangerous," Ranger said. And he hung up.

I was still contemplating the retraction when Dotty rolled in. She parked in her driveway, took two grocery bags from the backseat, and let herself into the house.

My phone rang again. I did an eye roll and snapped my phone open. "Yes."

"Have you been waiting long?" It was Jeanne Ellen.

I whipped my head around, looking up and down the street. "Where are you?"

"Behind the blue van. You'll be happy to know you didn't miss anything this afternoon. Dotty had a full day of housewifey things to do."

"Did she know you were following her?"

There was a pause where I assumed Jeanne Ellen was stunned that I might think she'd ever get made. "Of course not," Jeanne Ellen said. "She didn't have Evelyn in her day planner today."

"Well, cheer up," I said. "The day's not over."

"True. I thought I'd stay here a bit longer, but the street feels crowded with both of us sitting here."

"And?"

"And I thought it would be a good idea for you to leave."

"No way. *You* should leave."

"If anything happens I'll call you," Jeanne Ellen said.

"That's a big fib."

"True, again. Let me tell you something that isn't a fib. If you don't leave, I'll put a bullet hole in your car."

I knew from past experience that bullet holes were very bad for resale. I disconnected, put the car in gear, and drove away. I drove exactly two blocks and parked in front of a small white ranch. I locked up and walked around the block until I was directly behind Dotty's house, one street over. There was no activity on the street. Not a lot of life visible from

Dotty's neighbors. Everyone was still at the mall, the soccer game, the Little League game, the car wash. I cut between two houses and straddled the white picket fence that enclosed Dotty's backyard. I crossed the small yard, and knocked on Dotty's back door.

Dotty opened the door and stared out at me, surprised to find a strange woman on her property.

"I'm Stephanie Plum," I said. "I hope I didn't startle you by showing up at your back door like this."

Relief replaced surprise. "Of course, your parents live next to Mabel Markowitz. I went to school with your sister."

"I'd like to talk to you about Evelyn. Mabel is worried about her, and I said I'd do some inquiring around. I came to the back door because the front of your house is under surveillance."

Dotty's mouth dropped and her eyes widened. "Someone's watching me?"

"Steven Soder has hired a private detective to find Annie. The detective's name is Jeanne Ellen Burrows, and she's in a black Jaguar, behind the blue van. I spotted her when I drove up, and I didn't want her to see me, so I came through the back." Take that, Jeanne Ellen Burrows. Direct hit. *Kapow!*

"Omigod," Dottie said. "What should I do?"

"Do you know where Evelyn is?"

"No. Sorry. Evelyn and I sort of lost touch."

She was lying. She'd waited too long to say no. And now spots of color were blooming on her cheeks. She was possibly the worst liar I'd ever seen. She was a disgrace to Burg women. Burg women were *great* liars. No wonder Dotty had to move to South River.

I let myself into her kitchen and closed the door. "Listen," I said, "don't worry about Jeanne Ellen. She's not dangerous. You just don't want to lead her to Evelyn."

"You mean *if* I knew where Evelyn was then I should be careful about going there."

"Careful isn't good enough. Jeanne Ellen will follow you, and you'll never see her. Don't go anywhere near Evelyn. Stay away from her."

Dotty wasn't liking this advice. "Hmmm," she said. "Maybe we should talk about Evelyn."

She shook her head. "I can't talk about Evelyn."

I gave her my card. "Call me if you change your mind. If Evelyn gets in touch with you, and you need to go see her, please consider letting me help you. You can call Mabel and check me out."

Dotty looked at the card and nodded. "Okay."

I let myself out the back door and slipped through the yards to the street. I walked the half block back to my car and took off for home.

I STEPPED OUT OF THE ELEVATOR AND FELT MY heart sink at the sight of Kloughn camping in my hall. He was sitting with his back to the wall, legs outstretched, arms crossed over his chest. His face brightened when he saw me, and he scrambled to his feet.

"Boy," he said, "you've been gone all afternoon. Where were you? You didn't catch Bender, did you? You wouldn't catch him without me, would you? I mean, we're a team, right?"

"Right," I said. "We're a team." A team without handcuffs.

I let us into my apartment, and we both migrated to the kitchen. I slid a look at the answering machine. Nothing was blinking. No message from Morelli, pleading for a date. Not that Morelli ever pleaded for anything. Still, a girl could hope. Large mental sigh. I was going to spend Saturday night with Albert Kloughn. It felt like doomsday.

Kloughn was looking at me expectantly. He was like a puppy, eyes bright, tail wagging, waiting to be taken for a walk. Endearing . . . in an incredibly annoying sort of way.

"Now what?" he asked. "What do we do now?"

I needed to think about this. Usually the problem is *finding* the FTA. I never had a problem finding Bender. I had a problem hanging on to him.

I opened the refrigerator and stared inside. My motto has always been, When all else fails, eat something. "Let's make dinner," I said.

"Oh boy, a home-cooked meal. That would really hit the spot. I haven't eaten in hours. Okay, I had a candy bar just before you got here, but that doesn't count, does it? I mean, it's not like real food. And I'm still hungry. It's not like it's a meal, right?"

"Right."

"What should we cook? Pasta? You got some fish? We could have fish. Or a nice steak. I still eat meat. Lots of people don't eat meat anymore, but I still eat it. I eat everything."

"Do you eat peanut butter?"

"Sure. I love peanut butter. Peanut butter is a staple, right?"

"Right." I ate a lot of peanut butter. You don't have

to cook it. You only dirty one knife in the preparation. And you can count on it. It's always the same. As opposed to picking out a piece of fish, which in my experience is risky.

I made us peanut butter and bread-and-butter pickle sandwiches. And because I had company, I added a layer of potato chips.

"This is very creative," Kloughn said. "You get a lot of textures this way. And you don't get your fingers greasy by eating the potato chips separately. I'll have to remember this. I'm always looking for new recipes."

Alright, I was going to take another shot at capturing Bender. I was going to break into his house, one more time. As soon as I located a pair of handcuffs.

I dialed Lula's number.

"So," I said to Lula, "what's going on tonight?"

"I'm just trying to figure out what to wear, on account of it's Saturday. And it's not like I'm some loser who can't get a date. I'd be out of the house by now, but I can't make up my mind between two dresses."

"Do you have handcuffs?"

"Sure. I got handcuffs. You never know when you need handcuffs."

"Maybe I could borrow them. Just for a couple hours. I need to bring Bender in."

"You're gonna go get Bender tonight? You need help? I could cancel my date. Then I wouldn't have to decide on a dress. You have to come over here to get the cuffs anyway. You might as well take me with."

"You don't actually have a date, do you?"

"I could if I wanted."

"I'll pick you up in a half hour."

LULA WAS IN THE FRONT SEAT, AND KLOUGHN WAS in the backseat. We were parked in front of Bender's apartment, trying to decide on the best approach.

"You watch the back door," I said to Lula. "And Albert and I will go in the front door."

"I don't like that plan," Lula said. "I want to go in the front door. And I want to be the one holding the cuffs."

"I think Stephanie should hold the cuffs," Kloughn said. "She's the bounty hunter."

"Hunh," Lula said. "What am I, chopped liver? And besides, they're my cuffs. I should get to hold them. Either I hold them, or you haven't got no cuffs."

"Fine!" I said to Lula. "*You* go in the front door, and *you* hold the cuffs. Just make sure you get them on Bender."

"What about me?" Kloughn wanted to know. "Where do I go? Do I take the back door? What do I do back there? Do I bust in the door?"

"No! No door busting. You stand there and wait. Your job is to make sure Bender doesn't escape from the back door. So if the back door opens and Bender runs out, you have to stop him."

"You can count on me. He won't get past me. I know I look pretty tough, but I'm even tougher than that. I'm *real* tough."

"Right," Lula and I said in unison.

Kloughn went around back, and Lula and I marched up to the front door. I rapped on the door and Lula and I stood to either side. There was the unmistakable sound of a shotgun ratcheting back, Lula and I gave each other an *oh shit* look, and Bender blasted a two-foot hole in his front door.

Lula and I took off, running. We dove into the car headfirst, there was another shotgun blast, I scrambled behind the wheel and took off, tires smoking. I whipped the car around the side of the building, jumped the curb, and skidded to a stop inches from Kloughn. Lula grabbed Kloughn by the front of his shirt, pulled him into the car, and I rocketed away.

"What happened?" Kloughn asked. "Why are we leaving? Wasn't he home?"

"We changed our mind about getting him tonight," Lula said. "We could have got him if we really wanted, but we changed our mind."

"We changed our mind because he shot at us," I said to Kloughn.

"I'm pretty sure that's illegal," Kloughn said. "Did you shoot back?"

"I was thinking about it," Lula said, "but you gotta fill out a lot of papers when you shoot someone. I didn't want to take the time tonight."

"At least you got to hold the cuffs," Kloughn said.

Lula looked down at her hands. No cuffs. "Uh-oh," Lula said. "I must have dropped the cuffs in the excitement of the moment. It wasn't that I was scared, you know. I just got excited."

On the way through town I stopped at Soder's bar.

"This will only take a minute," I told everyone. "I need to talk to Steven Soder."

"Fine by me," Lula said. "I could use a drink." She looked over at Kloughn. "How about you, Pufnstuf?"

"Sure, I could use a drink, too. It's Saturday night, right? You gotta go out and have a drink on Saturday night."

"I could have had a date," Lula said.

"Me, too," Kloughn said. "There are lots of women who want to go out with me. I just didn't feel like being bothered. Sometimes it's good to take a night off from all that stuff."

"Last time I was in this bar I sort of got thrown out," Lula said. "You don't suppose they're gonna hold a grudge, do you?"

Soder saw me when I walked in. "Hey, it's Little Miss Loser," he said. "And her two loser friends."

"Sticks and stones," I said.

"Have you found my kid yet?" A taunt, not a question.

I shrugged. The shrug said *maybe I have, but then again maybe I haven't.*

"*Looooser,*" Soder sang.

"You should learn some people skills," I said to him. "You should be more civil to me. And you should have been nicer to Dotty earlier today."

That got him standing up straighter. "How do you know about Dotty?"

Another shrug.

"Don't give me another one of them shrugs," he said. "That birdbrain ex-wife of mine is a kidnapper. And you better tell me if you know anything."

I had him wondering about the extent of my knowledge. Probably not smart, but definitely satisfying.

"I've changed my mind about wanting a drink," I said to Lula and Kloughn.

"Okay by me," Lula said. "I don't like the atmosphere in this bar anyway."

Soder took another look at Kloughn. "Hey, I remember you. You're the jerk-off lawyer who represented Evelyn."

Kloughn beamed. "You remember me? I didn't think anyone would remember. Boy, how about that."

"Evelyn got control of the kid because of you," Soder said. "You made a big issue about this bar. You put my kid with a drugged-up moron, you incompetent fuck."

"She didn't look drugged-up to me," Kloughn said. "Maybe a little . . . distracted."

"How about if I distract my foot up your ass," Soder said, making for the end of the long oak bar.

Lula shoved her hand into her big leather shoulder bag. "I got Mace in here, somewhere. I got a gun."

I turned Kloughn around and pushed him toward the door. "*Go*," I yelled in his ear. "Run for the car!"

Lula still had her head down, rummaging in her bag. "I *know* I've got a gun in here."

"Forget the gun!" I said to Lula. "Let's just get out of here."

"The hell," Lula said. "This guy deserves to get shot. And I'd do it if I could just find my gun."

Soder rounded the bar and charged after Kloughn. I stepped in front of Soder, and he gave me a two-handed shove.

"Hey, you can't shove her like that," Lula said. And she smacked Soder in the back of his head with her bag. He whirled around, and she hit him again, this time catching him in the face, knocking him back a couple feet.

"What?" Soder said, dazed and blinking, swaying slightly.

Two goons started at us from the other end of the bar, and half the room had guns drawn.

"Uh-oh," Lula said. "Guess I left my gun in my other handbag."

I grabbed Lula by the sleeve and gave her a yank toward the door, and we both took off running. I beeped the car open with my remote, we all jumped in, and I zoomed away.

"Soon as I find my gun, I've got a mind to go back there and pop a cap up his ass," Lula said.

In all the time I've known Lula, I've never known her to pop a cap up anyone's ass. Unjustified bravado was high on our list of bounty hunter talents.

"I need a day off," I said. "I especially need a day without Bender."

ONE OF THE GOOD THINGS ABOUT HAMSTERS IS THAT you can tell them anything. Hamsters are nonjudgmental as long as you feed them.

"I have no life," I said to Rex. "How did it come to this? I used to be such an interesting person. I used to be fun. And now look at me. It's two o'clock on a Sunday afternoon, and I've watched *Ghostbusters* twice. It's not even raining. There's no excuse, except that I'm boring."

I glanced over at the answering machine. Maybe it was broken. I lifted the phone receiver and got a dial tone. I pushed the message button and the voice told me I had no messages. Stupid invention.

"I need a hobby," I said.

Rex sent me a *yeah, right* look. Knitting? Gardening? Decoupage? I don't think so.

"Okay, then how about sports? I could play tennis." No, wait a minute, I'd tried tennis and I sucked. What about golf? Nope, I sucked at golf, too.

I was wearing jeans and a T-shirt and the top button was open on jeans. Too many cupcakes. I got to thinking about Steven Soder calling me a loser. Maybe he was right. I scrinched my eyes closed to see if I could pop out a pity tear for myself. No luck. I sucked my stomach in and buttoned my pants. Pain. And there was a roll of fat hanging over the waistband. Not attractive.

I stomped into my bedroom and changed into running shorts and shoes. I was *not* a loser. I had a small roll of fat hanging over my waistband. No big deal. A little exercise and the fat would disappear. And there'd be the added benefit of endorphins. I didn't exactly know what endorphins were but I knew they were good and you got them from exercise.

I got into the CR-V and drove to the park in Hamilton Township. I could have gone running from my back door but where's the fun in that? In Jersey we never miss an opportunity for a car trip. Besides, the driving gave me prep time. I needed to psych myself up for this exercise stuff. I was going to really get into it this time. I was going to run. I was going to sweat. I was going to look great. I was going to *feel* great. Maybe I'd actually *take up* running.

It was a glorious blue-sky day, and the park was crowded. I got a spot toward the back of the lot, locked the CR-V up, and walked to the jogging path. I did some warm-up stretches and took off at a slow run. After a quarter mile I remembered why I never did this. I *hated* it. I hated running. I hated sweating. I hated the big, ugly running shoes I was wearing.

I pushed through to the half-mile mark where I had to stop, thank God, for a stitch in my side. I looked down at the fat roll. It was still there.

I made it to a mile and collapsed onto a bench. The bench looked out over the lake where people were rowing around in boats. A family of ducks floated close to the shore. Across the lake, I could see the parking lot and a concession stand. There was water at the concession stand. There was no water by my bench. Hell, who was I kidding? I didn't want water, anyway. I wanted a Coke. And a box of Cracker Jacks.

I was looking out at the ducks, thinking there were times in history when fat rolls were considered sexy, and wasn't it too bad I didn't live during one of those times. A huge, shaggy, prehistoric, orange beast bounded over to me and buried his nose in my crotch. Yipes. It was Morelli's dog, Bob. Bob had originally come to live at my house but after some shifting around had decided he preferred living with Morelli.

"He's excited to see you," Morelli said, settling next to me.

"I thought you were taking him to obedience school."

"I did. He learned how to sit and stay and heel. The course didn't address crotch sniffing." He looked me over. "Flushed face, the hint of sweat at the hairline, hair pulled into a ponytail, running shoes. Let me take a guess here. You've been exercising."

"And?"

"Hey, I think it's great. I'm just surprised. Last time I went running with you, you took a detour into a bakery."

"I'm turning over a new leaf."

"Can't button your jeans?"

"Not if I want to breathe at the same time."

Bob spotted a duck on the bank and raced after it. The duck took to the water, and Bob splashed in up to his eyeballs. He turned and looked at us, panic stricken. He was possibly the only retriever in the entire world who couldn't swim.

Morelli waded into the lake and dragged Bob back to the shore. Bob slogged onto the grass, gave himself a shake, and immediately ran off, chasing a squirrel.

"You're such a hero," I said to Morelli.

He kicked his shoes off and rolled his slacks to his knees. "I hear you've been up to some heroics, too. Butch Dziewisz and Frankie Burlew were in Soder's bar last night."

"It wasn't my fault."

"Of course it was your fault," Morelli said. "It's always your fault."

I did an eye roll.

"Bob misses you."

"Bob should call me sometime. Leave a message on my machine."

Morelli slouched back on the bench. "What were you doing in Soder's bar?"

"I wanted to talk to him about Evelyn and Annie, but he wasn't in a good mood."

"Did his mood take a downturn before or after he got clocked with the shoulder bag?"

"He was actually more mellow after Lula hit him."

"*Dazed*, was the word Butch used."

"Dazed could be accurate. We didn't stay around long enough to find out."

Bob returned from the squirrel chase and woofed at Morelli.

"Bob's restless," Morelli said. "I promised him we'd walk around the lake. Which direction are you headed?"

It was one mile if I retraced my steps and three miles if I continued around the lake with Morelli. Morelli looked very fine with his pants rolled up, and I was sorely tempted. Unfortunately, I had a blister on my heel, I still had a cramp in my side, and I suspected I wasn't at my most attractive. "I'm headed for the lot," I said.

There was an awkward moment where I waited for Morelli to prolong our time together. I would have liked him to walk back to the car with me. Truth is, I missed Morelli. I missed the passion, and I missed the affectionate teasing. He never tugged at my hair anymore. He didn't try to look down my shirt or up my skirt. We were at an impasse, and I was at a loss as to how to end it.

"Try to be careful," Morelli said. We stared at each other for a moment, and we each went our own way.

SEVEN

I LIMPED BACK TO THE CONCESSION STAND AND GOT a Coke and a box of Cracker Jacks. Cracker Jacks don't count as junk food because they're corn and peanuts, which we know to be high in nutrition. And they have a prize inside.

I walked the short distance to the water's edge, opened the box of Cracker Jacks, and a goose rushed up to me and pecked me in the knee. I jumped back, but he kept coming at me, honking and pecking. I threw a Cracker Jack as far as I could, and the goose scrambled after it. Big mistake. Turns out, tossing a Cracker Jack is the goose equivalent to a party invitation. Suddenly geese were rushing at me from every corner of the park, running on their stupid goose webbed feet, waggling their fat goose asses, flapping their big goose wings, their beady, black goose eyes fixed on my Cracker Jacks. They fought among themselves as they charged me, squawking, honking, viciously snapping, jockeying for position.

"Run for your life, honey! Give them the Cracker Jacks," an old lady yelled from a nearby bench. "Throw them the box, or those honkers'll eat you alive!"

I held tight to my box. "I didn't get to the prize. The prize is still in the box."

"Forget the prize!"

There were geese flying in from across the lake. Hell, for all I knew they could have been flying in from Canada. One of them hit me square in the chest and sent me sprawling. I let out a shriek and lost my grip on the box. The geese attacked with no regard for human or goose life. The noise was deafening. Goose wings beat against me, and goose toenails ripped holes in my T-shirt.

It seemed like the feeding frenzy lasted for hours, but in fact it was maybe a minute. The geese departed as quickly as they came, and all that was left were goose feathers and goose poop. Huge, gelatinous gobs of goose poop . . . as far as the eye could see.

An old man was on the bench with the old woman. "You don't know much, do you?" he said to me.

I picked myself up, crept to my car, opened the door with the remote, and numbly wedged myself behind the wheel. So much for exercise. I drove on autopilot out of the lot and somehow found my way to Hamilton Avenue. I was a couple blocks from my apartment building when I sensed movement on the seat next to me. I turned my head to look, and a spider the size of a dinner plate jumped at me.

"*Eeeeyow!* Holy shit! *HOLY SHIT!*" I sideswiped a parked car, took the curb, and came to a stop on a patch of lawn. I threw my door open and hurled myself out of the car. I was still jumping around, shaking my hair out, when the first cops arrived.

"Let me get this straight," one of the cops said. "You almost totaled the Toyota that's parked at the curb, not to mention major damage on your CR-V, because you were attacked by a spider?"

"Not just *a* spider. We're talking more than one. And big. Possibly *mutant* spiders. A herd of mutant spiders."

"You look familiar," he said. "Aren't you a bounty hunter?"

"Yes, and I'm very brave. Except for spiders." And except for Eddie Abruzzi. Abruzzi knew how to frighten a woman. He knew all the creepy crawly things that were demoralizing and irrationally frightening. Snakes and spiders and ghosts on fire escapes.

The cops exchanged a glance that said *girls* . . . and swaggered off to the CR-V. They poked their heads inside and a moment later there was a double shriek, and the car door was slammed shut.

"Jesus freaking Christ," one of them yelled. "Holy crap!"

After a brief discussion it was decided this was beyond the ability of a simple exterminator and, once again, Animal Control was called. An hour later, the CR-V was pronounced spider-free, I possessed a ticket for reckless driving, and I'd exchanged insurance information with the owner of the parked car.

I drove the remaining couple blocks, parked the CR-V, and stumbled into my building. Mr. Kleinschmidt was in the lobby.

"You look terrible," Mr. Kleinschmidt said. "What happened to you? Are those goose feathers stuck to your shirt? And how'd your shirt get all ripped and grass stained?"

"You don't want to know," I told him. "It's really ugly."

"I bet you were feeding the geese at the park," he said. "You never want to do that. Those geese are animals."

I gave up a sigh and stepped into the elevator. When I let myself into my apartment I realized something was different. My message light was blinking. *Yes.* Finally! I punched the button and leaned forward to listen.

"Did you like the spiders?" the voice asked.

I was still standing in the kitchen, sort of dumbstruck by the day, when Morelli showed up. He rapped once on the front door, and the unlocked door swung open. Bob bounded in and began running around, investigating.

"I understand you had a spider problem," Morelli said.

"That's an understatement."

"I saw your CR-V in the lot. You trashed the whole right side."

I played the phone message for him.

"It's Abruzzi," I said. "It's not his voice on the

tape, but he's behind this. He thinks this is some *war game*. And someone must have followed me to the park. Then they unlocked my car and dumped a load of spiders into it while I was running."

"How many spiders?"

"Five large tarantulas."

"I could talk to Abruzzi."

"Thanks, but I can handle it." Yeah, right. That's why I ripped the door off a parked car. Truth is, I'd love to have Morelli step in and make Abruzzi go away. Unfortunately, it would send a bad message: Dopey, helpless female needs big strong man to get her out of unfortunate mess.

Morelli gave me the once-over, taking in the grass stains, goose feathers, and rips in my shirt. "I got Bob a hot dog after we walked around the lake, and there was a lot of talk at the concession stand about a woman who'd been attacked by a flock of geese."

"Hmm. Imagine that."

"They said she provoked the attack by feeding one of the geese a Cracker Jack."

"It wasn't my fault," I said. "Damn stupid geese."

Bob had been roaming the apartment. He came into the kitchen and smiled up at us. A piece of toilet paper dangled from his lips. He opened his mouth and stuck his tongue out. *"Kack!"* His mouth opened wider, and he horked up a hot dog, a bunch of grass, a lot of slime, and a wad of toilet paper.

We both stared at the steaming pile of dog barf.

"Well, I guess I should be going now," Morelli said, looking to the door. "I just wanted to make sure you were okay."

"Wait a minute. Who's going to clean this up?"

"I'd like to help, but . . . oh man, that smells really bad." He had his hand over his nose and mouth. "Gotta go," he said. "Late. Something to do." He was in the hall. "Maybe you should just leave and rent a new apartment."

Another opportunity to use the bitch look.

I DIDN'T SLEEP WELL . . . WHICH I'M SURE IS NORMAL after you've been attacked by killer geese and mutant spiders. At six o'clock I finally hauled myself out of bed, took a shower, and got dressed. I decided I needed a treat after the crappy night, so I packed myself off in the CR-V and drove into town to Barry's Coffees. There was always a line at Barry's but it was worth it because he had forty-two different kinds of coffee, plus all the exotic espresso drinks.

I ordered a double skinny caramel mochaccino and took my drink to the window bar. I squeezed in next to an old lady with chopped-off, spikey hair dyed flame red. She was short and round, with apple cheeks and an apple shape. She was wearing large turquoise and silver earrings, elaborate rings on every gnarled finger, a white polyester warm-up suit, and platform Skechers. Her eyes were heavily gunked with mascara. Her dark red lipstick had been transferred to her cappuccino cup.

"Hey, honey," she said in a two-pack-a-day voice. "Is that a caramel mochaccino? I used to drink them but they gave me the shakes. Too much sugar. You keep drinking them you're gonna get diabetes. My brother has diabetes and they had to cut his foot off.

It was real ugly. First his toes turned black, and then the whole foot, and then his skin started falling off in big clumps. It was like a shark had got hold of him and ripped off chunks of meat."

I looked around for another place to stand while I drank my coffee, but the place was packed.

"He's in a nursing home now on account of he can't get around so good," she said. "I visit him when I can, but I got things to do. You get to be my age and you don't want to sit around wasting time. I could wake up any morning and be dead. Of course I keep myself in real good shape. How old do you think I am?"

"Eighty?"

"Seventy-four. I look better some days than others," she said. "What's your name, honey?"

"Stephanie."

"My name's Laura. Laura Minello."

"Laura Minello. That sounds familiar. Are you from the Burg?"

"Nope. I've lived all my life in North Trenton. Cherry Street. I used to work at the Social Security office. Worked there for twenty-three years, but you wouldn't remember me from there. You're too young."

Laura Minello. I knew her from somewhere, but I couldn't place it.

Laura Minello gestured at a red Corvette parked in front of Barry's. "See that fancy red car? That's my car. Pretty slick, hunh?"

I looked at the car. And then I looked at Laura Minello. Then I looked at the car again. Holy cow. I dug around in my shoulder bag, searching for the papers Connie had given me.

"Have you had the car long?" I asked Laura.

"Couple days."

I pulled the papers out of my bag and scanned the top page. Laura Minello, accused of grand theft auto, age seventy-four. Residence on Cherry Street.

God works in mysterious ways.

"You stole that Corvette, didn't you?" I asked Minello.

"I borrowed it. Old people are allowed to do things like that so they can go for the gusto before they croak."

Oh boy. I should have looked at the bond agreement before I accepted the file from Connie. Never take on old people. It's always a disaster. Old people think conveniently. And you look like a jerk when you apprehend them.

"This is a strange coincidence," I said. "I work for Vincent Plum, your bail bondsman. You missed a court date, and you need to reschedule."

"Okay, but not today. I'm going to Atlantic City. Just pencil something in for me next week."

"It doesn't work that way."

A blue-and-white cruised by Barry's. It stopped just beyond the red Vette and two cops got out.

"Uh-oh," Laura said. "This don't look good."

One of the cops was Eddie Gazarra. Gazarra was married to my cousin, Shirley the Whiner. Gazarra checked the plate on the Vette, and then he walked around the car. He went back to the blue-and-white and made a call.

"Damn cops," Laura said. "Haven't got anything better to do than to go around and bust senior citizens. There should be a law against it."

I rapped on the coffeehouse window and caught Gazarra's attention. I pointed to Laura sitting next to me and smiled. *Here she is,* I mouthed to Gazarra.

IT WAS CLOSE TO NOON, AND I WAS PARKED IN FRONT of Vinnie's office, trying to muster the courage to go inside. I'd followed Gazarra and Laura Minello back to the station, and I'd gotten a body receipt for Minello. The body receipt would get me fifteen percent of Minello's bond. And the fifteen percent would make an essential contribution toward this month's rent. Ordinarily the delivery of a body receipt is a happy occasion. Today it would be marred by the fact that in the pursuit of Andrew Bender I'd lost four pairs of cuffs. Not to mention that on all occasions I'd looked like a complete idiot. And Vinnie was in residence, lurking in his lair, anxious to remind me of all this.

I set my teeth, grabbed my bag, and headed for the door.

Lula stopped filing when I walked in. "Hey, jelly-bean," Lula said. "What's new?"

Connie looked up from her computer. "Vinnie's in his office. Break out the garlic and crosses."

"What kind of mood is he in?"

"Are you here to tell me you captured Bender?" Vinnie yelled from the other side of his closed door.

"No."

"Then I'm in a *bad* mood."

"How can he hear with the door closed?" I asked Connie.

She raised her hand, middle finger extended.

"I saw that," Vinnie yelled.

"He had video and sound installed so he doesn't miss something," Connie said.

"Yeah, it's secondhand," Lula said. "It came out of the adult video store that closed. I wouldn't touch it without rubber gloves."

Vinnie's door opened, and Vinnie stuck his head out. "Andy Bender is a drunk, for crissake. He wakes up in the morning, falls into a can of beer, and never climbs out. He should have been a gift. Instead, he's making you look like a moron."

"He's one of them crafty drunks," Lula said. "He can even *run* when he's drunk. And he shot at us last time. You're gonna have to pay me more if I'm gonna get shot at."

"You two are pathetic," Vinnie said. "I could catch this guy with one hand tied behind my back. I could catch this guy blindfolded."

"Hunh," Lula said.

Vinnie leaned forward. "You don't believe me? You think I couldn't bring this guy in?"

"Miracles happen," Lula said.

"Oh yeah? You think it would take a miracle? Well, I'll show you a miracle. You two losers be here at nine tonight, and we'll take this guy down."

Vinnie pulled his head back inside his office and slammed the door shut.

"Hope he's got cuffs," Lula said.

I gave Connie the body receipt for Laura Minello

and waited while she wrote my check. We all turned and looked when the front door opened.

"Hey, I know you," Lula said to the woman who walked into the office. "You tried to kill me."

It was Maggie Mason. We'd met her on a previous case. Our relationship with Maggie had started out bad, but had ended up good.

"You still mud wrestling at The Snake Pit?" Lula asked.

"The Snake Pit closed down." Maggie did a *shit happens* shrug. "It was time for me to get out anyway. Wrestling was fun for a while, but my dream was always to open a bookstore. When the Pit folded I persuaded one of the owners to go into business with me. That's why I stopped in. We're going to be neighbors. I just signed a lease on the building next door."

I WAS SITTING IN FRONT OF VINNIE'S OFFICE, IN MY wrecked car, wondering what to do next, and my cell phone rang.

"You gotta do something," Grandma Mazur said. "Mabel was just over, for the fortieth time. She's driving us nuts. First off, she bakes all day, and now she's giving the stuff to us because she hasn't got any more room in her house. She's wall-to-wall bread. And this last time, she started crying. *Crying.* You know how we don't do good with crying here."

"She's worried about Evelyn and Annie. They're the only family she has left."

"Well, find them," Grandma said. "We don't know what to do with all these coffee cakes."

I drove to Key Street and parked across from Evelyn's house. I thought about Annie sleeping in her bedroom upstairs, playing in the small backyard. A little girl with curly red hair and large serious eyes. A kid who was best friends with my niece, the horse. What kind of a kid would buddy up with Mary Alice? Not that Mary Alice isn't a great kid, but let's face it, she's a couple inches off average. Probably Mary Alice and Annie were both on the outside looking in, needing a friend. And they found each other.

Talk to me, I said to the house. *Tell me a secret.*

I was sitting there, waiting for the house to say something, and a car pulled up behind me. It was the big black Lincoln with two men in the front. I didn't have to think too long or hard to figure out it was Abruzzi and Darrow.

The smart thing would be to take off and not look back. Since I had a long history of rarely doing the smart thing, I locked my door, cracked the window on the driver's side, and waited for Abruzzi to come talk to me.

"You've got your door locked," Abruzzi said when he walked over. "Are you afraid of me?"

"If I was afraid of you, I'd have the motor running. Do you come here often?"

"I like to keep an eye on my properties," he said. "What are you doing here? You aren't planning on breaking in again, are you?"

"Nope. I'm just sightseeing. Strange coincidence that you always show up when I'm here."

"It's not a coincidence," Abruzzi said. "I have informants everywhere. I know everything you do."

"Everything?"

He shrugged. "Many things. For instance, I know you were at the park on Sunday. And then you had an unfortunate accident with your car."

"Some moron thought it would be cute to put spiders in my car."

"Do you like spiders?"

"They're okay. Not as much fun as bunnies, for instance."

"I understand you hit a parked car."

"One of the spiders took me by surprise."

"The element of surprise is important in a battle."

"This isn't a battle. I'm trying to put an old woman's mind at ease by finding a little girl."

"You must think I'm stupid. You're a bounty hunter. A mercenary. You know perfectly well what this is about. You're in this for the money. You know what the stakes are. And you know what I'm trying to recover. What you don't know is who you're dealing with. I'm toying with you now, but at some point the game will get boring for me. If you haven't come over to my side by the time I get bored with the game, I'll come after you with a vengeance, and I'll rip the heart out of your body while it's still beating."

Yikes.

He was dressed in a suit and tie. Very tasteful. Looked expensive. No gravy stains on the tie. He was insane, but at least he dressed well.

"Guess I'll go now," I said. "You probably want to go home and get medicated."

"Nice to know you like bunnies," he said.

I cranked the engine over and took off. Abruzzi stood there, staring after me. I checked my rearview mirror for a tail. Didn't see anyone. I wiggled around a couple streets. Still no tail. I had a bad feeling in my stomach. It felt a lot like horror.

I drove past my parents' house and noticed Uncle Sandor's Buick was parked in the driveway. My sister was using the Buick until she saved enough money to get her own car. But my sister was supposed to be at work. I pulled in behind her and popped into the house. Grandma Mazur, my mom, and Valerie were all at the kitchen table. They had coffee in front of them but no one was drinking.

I opted for a soda and took the fourth chair. "What's up?"

"Your sister got fired from her job at the bank," Grandma Mazur said. "She got into a fight with her boss, and she got herself fired, on the spot."

Valerie fighting with someone? Saint Valerie? The sister with the disposition of vanilla pudding?

When we were kids Valerie always turned her homework in on time, made her bed before going to school, and was thought to bear an uncanny resemblance to the serene plaster statues of the Virgin Mary found on Burg lawns and in Burg churches. Even Valerie's period came and went with serenity, always arriving on schedule to the minute, the flow delicate, the mood swings going from nice to nicer.

I was the sister who got cramps.

"What happened?" I asked. "How could you get into a fight with your boss? You just started that job."

"She was unreasonable," Valerie said. "And mean. I made one tiny mistake, and she was horrible about it, yelling at me in front of everyone. And before I knew it I was yelling back. And then I got fired."

"You *yelled*?"

"I haven't been myself lately."

No shit. Last month she decided she was going to try being a lesbian, and this month she was yelling. What was next? Full head rotation?

"So what was the mistake?"

"I spilled some soup. That's all I did. I spilled a little soup."

"It was one of them Cup-a-Soup things," Grandma said to me. "It had them itty-bitty noodles in it. Valerie dumped the whole thing onto a computer, and it seeped between the cracks and blew out the system. They just about had to shut the bank down."

I didn't want bad things to happen to Val. Still, it was kind of nice to see her screw up after a lifetime of perfection.

"I don't suppose you remember anything new about Evelyn?" I asked Valerie. "Mary Alice said she and Annie were best friends."

"They were school friends," Valerie said. "I don't remember ever seeing Annie."

I looked over at my mother. "Did you know Annie?"

"Evelyn used to bring her around when she was younger, but they stopped visiting a couple years ago when Evelyn started having problems. And Annie never came to the house with Mary Alice. For that matter, I don't think Mary Alice ever talked about Annie."

"Least not so we could understand," Grandma said. "She might of said something in horse talk."

Valerie was looking depressed, pushing a cookie around on the kitchen table with her finger. If *I* was depressed, the cookie would be history. Come to think of it . . .

"Do you want that cookie?" I asked Valerie.

"I bet those little soup noodles looked like worms," Grandma said. "Remember when Stephanie got worms? The doctor said they came off the lettuce. He said we didn't wash the lettuce good enough."

I'd forgotten about the worms. Not one of my favorite childhood memories. Right up there with the day I vomited spaghetti and meatballs on Anthony Balderri.

I finished my soda, ate Valerie's cookie, and went next door and checked in with Mabel.

"Anything new?" I asked Mabel.

"I got another call from the bail bonds company. They won't just come in here and throw me out, will they?"

"No. It'll have to go through legal channels. And the bond company involved is reputable."

"I haven't heard from Evelyn since she left," Mabel said. "I thought for sure I'd hear from her by now."

I returned to my car, and I tapped a call in to Dotty.

"It's Stephanie Plum," I said. "Is everything okay?"

"That woman you told me about is still sitting in front of my house. I even took the day off because she's creeping me out. I called the police, but they said they couldn't do anything."

"Do you have my card with my pager number?"

"Yes."

"Call me if you need to see Evelyn. I'll help you get past Jeanne Ellen."

I disconnected and did a palms-up in the car, all by myself. What more could I do?

I jumped when my phone rang. It was Dotty calling back. "Okay, I need help. I'm not saying I know where Evelyn is staying. I'm just saying I need to go somewhere, and I can't be followed."

"Understood. I'm about forty minutes away."

"Come in through the back again."

So maybe Jeanne Ellen was doing me a favor. She'd put Dotty into a situation where she needed me. How bizarre is that?

First thing I did was stop by the office and get Lula.

"Let's rock and roll," Lula said. "I'll distract the heck out of Jeanne Ellen. I'm the queen of distraction."

"Great. Just remember, no shooting."

"Maybe a tire," Lula said.

"Not a tire. Nothing. *No shooting.*"

"I hope you realize this puts a big crimp in my distracting."

Lula was wearing the new boots with a lemon yellow spandex miniskirt. I didn't think she'd have a distraction problem.

"This is the plan," I said when we got to South River. "I'm going to park one street over from Dotty, and we'll go in through the back. Then you can keep Jeanne Ellen busy while I take Dotty to Evelyn."

I took the shortest path through the yards and knocked once on Dotty's back door.

Dotty opened the door and stifled a scream. "Holy

Jesus," she said. "I wasn't expecting . . . two people."

What she wasn't expecting was a plus-size black woman bulging out of a tiny yellow skirt.

"This is my partner, Lula," I said. "She's good at creating a distraction."

"No kidding." Dotty was dressed in jeans and sneakers. She had a bag of groceries on the kitchen table and a two-year-old under her arm.

"This is my problem," Dotty said. "I have *a friend* who has no food in the house and can't go out to get any. I want to take these groceries to her."

"Is Jeanne Ellen out front?"

"She left about ten minutes ago. She does that. She'll sit there for hours, and then she'll go away for a while, but she always comes back."

"Why don't you take the groceries to *your friend* when Jeanne Ellen leaves?"

"You said not to do that. You said even if I didn't see her she'd follow me."

"Good point. Okay, here's the plan. You and I will cut through the back and take my car. And Lula will drive your car. Lula will make sure we're not followed, and she'll decoy Jeanne Ellen off, if Jeanne Ellen appears."

"No good," Dotty said. "I have to go alone. And I need someone to sit with the kids. My sitter just punked out on me. It's going to have to be that I cut through the yard and use your car, and you take care of the kids. I won't be long."

Lula and I shouted no simultaneously.

"Not a great idea," I said. "We don't baby-sit. We don't actually know anything about kids." I looked over at Lula. "Do you know anything about kids?"

Lula shook her head vigorously. "I don't know nothing about kids. I don't *want* to know nothing about kids, either."

"If I don't get this food to Evelyn she's going to go out and get it herself. If she's recognized, she'll have to move on."

"Evelyn and Annie can't stay hidden forever," I said.

"I know that. I'm trying to straighten things out."

"By talking to Soder?"

The surprise was obvious on her face. "You were watching me, too."

"Soder didn't look happy. What were you arguing about?"

"I can't tell you. And I need to go. Please let me go."

"I want to talk to Evelyn on the phone. I need to know she's okay. If I can talk to her on the phone, I'll let you go. And Lula and I will baby-sit."

"Hold on here," Lula said. "That don't sound like a deal to me. Kids spook me out."

"Okay," Dottie said. "I don't see where it'll harm anything to let you talk to Evelyn."

She went to the living room to dial. There was a brief conversation, Dottie returned, and passed the phone to me.

"Your grandmother is worried," I told Evelyn. "She's worried about you and Annie."

"Tell her we're alright. And please stop looking for us. You're just making things more complicated."

"I'm not the person you have to worry about.

Steven's hired a private investigator, and she's good at finding people."

"Dotty told me."

"I'd like to talk to you."

"I can't talk now. I have to get things straightened out first."

"What things?"

"I can't talk about it." And she hung up.

I gave Dotty the keys to my car. "Keep your eyes open for Jeanne Ellen. Check your rearview mirror for a tail."

Dotty grabbed the bag of groceries. "Don't let Scotty drink out of the toilet," she said. And then she took off.

The two-year-old was standing in the middle of the kitchen floor, looking at Lula and me like he'd never seen humans before.

"You think that's Scotty?" Lula asked.

A little girl appeared in the doorway leading to the bedrooms. "Scotty is a dog," she said. "My brother's name is Oliver. Who are you?"

"We're the baby-sitters," Lula said.

EIGHT

"WHERE'S BONNIE?" THE LITTLE GIRL ASKED. "BON-nie always baby-sits for Oliver and me."

"Bonnie punked out," Lula said. "So you get us."

"I don't want you to baby-sit for me. You're fat."

"I'm not fat. I'm a *substantial woman*. And you better watch what you say on account of you say things like that in first grade and they'll kick your ass out of school. I bet they don't put up with that kind of talk in first grade."

"I'm going to tell my mother you said *ass*. She won't pay you after she finds out you said *ass*. And she won't ever have you baby-sit again."

"And what's the *bad* news?" Lula asked.

"This is Lula. And I'm Stephanie," I said to the little girl. "What's your name?"

"My name is Amanda, and I'm seven years old. And I don't like *you*, either."

"Bet she's gonna be a treat when she's old enough for PMS," Lula said.

"Your mom shouldn't be long," I said to Amanda. "How about we put the television on?"

"Oliver won't like that," Amanda said.

"Oliver," I said, "do you want to watch television?"

Oliver shook his head. "No," he yelled. "No, no, no!" And he started crying. Loud.

"Now you did it," Lula said. "Why's he crying? Man, I can't hear myself think. Somebody get him to stop."

I bent down to Oliver's level. "Hey, big guy," I said. "What's the matter?"

"No, no, no!" he yelled. His face was brick red, scrinched up in anger.

"He keep frowning like that and he's gonna need Botox," Lula said.

I felt around in the diaper area. He didn't seem wet. He didn't have a spoon stuck up his nose. No limbs seemed to be severed. "I don't know what's wrong," I said. "I mostly know about hamsters."

"Well, don't look at me," Lula said. "I don't know nothing about kids. I never even was one. I was born in a crack house. Being a kid wasn't an option in my neighborhood."

"He's hungry," Amanda said. "He's going to cry like that until you feed him."

I found a box of cookies in the cupboard and held one out to Oliver.

"No," he yelled, and he knocked the cookie out of my hand.

A scruffy-looking dog rushed in from the bedroom area and ate the cookie before it hit the floor.

"Oliver doesn't want to eat a cookie," Amanda said.

Lula had her hands over her ears. "I'm gonna go deaf if he don't stop this howling. I'm getting a headache."

I got a bottle of juice out of the refrigerator. "Do you want this?" I asked.

"No!"

I tried ice cream.

"No!"

"How about a leg of lamb?" Lula asked. "I wouldn't mind having some leg of lamb."

He was on the floor now, on his back, kicking his heels against the tile. "No, no, no!"

"This here's a full-blown tantrum," Lula said. "This kid needs a time-out."

"I'm telling my mother you made Oliver cry," Amanda said.

"Hey, give me a break," I said. "I'm trying. You're his sister. Help me out here."

"He wants a grilled cheese sandwich," Amanda said. "It's his favorite food."

"Good thing he didn't want the leg of lamb," Lula said. "We wouldn't know how to cook that."

I found a pan and some butter and cheese, and I started the bread frying in the pan. Oliver was still bellowing at the top of his lungs, and now the dog was yapping, running in circles around him.

The doorbell rang, and I figured with the sort of luck I was having it was probably Jeanne Ellen. I left Lula in charge of the grilled cheese sandwich, and I went to answer the door. I was wrong about it being Jeanne Ellen, but I was right about my luck. It was Steven Soder.

"What the hell?" he said. "What are you doing here?"

"Visiting."

"Where's Dotty? I need to talk to her."

"Hey," Lula called from the kitchen, "I need an opinion on this grilled cheese."

"Who's that?" Soder wanted to know. "That doesn't sound like Dotty. That sounds like the fatso who hit me with her purse."

"We're in the middle of something right now," I said to Soder. "Maybe you could come back later."

He muscled his way past me and stalked into the kitchen. "You!" he shouted at Lula. "I'm going to kill you."

"Not in front of the k-i-d," Lula said. "You don't want to use that kind of violent talk. It stirs up all kinds of latent shit when they get to be teenagers."

"I'm not stupid," Amanda said. "I can spell. And I'm telling my mother you said *shit.*"

"Everybody says *shit,*" Lula said. She looked to me. "Doesn't everybody say *shit?* What's wrong with *shit?*"

The grilled cheese looked perfect in the fry pan, so I lifted it out with a spatula, slid it onto a plate, and gave it to Oliver. The dog stopped running in circles, snatched the sandwich off the plate, and ate it. And Oliver went back to howling.

"Oliver has to eat at the table," Amanda said.

"There's a lot of stuff to remember in this house," Lula said.

"I want to talk to Dotty," Soder said.

"Dotty isn't here," I yelled over Oliver's screaming. "Talk to me."

"In your dreams," Soder said. "And for crissake, somebody get this kid to shut up."

"The dog ate his sandwich," Lula said. "And it's all your fault on account of you distracted us."

"So do your Aunt Jemima thing and make him another sandwich," Soder said.

Lula's eyes bugged out of her head. "Aunt Jemima? Excuse me? Did you say Aunt Jemima?" She leaned forward so her nose was inches from Soder's, hands on hips, one hand still holding tight to the fry pan. "Listen to me, you punk-ass loser, you don't want to call me no Aunt Jemima or I'm gonna *give* you Aunt Jemima in the face with this fry pan. Only thing stopping me is I don't want to k-i-l-l you in front of the b-r-a-t-s."

I saw Lula's point, but being working-class white I had a totally different perspective on Aunt Jemima. Aunt Jemima conjured nothing but good memories of steaming pancakes dripping with syrup. I loved Aunt Jemima.

"Knock, knock," Jeanne Ellen said at the open door. "Can anyone come to this party?"

Jeanne Ellen was back to being dressed in the black leather outfit.

"Wow," Amanda said, "are you Catwoman?"

"Michelle Pfeiffer was Catwoman," Jeanne Ellen said. She looked down at Oliver. He was on his back again, kicking and screaming. "Stop," Jeanne Ellen said to Oliver.

Oliver blinked twice and stuck his thumb in his mouth.

Jeanne Ellen smiled at me. "Baby-sitting?"

"Yep."

"Nice."

"Your client is being intrusive," I said.

"My apologies," Jeanne Ellen said. "We're leaving now."

Amanda, Oliver, Lula, and I all stood like statues until the front door closed behind Jeanne Ellen and Soder. Then Oliver went back to his screaming.

Lula tried the stop thing but Oliver only screamed louder. So we made him another grilled cheese.

Oliver was finishing his sandwich when Dotty returned.

"How'd it go?" Dotty asked.

Amanda looked at her mother. Then she took a long look at Lula and me. "Fine," Amanda said. "I'm going to watch television now."

"Steven Soder stopped by," I said.

Dotty's face went ashen. "He was here? Soder came here?"

"He said he wanted to talk to you."

Color flamed on her cheekbones. She put a hand to Oliver. A mother's protective gesture. She smoothed the baby-fine hair back from Oliver's forehead. "I hope Oliver wasn't too much trouble."

"Oliver was terrific," I said. "It took us a while to figure out he wanted a grilled cheese sandwich, but after that he was terrific."

"Sometimes being a single mom gets a little over-whelming," Dotty said. "The responsibility of it. And the alone part. It's okay when everything's going nor-mal, but sometimes you wish there was another adult in the house."

"You're afraid of Soder," I said.

"He's a terrible person."

"You should tell me what's going on. I could help." At least I *hoped* I could help.

"I need to think," Dotty said. "I appreciate your offer, but I need to think."

"I'll stop around tomorrow morning to make sure you're okay," I said. "Maybe we can straighten this out tomorrow."

LULA AND I WERE HALFWAY TO TRENTON BEFORE either of us spoke.

"Life just gets weirder and weirder," Lula finally said.

That pretty much summed it up as far as I was concerned. I suppose I'd made progress. I'd spoken to Evelyn. I knew she was safe for now. And I knew she wasn't all that far away. Dotty had been gone less than an hour.

Soder was bothersome, but I could understand his actions. He was a jerk, but he was also a distraught dad. Most likely Dotty was negotiating some sort of truce between Soder and Evelyn.

What I couldn't understand was Jeanne Ellen. The fact that Jeanne Ellen was still doing surveillance bothered me. The surveillance seemed pointless now that Dotty knew about Jeanne Ellen. So why was Jeanne Ellen sitting across from Dotty's house when we left? It was possible that Jeanne Ellen was exerting pressure in the form of harassment. Make Dotty's life unpleasant and try to get her to cave. There was another possibility that felt pretty far out but had to be considered. Protection. Jeanne Ellen was sitting out there like the Queen's Guard. Maybe Jeanne Ellen was guarding the link to Evelyn and Annie. This led to a bunch of questions I couldn't answer. Such as, *who* was Jeanne Ellen guarding Dotty *from?* Abruzzi?

"You gonna show up at nine?" Lula asked when I pulled to a stop in front of the bonds office.

"I guess so. How about you?"

"Wouldn't miss it for anything."

I stopped at the store on the way home and picked up a few groceries. By the time I reached my apartment it was dinnertime and the building was filled with cooking smells. Minestrone soup simmering behind Mrs. Karwatt's door. Burritos from the other end of the hall.

I approached my door with my key in my hand, and I froze. If Abruzzi could get into my locked car, he could get into my locked apartment. I needed to be careful. I put the key in the lock. I turned the key. I opened the door. I stood in the hall with the door open for a moment, taking in the feel of my apart-

ment. Listening to the silence. Reassured by my heart-
beat and the fact that a pack of wild dogs didn't rush
out to devour me.

I crossed the threshold, left my front door wide
open, and walked through the rooms, carefully opening drawers and closet doors. No surprises, thank
God. Still, my stomach felt icky. I was having a hard
time pushing Abruzzi's threat out of my head.

"Knock, knock," a voice called from the open doorway.

Kloughn.

"I was in the neighborhood," he said, "so I thought
I'd say hello. I have some Chinese food with me, too.
I got it for myself, but I got too much. I thought you
might want some. But you don't have to eat it if you
don't want to. But then if you want to eat it, that
would be great. I didn't know if you liked Chinese
food. Or if you liked to eat alone. Or . . ."

I grabbed Kloughn and pulled him into my apartment.

"WHAT'S THIS?" VINNIE SAID WHEN I SHOWED UP
with Kloughn.

"Albert Kloughn," I told him, "attorney at law."

"And?"

"He brought me supper, so I invited him along."

"He looks like the Pillsbury Doughboy. What'd he
bring you to eat, dinner rolls?"

"Chinese," Kloughn said. "It was one of those last-
minute things that I just felt like eating Chinese."

"I'm not crazy about taking a lawyer along on a
bust," Vinnie said.

"I won't sue you, I swear to God," Kloughn said. "And look, I have a flashlight and defense spray and everything. I'm thinking about getting a gun, but I can't decide if I want a six shooter or a semiautomatic. I'm sort of leaning to the semiautomatic."

"Go with the semiautomatic," Lula said. "It holds more bullets. You can never have too many bullets."

"I want a vest," I said to Vinnie. "Last time I did a takedown with you, you shot everything to smithereens."

"That was an unusual circumstance," Vinnie said.

Yeah, right.

I got Kloughn and myself suited up in Kevlar, and we all packed off in Vinnie's Cadillac.

A half hour later we were parked around the corner from Bender. "Now you're going to see how a professional operates," Vinnie said. "I have a plan, and I expect everyone to do their part, so listen up."

"Oh boy," Lula said. "A plan."

"Stephanie and I will take the front door," Vinnie said. "Lula and the clown will take the back door. We all enter at the same time and subdue the rat bastard."

"That's some plan," Lula said. "I would never have thought of that one."

"K-l-o-u-g-h-n," Albert said.

"All you have to do is listen for me to yell 'bond enforcement,' " Vinnie said. "Then we crash down the doors and rush in with everyone yelling 'freeze . . . bond enforcement.' "

"I'm not doing that," I said. "I'll feel like an idiot. They only do that on television."

"I like it," Lula said. "I always wanted to crash down a door and yell stuff."

"I could be wrong," Kloughn said, "but crashing down doors might be illegal."

Vinnie buckled himself into a nylon webbed gun belt. "It's only illegal if it's the wrong house."

Lula took a Glock out of her purse and shoved it into the waistband of her spandex miniskirt. "I'm ready," she said. "Too bad we don't have a TV crew with us. This yellow skirt would show up real good."

"I'm ready, too," Kloughn said. "I've got a flashlight in case the lights go off."

I didn't want to alarm him, but that's not why bounty hunters carry two-pound Mag lights.

"Has anyone checked to make sure Bender is home?" I asked. "Anyone talk to his wife?"

"We'll listen under the window," Vinnie said. "It looks like someone's watching television in there."

We all tiptoed across the lawn and pressed ourselves against the building and listened under the window.

"Sounds like a movie," Kloughn said. "Sounds like a *dirty* movie."

"Then Bender's gotta be here," Vinnie said. "His wife isn't going to be sitting around all by herself, watching a porno flick."

Lula and Kloughn went around to the back door, and Vinnie and I went to the front door. Vinnie drew his gun and rapped on the door, which had been patched with a big piece of plywood.

"Open up," Vinnie shouted. "Bond enforcement!" He took a step back and was ready to give the door a kick with his boot when we heard Lula break into the house from the rear, yelling at the top of her lungs.

Before we had a chance to react, the front door burst open and a naked guy rushed out at us, almost knocking me off the stoop. Inside the house there was pandemonium. Men were scrambling to leave, some of them naked, some of them dressed, all of them waving guns, shouting, "Outta my way, muthafucka!"

Lula was in the middle of it. "Hey," she was yelling, "this here's a bond enforcement operation! Everybody stop running!"

Vinnie and I had worked our way into the middle of the room, but we couldn't find Bender. Too many men in too small a space, all trying to get out of the house. No one cared that Vinnie had his gun drawn. I'm not sure anyone noticed in the mayhem.

Vinnie got off a round and a chunk of ceiling fell down. After that, it was quiet because no one was left in the room but Vinnie, Lula, Kloughn, and me.

"What happened?" Lula asked. "What just happened here?"

"I didn't see Bender," Vinnie said. "Is this the right house?"

"Vinnie?" A female voice called from the bedroom. "Vinnie, is that you?"

Vinnie's eyes opened wide. "Candy?"

A naked woman somewhere in age between twenty and fifty bounced out of the bedroom. She had gigantic breasts and her pubic hair cut into the shape of a thunderbolt. She held her arms out to Vinnie. "Long time no see," she said. "What's up?"

A second woman straggled from the bedroom. "Is

it really Vinnie?" she asked. "What's he doing here?"

I eased into the bedroom behind the women and looked for Bender. The bedroom was set with lights and a discarded camera. They hadn't been watching a porno . . . they'd been making one.

"Bender isn't in the bedroom or bathroom," I said to Vinnie. "And that's the whole house."

"You looking for Andy?" Candy asked. "He split earlier. He said he had work to do. That's why we borrowed his place. Nice and private. At least until you showed up."

"We thought we was getting busted," the other woman said. "We thought you was the cops."

Kloughn gave each of the women his card. "Albert Kloughn, attorney at law," he said. "If you ever need a lawyer."

An hour later, I pulled into my lot with Kloughn yammering away alongside me. I had Godsmack plugged into my CD player, but I couldn't get the volume loud enough to totally drown out Kloughn.

"Boy, that was something," Kloughn said. "I've never seen a movie star up close before. And especially naked ones. I didn't look too much, did I? I mean, you couldn't help looking, right? Even *you* looked, right?"

Right. But *I* didn't get down on my knees to examine the pubic hair thunderbolt.

I parked and walked Kloughn to his car, making sure he got safely out of the lot. I turned to go into the building and let out a yelp when I bumped into Ranger.

He was standing close, and he was smiling. "Big date?"

"It's been a strange day."

"How strange?"

I told him about Vinnie and the porno movie.

Ranger tipped his head back and laughed out loud. Not something I see very often.

"Is this a social visit?" I asked.

"As social as I get. I'm on my way home from a job."

"Home to the Bat Cave." No one knew where Ranger lived. The address on his driver's license was a vacant lot.

"Yeah. The Bat Cave," Ranger said.

"I'd like to see the Bat Cave sometime."

Our eyes held.

"Maybe someday," he said. "Looks like you could use some bodywork on your car."

I told him about the spiders and about Abruzzi suggesting to me that at some point in time he'd rip my heart out.

"Let me get this straight," Ranger said. "You were driving along after being attacked by a flock of geese, and a spider jumped at you and caused you to smash into a parked car."

"Stop smiling," I said. "It isn't funny. I *hate* spiders."

He slung an arm around my shoulders. "I know you do, babe. And you're worried Abruzzi will make good on his threat."

"Yes."

"You have too many dangerous men in your life."

I looked at him sideways. "Do you have any suggestions on how I can cut the list down?"

"You could kill Abruzzi."

I raised my eyebrows.

"No one would mind," Ranger said. "He's not a popular guy."

"And the other dangerous men in my life?"

"Not life threatening. You might get your heart *broken*, but you won't get it ripped out of your body."

Oh boy. That's supposed to make me feel relaxed?

"Aside from your suggestion of killing Abruzzi, I don't know how to get him to stop," I said to Ranger. "Soder might want his daughter back, but Abruzzi is after something else. And whatever it is that Abruzzi is after, he thinks I'm after it, too." I looked up at my window. I wasn't real crazy about entering my apartment alone. The heart-ripping-out thing still had me feeling spooked. And every now and then I felt non-existent spiders crawling on me. "So," I said, "as long as you're here, I don't suppose you'd want to come up and have a glass of wine?"

"Are you inviting me for more than wine?"

"Sort of."

"Let me take a guess. You want me to make sure your apartment is secure."

"*Yes.*"

He beeped his car locked, and when we got to the second floor, he took my key and he opened my apartment door. He flipped the lights on and looked around. Rex was running on his wheel.

"Maybe you should teach him to bark," Ranger said.

He prowled through my living room, into my bedroom. He flipped the light on and looked around. He raised the dust ruffle and looked under the bed. "You need to get a mop under there, babe," he said. He moved to the dresser and opened each drawer. Nothing jumped out. He stuck his head into the bathroom. All clear.

"No snakes, no spiders, no bad guys," Ranger said. He reached out, grasped the collar on my denim jacket with both hands, and pulled me to him, his fingers lightly brushing my neck. "You're running up a bill. I assume you'll tell me when you're ready to settle your account."

"Sure. Absolutely. You'll be the first to know." God, I was being such a dork!

Ranger grinned down at me. "You have cuffs, right?"

Ulk. "Actually, no. I'm currently cuffless."

"How are you going to catch the bad guys if you haven't got cuffs?"

"It's a problem."

"I have cuffs," Ranger said, touching his knee to mine.

My heart was up to about two hundred beats per minute. I wasn't exactly a handcuff-me-to-the-bed kind of person. I was more a turn-out-all-the-lights-and-hope-for-the-best kind of person. "I think I'm hyperventilating," I said. "If I pass out just hold a paper bag over my nose and mouth."

"Babe," Ranger said, "it's not the end of the world to sleep with me."

"There are issues."

He raised an eyebrow. "Issues?"

"Well, actually, relationships."

"Are you in a relationship?" Ranger asked.

"No. Are you?"

"My lifestyle doesn't lend itself to relationships."

"Do you know what we need? Wine."

He released my jacket collar and followed me into the kitchen. He lounged against the counter while I took two wineglasses from the cupboard and grabbed the bottle of merlot that I'd just bought. I poured out two glasses, gave one to Ranger, and kept one for myself.

"Cheers," I said. And I chugged the wine.

Ranger took a sip. "Feel better?"

"I'm getting there. I hardly feel like fainting any-more. And most of the nausea is gone." I refilled my glass and carted the bottle into the living room. "So," I said, "would you like to watch television?"

He picked the remote off the coffee table and re-laxed into the couch. "Let me know when you're nausea-free."

"I think it was the handcuff thing that pushed me over the edge."

"I'm disappointed. I thought it was the idea of me naked." He searched through the sports and settled on basketball. "Are you okay with basketball? Or would you rather I search for a violent movie?"

"Basketball is good."

Okay, I know I was the one who suggested television, but now that I had Ranger on my couch it felt too weird. He had his dark hair slicked back into a ponytail. He was dressed in SWAT blacks, fully loaded gun belt removed but a nine-millimeter at the small of his back, Navy SEAL watch on his wrist. And he was slouched on my couch, watching basketball.

I noticed my wineglass was empty, and I poured myself a third glass.

"This feels odd," I said. "Do you watch basketball in the Bat Cave?"

"I don't have a lot of free time for television."

"But the Bat Cave *has* a television?"

"Yeah, the Bat Cave has a television."

"Just curious," I said.

He drank some wine, and he watched me. He was different from Morelli. Morelli was a tightly coiled spring. I was always aware of contained energy with Morelli. Ranger was a cat. Quiet. Every muscle relaxed on command. Probably did yoga. Might not be human.

"*Now* what are you thinking?" he asked.

"I was wondering if you were human."

"What are the other choices?"

I knocked back my glass of wine. "I didn't have anything else specifically in mind."

I WOKE UP WITH A HEADACHE AND MY TONGUE stuck to the roof of my mouth. I was on my couch, tucked under the quilt from my bed. The television was silent, and Ranger was gone. From what I could remember, I'd seen about five minutes of basketball before falling asleep. I'm a cheap drunk. Two and a half glasses of wine and I'm comatose.

I stood under a hot shower until I was pruney and the throbbing behind my eyes had partially subsided. I got dressed and made tracks to McDonald's. I got a large fries and a Coke at the drive-thru and ate in the parking lot. This is the Stephanie Plum cure for a hangover. My cell phone rang when I was halfway through with the fries.

"Did you hear about the fire?" Grandma asked. "Do you know anything about it?"

"What fire?"

"Steven Soder's bar burned to the ground last night. Technically, I guess it burned this morning, since it was after closing when it caught fire. Lorraine Zupek just called. Her grandson is a firefighter, you know. He told her they had every truck in the city there but there wasn't anything they could do. I guess they're thinking it might have been arson."

"Was anyone hurt?"

"Lorraine didn't say."

I shoved a handful of fries into my mouth and cranked the engine over. I wanted to see the fire scene. I'm not sure why. Ghoulish curiosity, I guess. If Soder had *partners*, then this wasn't entirely unexpected. Partners were known to come into a business sometimes, drain it of all profits, and then destroy it.

It took me twenty minutes to get through town. The street in front of The Foxhole was closed to traffic, so I parked two blocks away and walked. A fire truck was still on the scene, and a couple cop cars were angled into the curb. A photographer from the *Trenton*

Times was taking pictures. Crime-scene tape hadn't been stretched, but sightseers were kept at a distance by the police.

The brick face was blackened. Windows were gone. There were two levels of apartments above the bar. They looked totally destroyed. Sooty water pooled on the street and sidewalk. A hose snaked into the building from the one remaining truck but it wasn't in use.

"Was anyone hurt?" I asked one of the bystanders.

"Doesn't look like it," he said. "It was after-hours for the bar. And the apartments were empty. There were some code violations, so they were being renovated."

"Do they know how the fire got started?"

"Nobody's said."

I didn't recognize any of the cops or firefighters. I didn't see Soder anywhere. I took one last look, and I left. A quick stop at the office was next on my list. Connie should have the more complete background check on Evelyn by now.

"Jeez," Lula said when I walked in, "you don't look so good."

"Hangover," I said. "I ran into Ranger after I dropped Kloughn off, and we had a couple glasses of wine."

Connie and Lula stopped what they were doing and stared at me.

"Well?" Lula said. "You're not going to stop there, are you? What happened?"

"Nothing happened. I was sort of creeped out about the spiders and stuff, so Ranger came in with me to make sure everything was okay. We had a couple glasses of wine. And he left."

"Yeah, but what about the part between the *drinking* and the *leaving?* What happened there?"

"Nothing happened."

"Hold on here," Lula said. "You're telling me you had Ranger in your apartment, the two of you are drinking wine, and nothing happened. No fooling around at all."

"That makes no sense," Connie said. "Anytime the two of you are in this office, he's looking at you like you're lunch. There has to be some explanation. Your grandma was there, right?"

"It was just the two of us. Just Ranger and me."

"Did you put him off? You smack him, or something?" Lula asked.

"It wasn't like that. It was friendly." In an uncomfortably tense sort of way.

"Friendly," Lula said. "Hunh."

"So how do you feel about that?" Connie asked me.

"I don't know," I said. "I guess friendly is good."

"Yeah, except naked and sweaty would be better," Lula said.

We all thought about that for a moment.

Connie fanned herself with a steno pad. "Whew," she said. "Hot flash."

I resisted looking down to see if my nipples were hard. "Did Evelyn's report come in?"

Connie leafed through a stack of folders on her desk and pulled one out. "Just got it this morning."

I took the folder and read down the first page. I turned to the second page."

"Not a lot there," Connie said. "Evelyn stuck pretty close to home. Even as a kid."

I stuffed the folder into my bag and looked up at the video camera. "Is Vinnie here?"

"He hasn't come in yet. Probably got Candy inflating his ego," Lula said.

NINE

I READ THROUGH EVELYN'S FILE ONE MORE TIME when I got to my car. Some of the information seemed invasive, but this is the age of data for anyone interested. I had a credit report and some medical history. Nothing struck me as incredibly helpful.

A rap on my passenger-side window pulled me away from the file. It was Morelli. I unlocked the door, and he slid in next to me.

"Hung over?" he asked, but it was more of a statement than a question.

"How'd you know?"

He poked at the fast-food carton. "McDonald's french fries and Coke for breakfast. Dark circles under your eyes. Hair from hell."

I checked out my hair in the rearview mirror. *Yow.* "I overdid the wine last night."

He took that in. Nothing was said for a long moment. I didn't volunteer more. He didn't ask.

He looked at the file in my hand. "Are you getting any closer to Evelyn?"

"I've made some progress."

"You heard about Soder's bar."

"I just came from there," I said. "It looked bad. Lucky no one was in the building."

"Yeah, except so far we haven't been able to locate Soder. His girlfriend said he never came home."

"Do you think he could have been in the bar when the fire broke out?"

"The guys are in there checking. They had to wait for the building to cool. No sign of him so far. I thought you'd want to know." Morelli had his hand on the door handle. "I'll let you know if we find him."

"Wait a minute. I have a theoretical question. Suppose you were watching television with me. And we were alone in my apartment. And I had a couple glasses of wine, and I sort of passed out. Would you try to make love to me, anyway? Would you do a little *exploring* while I was asleep?"

"What are we watching? Is it the play-offs?"

"You can leave now," I said.

Morelli grinned and got out of the car.

I dialed Dotty's number on my cell phone. I was anxious to tell her the news about the bar and about Soder going missing. The phone rang a bunch of times and the machine picked it up. I left a message for a callback and tried her work number. I got her voice mail at work. Dotty was on vacation, scheduled to return in two weeks.

The voice mail message sent a strange emotion curling through my stomach. I searched for a name for the emotion. Unease was the closest I could come.

In less than an hour, I was parked in front of Dotty's house. No sign of Jeanne Ellen. And no sign of life in Dotty's house. No car in the driveway. No doors or windows opened. Nothing wrong with that, I told myself. The kids would be in school and day care at this time of day. And Dotty was probably out shopping.

I walked to the door and rang the bell. No one answered. I looked in the front window. The house looked at rest. No lights on. No television blaring. No kids running around. The bad feeling crept into my stomach again. Something was wrong. I walked around and looked in the back window. The kitchen was tidy. No signs of breakfast. No bowls in the sink. No cereal boxes left out. I tried the doorknob. Locked. I knocked on the door. No response. That's when it hit me. No dog. The dog should be running around, barking at the door. It was a one-story ranch. I circled the house and looked in every window. No dog.

Okay, so she's walking the dog. Or maybe she took the dog to the vet. I tried Dotty's two closest neighbors. Neither knew what had happened to Dotty and the dog. Both had noticed they were missing this morning. The consensus was that Dotty and her family vacated the house sometime during the night.

No Dotty. No dog. No Jeanne Ellen. I had other names for the thing in my stomach now. Panic. Fear.

With a touch of nausea from the hangover.

I went back to my car and sat in front of the house for a while, taking it all in. At some point I looked down at my watch and realized an hour had passed. I suppose I was hoping Dotty would return. And I suppose I knew it wasn't going to happen.

When I was nine years old I persuaded my mom to let me get a parakeet. On the way home from the pet store the door to the cage came open somehow, and the bird flew away. That's what this felt like. It felt like I left the door open.

I put the car in gear and drove back to the Burg. I went straight to Dotty's parents' house. Mrs. Palowski answered my knock, and Dotty's dog came running from the kitchen, yapping the whole way.

I dredged up my biggest and best phony smile for Mrs. Palowski. "Hi," I said, "I'm looking for Dotty."

"You just missed her," Mrs. Palowski said. "She dropped Scotty off early this morning. We're baby-sitting him while Dotty and the children are on vacation."

"I really need to talk to her," I said. "Do you have a phone number where she can be reached?"

"I don't. She said she was going camping with a friend. A cabin in the woods somewhere. She said she'd be in touch, though. I could give her a message."

I gave Mrs. Palowski my card. "Tell Dotty I have very important information for her. And ask her to call me."

"Dotty isn't in any kind of trouble, is she?" Mrs. Palowski asked.

"No. This is information about one of Dotty's friends."

"It's Evelyn, isn't it? I heard Evelyn and Annie were missing. That's such a shame. Evelyn and Dotty used to be such good friends."

"Do they still get together?"

"Not for years, now. Evelyn kept to herself after she married. I think Steven made it difficult for her to have friends."

I thanked Mrs. Palowski for her time and returned to my car. I reread the report on Evelyn. No mention of a secret cabin in the woods.

My phone chirped, and I wasn't sure what I hoped for . . . a date was high on the list. Next might be news about Soder or a friendly call from Evelyn.

Close to last on the list was a call from my mother. "Help," she said.

Then my grandmother got on the phone. "You gotta come over and see this," she said.

"See what?"

"You gotta see for yourself."

My parents' house was less than five minutes away. My mother and grandmother were at the door, waiting for me. They stepped aside and motioned me into the living room. My sister was there, slouched in my father's favorite chair. She was dressed in a rumpled long flannel nightgown and furry bedroom slippers. Yesterday's mascara hadn't been removed but had been smudged by sleep. Her hair was snarled and untamed. Meg Ryan meets Beetlejuice. California girl goes to Transylvania. She had the television remote in her hand, her attention glued to a game show. The floor around her was littered with candy bar wrappers and empty soda cans. She didn't acknowledge our presence. She burped and scratched her boob and changed the channel.

This was my perfect sister. Saint Valerie.

"I see that smile," my mother said to me. "It's not funny. She's been like that ever since she lost her job."

"Yeah, we had to vacuum around her this morning," Grandma said. "I came too close and almost sucked up one of those bunny slippers."

"She's depressed," my mother said.

No shit.

"We thought maybe you could help get her a job," Grandma said. "Something that would get her out of the house, on account of now *we're* getting depressed looking at her. Bad enough we got to look at your father."

"You're always the one with the jobs," I said to my mother. "You always know when they're hiring at the button factory."

"She ran through all my contacts," my mother said. "I'm left with nothing. And unemployment is up. I can't get her a job boxing tampons."

"Maybe you could take her along with you on a bust," Grandma said. "Maybe that'd perk her spirits up."

"No way," I said. "She already tried being a bounty hunter, and she fainted the first time someone held a gun to her head."

My mother made the sign of the cross. "Dear God," she said.

"Well, you gotta do something," Grandma said. "I'm missing all my TV shows. I tried to change the channel, and she growled at me."

"She growled at you?"

"It was scary."

"Hey, Valerie," I said. "Is there a problem?"

No response.

"I got an idea," Grandma said. "Why don't we give her a zap with your stun gun? Then when she's out cold we can get the remote."

I thought about the stun gun in my bag. I wouldn't mind testing it. I wouldn't even mind zapping Valerie. Truth is, I've secretly wanted to zap Valerie for years. I slid a look at my mother and was instantly discouraged.

"Maybe I can get you a job," I said to Valerie. "Would you be willing to work for a lawyer?"

She kept focused on the television. "Is he married?"

"No."

"Gay?"

"I don't think so."

"How old is he?"

"I'm not sure. Sixteen, maybe." I hauled my cell phone out of my bag and called Kloughn.

"Wow, that would be great if your sister would work for me," Kloughn said. "She could have all the time she wants for lunch. And she could do her laundry while she works."

I severed the connection and turned to Valerie. "You have a job."

"Bummer," Valerie said. "I was just starting to get

the hang of this depression thing. Do you think this guy will marry me?"

I did some internal eye rolling, wrote Kloughn's name and address on a piece of paper, and gave it to Valerie. "You can start tomorrow at nine. If he's late, you can wait for him in the Laundromat. You won't have any trouble recognizing him. He's the guy with the two black eyes."

My mother did another sign of the cross.

I swiped a couple slices of baloney and a slice of cheese from the fridge and headed for the door. I wanted to get out of the house before I had to answer any more questions about Albert Kloughn.

The phone rang as I was leaving.

"Hold up," Grandma said to me. "This here's Florence Szuch, and she says she's at the mall, and she says Evelyn Soder is eating lunch in the food court."

I took off running, and Grandma was right behind me.

"I'm going, too," Grandma said. "I got a right, on account of how it was my snitch that called."

We jumped into the car, and I rocketed away. The mall was twenty minutes on a good day. I hoped Evelyn was a slow eater.

"Was she sure it was Evelyn?"

"Yep. Evelyn and Annie, and another woman and her two children."

Dotty and her kids.

"I didn't have time to get my purse," Grandma said. "So I haven't got a gun. I'm going to be real disappointed if there's shooting, and I'm the only one without a gun."

If my mother knew my grandmother was carrying a gun around in her purse she'd have a cow. "First off, *I* haven't got a gun," I said. "And second thing, there won't be any shooting."

I hit Route 1 and put my foot to the floor. This brought me into the flow of traffic. In Jersey we think the speed limit is merely a suggestion. No one in Jersey would actually *do* the speed limit.

"You should be a race car driver," Grandma said. "You'd be good at it. You could drive in them NASCAR races. I'd do it, but probably you need a driver's license, and I don't have one of those."

I saw the sign for the shopping center and took the off-ramp with my fingers crossed. What had started as a courtesy to Mabel had become a crusade. I *really* wanted to talk to Evelyn. Evelyn was critical to ending the crazy war game. And ending the war game was critical to not getting my heart ripped out.

I knew every square inch of the mall, and I parked at the entrance to the food court. I wanted to tell Grandma to wait in the car, but that would have been wasted energy.

"If Evelyn is still there, I need to talk to her alone," I said to Grandma. "You're going to have to stay out of sight."

"Sure," Grandma said. "I can do that."

We entered the mall together and quickly walked to the food court. I watched the people while I walked, looking for Evelyn or Dotty. The mall was moderately full. Not jammed like on weekends. Just enough people to give me cover. My breath caught when I recognized Dotty and her kids. I'd memorized the photo of Evelyn and Annie, and they were there, too.

"Now that I'm here, I wouldn't mind having a big pretzel," Grandma said.

"You get a pretzel, and I'll talk to Evelyn. Just don't leave the food court."

I stepped away from Grandma and the light suddenly dimmed in front of me. I was in the shadow of Martin Paulson. He didn't look much different than he had in the police station parking lot, rolling around on the ground, trussed up in shackles and handcuffs. I imagine fashion choices are limited when you're shaped like Paulson.

"Well, lookey here," Paulson said. "It's Little Miss Asshole."

"Not now," I said, moving around him.

He moved with me, blocking my way. "I have a score to settle with you."

What are the chances? I finally find Evelyn, and I run into Martin Paulson, itching for a fight. "Forget it," I said. "What are you doing here anyway?"

"I work here. I work at the drugstore, and I'm on my lunch break. I was falsely accused, you know."

Yeah, right. "Get out of my way."

"Make me."

I pulled the stun gun out of my bag, rammed it into Paulson's big belly, and hit the button. Nothing happened.

Paulson looked down at the stun gun. "What is that, a toy?"

"It's a stun gun." A worthless piece of crap stun gun.

Paulson took it from me and looked at it. "Cool," he said. He turned it off, and then he turned it on. And then he touched it to my arm. There was a flash of light in my head, and everything went black.

Before the blackness turned back to light, I could hear voices, far away. I struggled to get to the voices and they became louder, more distinct. I managed to get my eyes open, and faces swam into view. I tried to blink away the buzzing, and I took an assessment of the situation. Flat on my back on the floor. Paramedics hovering over me. Oxygen mask over my nose. Blood pressure cuff on my arm. Grandma beyond the paramedics, looking worried. Paulson beyond Grandma, peeking at me over her shoulder. *Paulson.* Now I remember. The son of a bitch knocked me out with my own stun gun!

I jumped up and lunged at Paulson. My legs gave out and I went down to my knees. "Paulson, you pig!" I yelled.

Paulson ducked back and disappeared.

I was trying to get the oxygen mask off, and the paramedics were trying to keep it on. It was the attack of the geese all over again.

"I thought you were dead," Grandma said.

"Not nearly. I accidentally came into contact with my stun gun when it was live."

"Now I recognize you," one of the paramedics said to me. "You're the bounty hunter who burned the funeral home down."

"I burned it down, too," Grandma said. "You should have been there. It was like fireworks."

I stood and tested my ability to walk. I was a little

creaky, but I didn't fall down. That was a good sign, right?

Grandma handed me my shoulder bag. "That nice round man gave me your stun gun. I guess it got dropped in all the excitement. I put it in your bag," she said.

First chance I got I was going to pitch the damn stun gun into the Delaware River. I looked around, but Evelyn was long gone. "I don't suppose you saw Evelyn or Annie?" I asked Grandma.

"No. I got myself one of those big soft pretzels, and I had them dip it in chocolate."

I DROPPED GRANDMA OFF AT MY PARENTS' HOUSE, and I went home to my apartment. I stood in the hall at the door for a moment before inserting the key in the lock. I took a deep breath, unlocked the door, and pushed it open. I stepped into the small foyer area, and I very softly sang, *who's afraid of the big bad wolf.* . . . I peeked into my kitchen and felt a sense of relief. Everything was okay in the kitchen. I moved into the living room and stopped singing. Steven Soder was sitting on my couch. He was listing slightly to one side, holding the remote in his right hand, but he wasn't watching television. He was dead, dead, dead. His eyes were milky and unseeing, his lips were parted, as if he'd been surprised, his skin was ghoulishly bloodless, and he had a bullet hole in the middle of his forehead. He was wearing a baggy sweater and khaki slacks. And he was barefoot.

Criminey, isn't it bad enough I have a dead guy

sitting on my couch? Does he have to be freaking barefoot?

I silently backed out of the room, and out of my apartment. I stood in the hall and tried to dial 911 on my cell phone, but my hands were shaking, and I had to try several times before I got it right.

I stayed in the hall until the police arrived. When my apartment was swarming with cops, I crept back into my kitchen, wrapped my arms around Rex's cage, and took Rex out of the apartment into the hall with me.

I was still in the hall, holding the hamster cage, when Morelli arrived. Mrs. Karwatt from next door and Irma Brown from upstairs were with me. Beyond Mr. Wolesky's door I could hear Regis. Not even for a homicide would Mr. Wolesky miss Regis. No matter it was a rerun.

I was sitting on the floor, back to the wall, hamster cage on my lap. Morelli squatted next to me and looked in at Rex. "Is he okay?"

I nodded yes.

"How about you?" Morelli asked. "Are you okay?"

My eyes filled with tears. I wasn't okay.

"He was sitting on the couch," Irma said to Morelli. "Can you imagine? Just sitting there with the remote in his hand." She shook her head. "That couch has death cooties now. I'd cry, too, if my couch had death cooties."

"There's no such thing as death cooties," Mrs. Karwatt said.

Irma looked over at her. "Would *you* sit on that couch, now?"

Mrs. Karwatt pressed her lips together.

"Well?" Irma asked.

"Maybe if it was washed real good."

"You can't wash away death cooties," Irma said. End of discussion. Voice of authority.

Morelli sat next to me, his back to the wall, too. Mrs. Karwatt left. And Irma left. And it was just Morelli and me and Rex.

"So what do you think about death cooties?" Morelli asked me.

"I don't know what the hell death cooties are, but I'm creeped out enough to want to get rid of the couch. And I'm going to boil the remote and dip it in bleach."

"This is bad," Morelli said. "This isn't fun and games anymore. Did Mrs. Karwatt hear or see anything unusual?"

I shook my head no. "Home is supposed to be the safe place," I said to Morelli. "Where do you go when your home doesn't feel safe anymore?"

"I don't know," Morelli said. "I've never had to face that."

It was hours before the body was removed, and the apartment was sealed.

"Now what?" Morelli asked. "You can't stay here tonight."

Our eyes locked, and we were both thinking the same thing. A couple months ago Morelli wouldn't have asked that question. I would have stayed with Morelli. Things were different now. "I'll stay with my parents," I said. "Just overnight, until I figure things out."

Morelli went in and grabbed some clothes for me and shoved the essentials in a gym bag. He loaded Rex and me into his truck and drove us to the Burg.

VALERIE AND THE KIDS WERE SLEEPING IN MY OLD bedroom, so I slept on the couch with Rex on the floor beside me. I have friends who take Xanax to help them sleep. I take macaroni and cheese. And if my mom is making it for me, so much the better.

I had macaroni and cheese at 11:00 and fell into a fitful sleep. I had more macaroni at 2:00 and more at 4:30. A microwave is a wonderful invention.

At 7:30 I woke up to a lot of yelling going on upstairs. My father was causing the usual morning bottleneck in the bathroom.

"I have to brush my teeth," Angie said. "I'm going to be late for school."

"What about me?" Grandma wanted to know. "I'm old. I can't hold it forever." She hammered on the bathroom door. "What are you doing in there anyway?"

Mary Alice was making snorting horse sounds, galloping in place and pawing the floor.

"Stop that galloping," Grandma shouted to Mary Alice. "You're giving me a headache. Go downstairs to the kitchen and get some pancakes."

"Hay!" Mary Alice said. "Horses eat hay. And I already ate. I have to brush my teeth. It's real bad when horses get cavities."

The toilet flushed, and the bathroom door opened. There was a brief scuffle, and the door slammed shut.

Valerie and the two girls groaned. Grandma beat them to the bathroom.

An hour later, my father was out to work. The girls were off to school. And Valerie was in a state.

"Is this too flirty?" she asked, standing in front of me in a gauzy little flowered dress and strappy heels. "Would a suit be better?"

I was scanning the paper, looking for mention of Soder. "It doesn't matter," I said. "Wear what you want."

"I need help," Valerie said, arms flapping. "I can't make these decisions all by myself. And what about the shoes? Should I wear these pink heels? Or should I wear the retro Weitzmans?"

I found a dead man sitting on my couch last night. I have couch cooties, and Valerie needs me to make a shoe decision.

"Wear the pink things," I said. "And take extra quarters, if you have any. Kloughn can always use extra quarters."

The phone rang, and Grandma ran to answer it. The calls would start now and would go on all day. The Burg loved a good murder.

"I have a daughter who finds men dead on her couch," my mother said. "Why me? Lois Seltzman's daughter *never* finds dead men on *her* couch."

"Isn't this something," Grandma said. "Three calls already, and it's not even nine. This could be bigger than the time your car got crushed by the garbage truck."

. . .

I HAD VALERIE DRIVE ME TO MY APARTMENT BUILD-
ing on her way to work. I needed my car, and my car
was parked in the lot. Upstairs, my apartment was
sealed. Fine by me. I was in no great rush to move
back in.

I got into the CR-V and sat there a moment, listening to the quiet. Quiet was in short supply at my
parents' house.

Mr. Kleinschmidt passed me on his way to his car.
"Nice going, chicky," he said. "We can always count
on you to keep things interesting. Did you really find
a dead guy on your couch?"

I nodded. "Yes."

"Boy, that must have been something. I wish I
could have seen him."

Mr. Kleinschmidt's enthusiasm dragged a smile out
of me. "Maybe next time."

"Yeah," Mr. Kleinschmidt said, happily. "Call me
first thing next time." He gave me a wave and went
off to his car.

Okay, so here we have a new point of view when
it comes to dead people. Dead people can be fun. I
thought about it for a couple minutes but had a hard
time buying into the concept. The best I could do was
an admission that Soder's death made my job easier.
Evelyn had no reason to flee with Annie now that
Soder was out of the picture. Mabel could stay in her
house. Annie could return to school. Evelyn could get
her life together.

Unless Eddie Abruzzi was part of the reason Evelyn had to hide. If Evelyn left because she had something Abruzzi wanted, nothing would change.

I looked at the blue-and-white and the crime-scene truck in my parking lot. The bright spot in all this was that unlike snakes in the hall and spiders in my car, this was a major crime and the police would work hard to solve it. And how hard could it be to solve? Someone had dragged a dead man into the foyer, up a flight of stairs, down the hall, and into my apartment . . . during daylight hours.

I dialed Morelli on my cell phone.

"I have some questions," I said. "How did they get Soder into my apartment?"

"You don't want to know."

"I do!"

"I'll meet you for coffee," Morelli said. "There's a new coffee shop across from the hospital."

I GOT A COFFEE AND A CROISSANT, AND I SAT ACROSS from Morelli. "Tell me," I said.

"Soder was sawed in half."

"What?"

"Someone used a power saw to cut Soder in half. And then they reassembled him on your couch. The baggy sweater was hiding the fact that they duct-taped Soder back together."

My lips went numb, and I could feel the coffee cup sliding from my grasp.

Morelli reached forward and pushed my head down, between my legs. "Breathe," he said.

The bells stopped clanging in my brain, and the dots went away. I sat up and took a sip of coffee. "I'm better now," I said.

Morelli did a sigh. "If only I could believe that."

"Alright, so they cut him in half. Then what?"

"We think they used a couple big duffel bags to bring him in. Hockey bags, maybe. Now that you've gotten over the gruesome part, the rest of the story is actually ingenious. Two guys, dressed in costume, carrying duffel bags and balloons, were seen entering the lobby and using the elevator. There were two tenants in the lobby at the time. They said they assumed someone was getting one of those singing birthday presents. Mr. Kleinschmidt had turned eighty the week before, and someone sent him two strippers."

"What sort of costume were these guys wearing?"

"One was a bear, and the other was a rabbit. No faces showing. About six foot tall, but hard to tell with the costume. We found the balloons in your closet. They took the bags back with them."

"Did anyone see them leave?"

"No one in your building. We're still canvassing the neighborhood. We're checking on costume rentals, too. So far we haven't come up with anything."

"It was Abruzzi. He was the one who left the snakes and the spiders. He was the one who put the cardboard cutout on my fire escape."

"Can you prove it?"

"No."

"That's the problem," Morelli said. "And probably Abruzzi didn't personally dirty his hands."

"There's a connection between Abruzzi and Soder. Abruzzi was the partner who took over the bar, right?"

"Soder lost his bar to Abruzzi because of a card game. Soder was playing some high stakes guys, and he needed money. He borrowed the money from Ziggy Zimmerli. And Zimmerli is owned by Abruzzi. Soder lost big time at the card game, couldn't repay the money he borrowed from Zimmerli, and Abruzzi took the bar."

"So what's the deal with the bar burning down, and Soder getting shot?"

"I'm not sure. Probably the bar and Soder moved from the asset column to the liability column and were liquidated."

"Did you pick up any prints in my apartment?"

"None that didn't belong there. With the exception of Ranger."

"I work with him."

"Yeah," Morelli said. "I know."

"I'm assuming Evelyn isn't a suspect," I said.

"Anyone can hire a rabbit and a bear to chop a guy up," Morelli said. "We aren't ruling anyone out yet."

I picked at my croissant. Morelli had his cop face on, and it didn't give much away. Still, I had a feeling there was more. "Is there something you're not telling me?"

"There was a detail we're not releasing to the press," Morelli said.

"A gruesome detail?"

"Yeah."

"Let me make a guess. Soder's heart was ripped out."

Morelli looked at me for a couple beats. "This guy is about as crazy as they come," he finally said. "I'd like to protect you, but I don't know how. I could chain you to my wrist. Or I could lock you up in a closet in my house. Or you could pack off for an extended vacation. Unfortunately, I don't think you're going to agree to any of those things."

Actually, I thought all of those options sounded kind of appealing. But Morelli was right, I couldn't agree to any of them.

TEN

I TOOK ANOTHER SIP OF COFFEE AND LOOKED AROUND the cafe. It had been nicely decorated with new black-and-white tile on the floor and round, wrought-iron soda fountain–style tables and chairs. Morelli and I were the only ones there. It took the Burg a while to warm up to new things.

"Thanks for being so nice to me last night," I said to Morelli.

He slouched back in his seat. "Against my better judgment, I love you."

I paused with the coffee cup midway to my mouth, and my heart did a flip-flop.

"Don't get all excited," Morelli said. "That doesn't mean I want a relationship."

"You could do worse," I said.

"With who? Lizzy Borden?"

"*You're* not perfect, either!"

"I don't find dead guys sitting on my couch."

"Well, I don't have a knife scar slicing through my eyebrow from a barroom brawl."

"That happened years ago."

"So? The dead guy was on my couch *yesterday*. It's been twenty-four hours since anything bad has happened."

Morelli pushed back from the table. "I have to get back to work. Try to stay out of trouble."

And he was gone, off to fight crime. I, on the other hand, had no crime to fight. Bender was my only open case, and I was willing to pretend he didn't exist. I was thinking about a second croissant when Les Sebring called on my cell phone.

"Could you stop by the office?" Sebring asked. "I'd like to talk to you."

I cut across town and got another call just as I was cruising the street in front of Sebring's office, looking for parking.

"He's a nerd," Valerie said. "You didn't tell me he was a nerd."

"Who?"

"Albert Kloughn. And what's with the hovering? Sometimes I can actually feel him breathing down my neck."

"He's insecure. Try thinking of him as a pet."

"A golden retriever."

"More like a giant hamster."

"I was sort of hoping he'd marry me," Valerie said. "I was hoping he'd be taller."

"Valerie, this isn't a date. This is a job. Where is he now?"

"He went next door. There's something wrong with the vending machine that dispenses detergent."

"He's a nice guy. A little annoying, maybe. But he won't fire you for spilling chicken soup. In fact, he'll buy you a replacement lunch. Think about it."

"And I shouldn't have worn these shoes," Valerie said. "I'm dressed all wrong."

I disconnected and found a place to park on the street across from Sebring. I put a quarter in the meter and made sure it registered. I didn't need another parking ticket. I still hadn't paid the last one.

Sebring's secretary walked me upstairs and led me into Sebring's private office. Sebring was waiting for me. And so was Jeanne Ellen Burrows.

I extended my hand to Sebring. "Nice to see you again," I said. I nodded to Jeanne Ellen. She smiled in return.

"I guess you're out of a job," I said to Jeanne Ellen.

"Yes. And I'll be flying to Puerto Rico later today to pick up an FTA for Les. I wanted to tell you about Soder before I left. For what it's worth, Soder claimed Annie was in danger. He never articulated that danger, but he felt Evelyn was incapable of protecting his daughter. I wasn't successful at locating Annie, but I realized Dotty was the conduit . . . the weak link. So I guarded Dotty."

"What about the back door? That was left un-guarded."

"I had the house wired," Jeanne Ellen said. "I knew you were in there."

"The house was wired, but you still couldn't find Evelyn?"

"Evelyn's location was never mentioned. You blew the whistle on me before I had a chance to follow Dotty to Evelyn."

"And what about Soder? The scene in the bookstore and at Dotty's house?"

"Soder was a fool. He thought he could bully Dotty into talking."

"Why are you telling me all this?"

Jeanne Ellen shrugged. "Professional courtesy."

I looked beyond her to Sebring. "Do you have an ongoing interest in this?"

"Not unless Soder comes back from the dead."

"What's your opinion? Do you think Annie's in danger?"

"Someone killed her father," Sebring said. "That's not a good sign. Unless, of course, it was Annie's mom who hired the hit. Then everything works out roses."

"Do either of you know how Eddie Abruzzi fits into this puzzle?"

"He owned Soder's bar," Jeanne Ellen said. "And Soder was afraid of him. If Annie actually was in danger, I thought the threat might be tied to Abruzzi. Nothing concrete, just a feeling I had."

"I hear you found Soder sitting on your couch," Sebring said to me. "Do you know what that means?"

"My couch has death cooties?"

Sebring smiled and his teeth almost blinded me.

"You can't wash away death cooties," he said. "Once they're on your couch, they're there to stay."

I left the office on that cheery note. I got into my car, and I took a moment to process the new information. What did it mean? It didn't mean much. It reinforced my fear that Evelyn and Annie were running, not just from Soder, but from Abruzzi, as well.

Valerie called again. "If I go out to lunch with Albert, would it be a date?"

"Only if he rips your clothes off."

I hung up and put the car in gear. I was going back to the Burg, and I was going to talk to Dotty's mom. She was the only connection I had to Evelyn. If Dotty's mom said Dotty and Evelyn were peachy fine and coming home, I'd feel like I was off the hook. I'd go to the mall and get a manicure.

MRS. PALOWSKI OPENED HER FRONT DOOR AND gasped at seeing me on her porch. "Oh dear," she said. As if the death couch cooties were contagious.

I sent her a reassuring smile and a little finger wave. "Hi. I hope I'm not imposing."

"Not at all, dear. I heard about Steven Soder. I don't know what to think."

"Me, either," I said. "I don't know why he was put on my couch." I did a grimace. "Go figure. At least he wasn't killed there. They packed him in." Even as I said it, I knew it was lame. Leaving a sawed-in-half corpse on a girl's couch is rarely a random act. "The thing is, Mrs. Palowski, I really do need to talk to Dotty. I was hoping she might have heard about Soder and gotten in touch with you."

"As a matter of fact, she did. She called this morning, and I told her you were asking after her."

"Did she say when she'd be home?"

"She said she might be gone a while. That was all she said."

There goes the manicure.

Mrs. Palowski wrapped her arms tight around herself. "Evelyn dragged Dotty into this, didn't she? It's not like Dotty to take off from work and pull Amanda out of school to go on a camping trip. I think something bad is going on. I heard about Steven Soder, and I went straight to mass. I didn't pray for Soder, either. He can go to hell for all I care." She crossed herself. "I prayed for Dotty," she said.

"Do you have any idea where Dotty might be? If she was trying to help Evelyn, where would she take her?"

"I don't know. I've tried to think, but I can't figure it out. I doubt Evelyn has much money. And Dotty is on a tight budget. So I can't see them flying off to someplace. Dotty said she had to stop at the mall yesterday to get some last-minute camping things, so maybe she really is camping. Sometimes, before the divorce, Dotty and her husband would go to a campground by Washington's Crossing. I can't think of the name, but it was right on the river, and you could rent a little trailer."

I knew the campground. I'd passed it a million times on the way to New Hope.

OKAY, NOW I WAS COOKING. I HAD A LEAD. I COULD check out the campground. Only thing, I didn't want

to check it out alone. It was too isolated at this time
of year. Too easy for Abruzzi to ambush me. So I
took a deep breath and called Ranger.

"Yo," Ranger said.

"I have a lead on Evelyn, and I could use some
backup."

Twenty minutes later, I was parked in the Washington's Crossing parking lot, and Ranger pulled in
beside me. He was driving a shiny black 4×4 pickup
with oversize tires and bug lights on the cab. I locked
my car and hoisted myself into his passenger seat. The
interior of the truck looked like Ranger regularly com-
municated with Mars.

"How's your mental health?" he asked. "I heard
about Soder."

"I'm rattled."

"I have a cure."

Oh, boy.

He put the truck in gear and headed for the exit. "I
know what you're thinking," he said. "And that
wasn't where I was going. I was going to suggest
work."

"I knew that."

He looked over at me and grinned. "You want me
bad."

I did. God help me. "We're going north," I said.
"There's a chance that Evelyn and Dotty are at the
campground with the little trailers."

"I know the campground."

The road was empty at this time of day. Two lanes
winding along the Delaware River and through the
Pennsylvania countryside. Patches of woods and clus-

ters of pretty houses bordered the road. Ranger was silent while he drove. He was paged twice and both times he read the message and didn't respond. Both times he kept the message to himself. Normal behavior for Ranger. Ranger led a secret life.

The pager buzzed a third time. Ranger unclipped it from his belt and looked at the readout. He cleared the screen, reclipped the pager, and continued to watch the road.

"Hello," I said.

He cut his eyes to me.

Ranger and I were oil and water. He was the Man of Mystery, and I was Ms. Curiosity. We both knew this. Ranger tolerated it with mild amusement. I tolerated it with teeth clenched.

I dropped my eyes to his pager. "Jeanne Ellen?" I asked. I couldn't help myself.

"Jeanne Ellen is on her way to Puerto Rico," Ranger said.

Our eyes held for a moment, and he turned his attention back to the road. End of conversation.

"It's a good thing you have a nice ass," I said to him. Because you sure as hell can be *annoying*.

"My ass isn't my best part, babe," Ranger said, smiling at me.

And that truly did end the conversation. I had no follow-up.

Ten minutes later we approached the campground. It sat between the road and the river and could easily go unnoticed. It didn't have a sign. And for all I knew, it didn't have a name. A dirt road slanted down to a couple acres of grass. Small ramshackle cabins and trailers were scattered along the river's edge, each with a picnic table and grill. It had an air of abandonment at this time of year. And it felt slightly disreputable, and intriguing, like a gypsy encampment.

Ranger idled at the entrance, and we scanned the surroundings.

"No cars," Ranger said. He eased the truck down the drive and parked. He reached under the dash, removed a Glock, and we got out of the truck.

We systematically went down the row of cabins and trailers, trying doors, looking in windows, checking the grills for recent use. The lock was broken on the front door to the fourth cabin. Ranger rapped once and opened the door.

The front room had a small kitchen area at one end. Not high-tech. Sink, stove, fridge circa 1950. The floor was covered with scuffed linoleum. There was a full-size couch at the far end of the room, a square wood table, and four chairs. The only other room to the cabin was a bedroom with two sets of bunks. The bunks had mattresses but no sheets or blankets. The bathroom was minuscule. A sink and a toilet. No shower or tub. The toothpaste in the sink looked fresh.

Ranger picked a pink plastic little girl's barrette off the floor. "They've moved on," he said.

We checked the refrigerator. It was empty. We went outside and investigated the remaining cabins and trailers. All the others were locked. We checked the Dumpster and found a single small bag of garbage.

"Do you have any other leads?" Ranger asked me.

"No."

"Let's walk through their houses."

I PICKED MY CAR UP AT WASHINGTON'S CROSSING and drove it across the river. I parked in front of my parents' house and got back into Ranger's truck. We went to Dotty's house first. Ranger parked in the driveway, removed the Glock from under the dash again, and we went to the front door.

Ranger had his hand on the doorknob and his handy-dandy lock-picking tool in his hand. And the door swung open. No lock picking necessary. It would appear we were coming in second in the breaking-and-entering race.

"Stay here," Ranger said. He stepped into the living room and did a quick survey. He walked through the rest of the house with his gun drawn. He returned to the living room and motioned me in.

I closed and locked the door behind me. "Nobody home?"

"No. There are drawers pulled out and papers scattered on the kitchen counter. Either someone's been through the house, or else Dotty left in a hurry."

"I was here after Dotty left. I didn't go into the house, but I looked in the windows and the house seemed neat. Do you think the house could have been burgled?" I knew in my heart it wasn't burglary, but one can hope.

"Don't think the motive was burglary. There's a computer in the kid's room and a diamond engagement ring in the jewelry box in the mother's room. The television is still here. My guess is, we're not the only ones looking for Evelyn and Annie."

"Maybe it was Jeanne Ellen. She had a bug planted here. Maybe she came back to get her bug before she left for Puerto Rico."

"Jeanne Ellen isn't sloppy. She wouldn't leave the front door open, and she wouldn't leave evidence of a break-in."

My voice inadvertently rose an octave. "Maybe she was having a bad day? Cripes, doesn't she ever have a bad day?"

Ranger looked at me and smiled.

"Okay, so I'm getting a little tired of the perfect Jeanne Ellen," I said.

"Jeanne Ellen isn't perfect," Ranger said. "She's just very good." He slung an arm around my shoulders and kissed me below my ear. "Maybe we can find an area where your skills exceed Jeanne Ellen's."

I narrowed my eyes at him. "Did you have something in mind?"

"Nothing I'd want to get into right now." He pulled a pair of disposable gloves out of his pocket. "I want to do a more thorough search. She didn't take a lot with her. Most of their clothes are still here." He moved into the bedroom and turned the computer on. He opened files that looked promising. "Nothing to help us," he finally said, shutting the computer off.

She didn't have caller ID, and there were no messages on her machine. Bills and shopping lists were scattered across the kitchen counter. We rifled through them, knowing it was probably wasted effort. If there had been anything good, the intruder would have taken it.

"Now what?" I asked.

"Now we look at Evelyn's house."

Uh-oh. "There's a problem with Evelyn's house. Abruzzi has someone watching it. Every time I stop by, Abruzzi shows up ten minutes later."

"Why would Abruzzi care that you're in Evelyn's house?"

"Last time I ran into him he said he knew I was in it for the money, that I knew what the stakes were. And that I knew what he was trying to recover. I think Abruzzi's after something, and it's tied to Evelyn somehow. I think it's possible that Abruzzi thinks this *thing* is hidden in the house, and he doesn't want me snooping around."

"Any ideas on what it is that he's trying to recover?"

"None. Not a clue. I've been through the house, and I didn't find anything unusual. Of course, I wasn't looking for secret hiding places. I was looking for something to direct me to Evelyn."

Ranger closed the front door behind us and made sure it was locked.

The sun was low in the sky when we got to Evelyn's house. Ranger did a drive-by. "Do you know the people on this street?"

"Almost everyone. Some I know better than others. I know the woman next door to Evelyn. Linda Clark lives two houses down. The Rojacks live in the corner house. Betty and Arnold Lando live across the street. The Landos are in a rental, and I don't know the family next to them. If I was looking for a snitch, my money would be on someone in the family next to the Landos. There's an old man who always seems to be home. Sits out on the porch a lot. Looks like he used to break kneecaps for a living, about a hundred years ago."

Ranger parked in front of Carol Nadich's half of the house. Then we walked around the house and entered Evelyn's half through the back door. Ranger didn't have to break a window to get in. Ranger inserted a small slender tool into the lock, and ten seconds later the door was open.

The house seemed just as I remembered. Dishes in the drain. Mail neatly stacked. Drawers closed. None of the signs of search that we'd seen in Dotty's house.

Ranger did his usual walk-through, starting in the kitchen, eventually moving upstairs into Evelyn's room. I was following behind him when I had a sudden flashback. Kloughn telling me about Annie's drawings. Scary drawings, Kloughn had said. Bloody.

I wandered into Annie's room and flipped pages on the pad on her desk. The first page contained a house drawing similar to the one downstairs. After that came a page of scribbles and doodles. And then the childish drawing of a man. He was laying on the ground. The ground was red. Red spurted from the man's body.

"Hey," I called to Ranger. "Come look at this."

Ranger stood beside me and stared at the drawing. He turned the page and found a second drawing with red on the ground. Two men were laying in the red. Another man pointed a gun at them. There were a lot of erasure marks around the gun. I guess guns are hard to draw.

Ranger and I exchanged glances.

"It could just be television," I said.

"It wouldn't hurt to take the pad with us, in case it isn't."

Ranger finished his search of Evelyn's room, moved to Annie's, and then to the bathroom. He stood hands on hips when he'd completed the search of the bathroom.

"If there's something here, it's well hidden," he said. "It would be easier if I knew what we were looking for."

We left the house the same way we came. Abruzzi wasn't waiting for us on the back porch. And Abruzzi wasn't waiting for us by Ranger's truck. I sat next to Ranger and I looked up and down the street. No sign of Abruzzi. I was almost disappointed.

Ranger rolled the engine over, drove to my parents' house, and parked behind my car. The sun had set and the street was dark. Ranger cut his lights and turned to see me better.

"Are you spending the night here again?"

"Yes. My apartment's still sealed. I imagine I'll get it back tomorrow." Then what? An involuntary shiver sent my lower back into spasm. My couch had death cooties.

"I see you're excited about returning," Ranger said.

"I'll figure it out. Thanks for helping me today."

"I feel cheated," Ranger said. "Usually when I'm with you a car explodes or a building burns down."

"Sorry to disappoint."

"Life is a bitch," Ranger said. He reached out and grabbed me by my jacket sleeves, hauled me across the console, and kissed me.

"*Now* you kiss me?" I said. "What was the deal when we were alone in my apartment?"

"You had three glasses of wine, and you fell asleep."

"Oh yeah. Now I remember."

"And you went into a panic attack at the thought of sleeping with me."

I was sprawled across the console, wedged behind the wheel, half sitting on Ranger's lap. His lips brushed against mine when he spoke and his hands were warm against my T-shirt.

"You weren't entirely responsible for the panic," I told him. "It was a sort of disastrous day."

"Babe, you have *a lot* of disastrous days."

"You sound like Morelli."

"Morelli is a good guy. And he loves you."

"And you?"

Ranger smiled.

I was racked with another spine shiver.

The porch light went on, and Grandma peered out at us from the living room window.

"Saved by the grandma," Ranger said, releasing me. "I'm going to wait for you to get in the house. I don't want anyone kidnapping you on my watch."

I opened the door and I jumped out. And I did a mental grimace because getting kidnapped and/or shot wasn't entirely off the radar screen.

Grandma was waiting for me when I walked through the door. "Who's the guy in the cool truck?"

"Ranger."

"That man is so hot," Grandma said. "If I was twenty years younger . . ."

"If you were twenty years younger you'd still be twenty years too old," my father said.

Valerie was in the kitchen, helping my mother frost cupcakes. I got a glass of milk and a cupcake, and I sat at the table. "How'd work go today?" I asked Valerie.

"I didn't get fired."

"That's great. Before you know it, he'll be proposing marriage."

"Do you think so?"

I slid her a sideways look. "I was joking."

"It could happen," Valerie said, dropping colored sprinkles on the cupcake.

"Valerie, you don't want to marry the first guy who comes along."

"Yes, I do. As long as he has a house with two bathrooms. I swear to God, I don't care if he's Jack the Ripper."

"I'm thinking about getting a computer so I can have cybersex," Grandma said. "Anybody know how that works?"

"You go into a chat room," Valerie said. "And you meet someone. And then you type dirty suggestions to each other."

"That sounds like fun," Grandma said. "How does the *sex* part happen?"

"You sort of have to do the sex part yourself."

"I knew it was too good to be true," Grandma said. "There's always a catch to everything."

IT WAS MORNING, I WAS LAST IN LINE FOR THE BATH-room, and I was beginning to appreciate Valerie's point of view. When faced with the choices of forever living with my parents, marrying Jack the Ripper, or going home to the cootie couch, I had to admit Jack the Ripper was looking pretty good. Okay, maybe not Jack the Ripper, but certainly Doug the Dullard could be tolerated.

I was dressed in my usual outfit of jeans and boots and a stretchy shirt. I had my hair brushed out in curls and my mascara on heavy. All my adult life I've hidden behind mascara. And if I'm *really* feeling insecure, I add eyeliner. Today was an eyeliner day. Plus, I painted my toenails. Bring out the heavy artillery, right? Morelli had called earlier and told me the crime scene tape was down. He'd made arrangements for a professional cleaning crew to go through the apartment, using full-strength Clorox wherever needed. He thought they'd be done around noon. For all I cared, they could be done around November.

I was in the kitchen, having a final cup of coffee before starting my day, and Mabel appeared at the back door.

"I just heard from Evelyn," she said. "She called me, and she said everyone was fine. She's staying with a friend, and she said not to worry." She put her hand to her heart. "I feel so much better. And I felt better knowing you were looking for Evelyn. It gave me peace of mind. Thank you."

"Did Evelyn say when she was coming home?"

"No. She said she wouldn't be back for Steven's funeral, though. I guess there are hard feelings."

"Did she say where she was? Did she mention the friend's name?"

"No. She was rushed. It sounded like she was calling from a store or a restaurant. There was a lot of noise in the background."

"If she calls again, tell her I'd like to talk to her."

"There isn't anything wrong, is there? Now that Steven's gone it seems like everything should be okay."

"I'd like to talk to her about her landlord."

"Are you interested in renting a house?"

"I might be." And that was the truth.

The phone rang, and Grandma ran for it. "It's for you," she said, holding the phone out to me. "It's Valerie."

"I need help," Valerie said. "You have to get over here in a hurry." And she hung up.

"Gotta go," I said. "Valerie's got a problem."

"She used to be so smart," Grandma said. "And then she moved to California. Think all that California sun dried her brain up like a raisin."

How bad could the problem be? I thought. More chicken soup in the computer? What would Kloughn care? He had no files to lose because he had no clients.

I pulled into the lot and parked nose first in front of Kloughn's office. I looked into the big plate glass windows but didn't see Valerie. I got out of the car, and Valerie came running from the Laundromat side.

"Over here," she said. "He's in the Laundromat."

"Who?"

"Albert!"

A row of turquoise plastic chairs lined the wall facing the dryers. Two old women sat side-by-side in the chairs, smoking, looking at Valerie. Taking it all in. No one else was in the room.

"Where?" I said. "I don't see him."

Valerie sucked in a sob and pointed to one of the large commercial dryers. "He's in there."

I looked more closely. She was right. Albert Kloughn was in the dryer. He was all scrunched up with his ass to the round porthole glass door, looking like Pooh stuck in the rabbit hole.

"Is he alive?" I asked.

"Yes! Of course he's alive." Valerie crept closer and knocked on the door. "At least, I *think* he's alive."

"What's he doing in there?"

"The lady in the blue sweater thought she lost her wedding ring in the dryer. She said it was wedged into the back of the drum. So Albert went in to get it. But then somehow the door slammed shut, and we can't get it to open."

"Jeez. Why didn't you call the fire department or the police?"

There was movement in the drum and a lot of muffled noise coming from Kloughn. The noise sounded like *no, no, no.*

"I think he's embarrassed," Valerie said. "I mean, how would it look? Suppose somebody took a picture, and it got in the paper? No one would ever hire him, and I'd be out of a job."

"No one hires him now," I said. I tried the door. I tried pushing buttons. I looked for a safety latch. "I'm scoring a big zero here," I said.

"There's something wrong with that dryer," the lady in the blue sweater said. "It's always getting stuck like that. There's something wrong with the lock. I wrote out a complaint about it last week, but nobody ever does nothing around here. The vending machine with the soap doesn't work, either."

"I really think we need help," I said to Valerie. "I think we should call the police."

There was more frantic movement and more of the *no, no, no*. And then there was something that sounded like a fart coming from inside the dryer.

Valerie and I took a step back.

"I think he's nervous," Valerie said.

Probably there was some sort of door release on the inside, but Kloughn was wedged in and couldn't turn to face the latch.

I fished around in the bottom of my bag and found some change. I dropped a quarter into the slot, turned the heat down to low, and started the dryer tumbling.

Kloughn's mumbling turned to shrieking, and Kloughn bounced around some, but for the most part he seemed fairly stable. After five minutes the dryer stopped tumbling. You don't get a heck of a lot for a quarter these days.

The door opened easy as anything, and Valerie and I pulled Kloughn out and stood him up. His hair was all fluffy. The kind of fluff you see on a baby robin. He was warm and smelled nice, like fresh ironing. His face was red, and his eyes were glassy.

"I think I farted," he said.

"You know what?" the lady in the blue sweater said. "I found my ring. It wasn't in the dryer after all. I put it in my pocket and forgot."

"That's nice," Kloughn said, his eyes unfocused, a little drool at the corner of his mouth.

Valerie and I had him propped up by his armpits.

"We're going to the office now," I said to Kloughn. "Try walking."

"Everything's still spinning. I'm out of the machine, right? I'm just dizzy, right? I can still hear the motor. I've got the motor in my head." Kloughn moved his legs like Frankenstein's monster. "I can't feel my feet," he said. "My feet fell asleep."

We half dragged, half pushed him back to the office and sat him in a chair.

"That was just like a ride," he said. "Did you see me going around in there? Like a fun house, right? Like an amusement park. I ride all those rides. I'm used to that sort of thing. I sit right up front."

"Really?"

"Well, no. But I think about it."

"Isn't he cute," Valerie said. And she kissed him on top of his fluffy head.

"Gosh," Kloughn said, smiling wide. "Gee."

ELEVEN

I DECLINED ON AN OFFER OF LUNCH FROM KLOUGHN, choosing instead to go to the bonds office.

"Anything new?" I asked Connie. "I'm all out of FTAs."

"What about Bender?"

"I wouldn't want to cut in on Vinnie."

"Vinnie doesn't want him, either," Connie said.

"It isn't that," Vinnie yelled from his inner office. "I've got things to do. Important things."

"Yeah," Lula said, "he's gotta slap his johnson around."

"You better get that guy," Vinnie yelled at me. "I'm not going to be happy if I'm out Bender's bond."

"I think there's something going on with Bender,"

Lula said. "He's one of them lucky drunks. It's like he's got a direct line to God. God protects the weak and the helpless, you know."

"God isn't protecting Bender," Vinnie yelled. "Bender is still out there because I have a couple of useless boobs on my payroll."

"Okay, fine," I said. "We'll go get Bender."

"We?" Lula asked.

"Yeah, you and me."

"Been there, done that," Lula said. "I'm telling you, he's under God's protection. And I'm not sticking my nose into God's business."

"I'll buy you lunch."

"I'll get my bag," Lula said.

"One thing," I said to Connie. "I need some cuffs."

"No more cuffs," Vinnie yelled. "What do you think, cuffs grow on trees?"

"I can't bring him in without cuffs."

"Improvise."

"Hey," Lula said, looking out the big plate glass front window, "check out the car that just stopped by Stephanie's car. It's got a big rabbit and a big bear in it. And the bear is driving."

We all stared out the window.

"Uh-oh," Lula said, "did that rabbit just throw something at Stephanie's car?"

There was a loud *barooooom,* the CR-V jumped several feet into the air and burst into flames.

"Guess it was a bomb," Lula said.

Vinnie came running out of his office. "Holy shit," he said. "What was that?" He stopped and gaped at the fireball in front of his office.

"It's just another one of Stephanie's cars got blown up," Lula said. "It got bombed by a big rabbit."

"Don't you hate when that happens," Vinnie said. And he went back into his office.

Lula and Connie and I migrated out to the sidewalk and watched the car burn. A couple blue-and-whites screamed onto the scene, followed by the EMT truck and finally two fire trucks.

Carl Costanza got out of one of the blue-and-whites. "Anyone hurt?"

"No."

"Good," he said, his face creasing into a grin. "Then I can enjoy this. I missed the spiders and the guy on the couch."

Costanza's partner, Big Dog, ambled over. "Way to go, Steph," he said. "We were all wondering when you'd trash another car. Can't hardly remember the last explosion."

Costanza bobbed his head in agreement. "It's been months," he said.

I saw Morelli angle in behind a fire truck. He got out of his truck and walked over.

"Christ," he said, looking at what was fast becoming a charred hunk of scrap metal.

"It was Steph's car," Lula told him. "It was fire-bombed by a big rabbit."

Morelli set his mouth to grim and glanced over at me. "Is that true?"

"Lula saw it."

"I don't suppose you'd reconsider taking a vacation," Morelli said to me. "Maybe go to Florida for a month or two."

"I'll think about it," I said to Morelli. "As soon as I bring Andy Bender in."

Morelli was still tuned to grim.

"I could bring him in easier if I had a pair of cuffs," I said.

Morelli reached under his sweater and pulled out a pair of cuffs. He handed them to me wordlessly, his expression unchanged.

"Kiss those cuffs good-bye," Lula mumbled behind me.

GENERALLY SPEAKING, A RED TRANS AM IS NOT A good choice for a surveillance car. Fortunately, with Lula's newly bleached canary yellow hair and my extra-heavy-on-the-mascara eyes we looked like businesswomen who belonged in a red Trans Am, on the street in front of Bender's house.

"Now what?" Lula asked. "You have any ideas?"

I had binoculars trained on Bender's front window. "I think someone's in there, but I can't see enough to identify anyone."

"We could call to see who answers," Lula said. "Except I ran out of money for a cell phone so I haven't got one no more, and your phone burned up in your car."

"I guess we could go knock on the door."

"Yeah, I like that idea. Maybe he'll shoot at us again. I was hoping someone would shoot at me today. That was the first thing I said when I got up: Boy, I hope I get shot at today."

"He only shot at me that one time."

"That makes me feel a lot better," Lula said.

"Well, what's your idea?"

"My idea is we go home. I'm telling you, God don't want us to get this guy. He even sent a rabbit to bomb your car."

"*God* didn't send a rabbit to bomb my car."

"What's your explanation? You think it's every day you see a rabbit driving down the street?"

I shoved the door open and got out of the Trans Am. I had the cuffs in one hand and pepper spray in the other. "I'm in a *bad* mood," I told Lula. "I'm up to here with snakes and spiders and dead guys. And now I don't even have a car. I'm going in, and I'm dragging Bender out. And after I drop his sorry ass off at the police station I'm going to Chevy's, and I'm going to get one of those margaritas they make in the gallon-size glass."

"Hunh," Lula said. "I guess you want me to go with you."

I was already halfway across the yard. "Whatever," I said. "Do whatever the hell you want."

I could hear Lula huffing along behind me. "Don't you pull no attitude with me," she was saying. "Don't you tell me to do whatever the hell I want. I already told you what I want. Did it count for anything? Hell, no."

I got to Bender's front door, and I tried the knob. The door was locked. I knocked loud, three times. There was no answer, so I banged three times with my fist.

"Open the door," I shouted. "Bond enforcement."

The door opened, and Bender's wife looked out at me. "This isn't a good time," she said.

I pushed her aside. "It's never a good time."

"Yes, but you don't understand. Andy is sick."

"You expect us to believe that?" Lula said. "What do we look, stupid?"

Bender lurched into the room. His hair was a wreck and his eyes were half-closed. He was wearing a pajama top and stained khaki work pants.

"I'm dying," he said. "I'm gonna die."

"It's just the flu," his wife said. "You should get back to bed."

Bender held his hands out. "Cuff me. Take me in. They got a doctor that comes around, right?"

I put the cuffs on Bender and looked over at Lula. "Is there a doctor?"

"They got a ward at St. Francis."

"I bet I got anthrax," Bender said. "Or smallpox."

"Whatever it is, it don't smell good," Lula said.

"I got diarrhea. And I'm throwing up," Bender said. "I got a runny nose and a scratchy throat. And I think I got a fever. Feel my head."

"Yeah, right," Lula said. "Looking forward to that opportunity."

He swiped at his nose with his sleeve and left a smear of snot on his pajama top. He hauled his head back and sneezed and sprayed half the room.

"Hey!" Lula yelled. "Cover up! You never heard of a hankie? And what's with that sleeve thing?"

"I'm gonna be sick," Bender said. "I'm gonna puke again."

"Get to the toilet!" his wife yelled. She grabbed a blue plastic bucket off the floor. "Use the bucket."

Bender stuck his head in the bucket and threw up.

"Holy crap," Lula said. "This is the House of Plague. I'm outta here. And you're not putting him in my car, either," she said to me. "You want to take him in, you can call a cab."

Bender pulled his head out of the bucket and held his shackled hands out to me. "Okay, I'm better now. I'm ready to go."

"Wait for me," I said to Lula. "You were right about God."

"IT WAS A DRIVE TO GET HERE, BUT IT WAS WORTH it," Lula said, licking salt off the rim of her glass. "This is the mother of all margaritas."

"It's therapeutic, too. The alcohol will kill any germs we might have picked up from Bender."

"Fuckin' A," Lula said.

I sipped my drink and looked around. The bar was filled with the after-work crowd. Most of them were my age. And most of them looked happier than me.

"My life sucks," I said to Lula.

"You're just saying that because you had to watch Bender throw up in a bucket."

This was partially true. Bender throwing up in a bucket did nothing to enhance my mood. "I'm thinking about getting a different job," I said. "I want to work where these people work. They all look so happy."

"That's because they got here ahead of us, and they're all snockered."

Or it could be that none of them were being stalked by a maniac.

"I lost another pair of handcuffs," I said to Lula. "I left them on Bender."

Lula tipped her head back and burst out laughing. "And you want to change jobs," she said. "Why would you want to do that when you're so good at this one?"

IT WAS ELEVEN O'CLOCK AND MOST HOUSES ON MY parents' street were dark. The Burg was early to bed and early to rise.

"Sorry about Bender," Lula said, letting the Trans Am idle at the curb. "Maybe we could tell Vinnie he died. We could say we were all set to bring Bender in, and he died. Bang. Dead as a doorknob."

"Better yet, why don't we just go back and kill him," I said. I opened the door to leave, caught my toe in the floor mat, and fell out of the car, face first. I rolled onto my back and stared up at the stars. "I'm fine," I said to Lula. "Maybe I'll sleep here tonight."

Ranger stepped into my line of sight, grabbed hold of my denim jacket, and pulled me to my feet. "Not a good idea, babe." He looked over at Lula. "You can go now."

The Trans Am laid rubber, and disappeared from view.

"I'm *not* drunk," I said to Ranger. "I only had *one* margarita."

His fingers were still curled into my jacket, but he softened his grip. "I understand you're having rabbit problems."

"Fucking rabbit."

Ranger grinned. "You are definitely drunk."

"I'm *not* drunk. I'm on the verge of being happy." I didn't exactly have the whirlies, but the world wasn't totally in focus, either. I leaned against Ranger for support. "What are you doing here?"

He released my jacket and wrapped his arms around me. "I needed to talk to you."

"You could have called."

"I tried calling. Your phone isn't working."

"Oh yeah. I forgot. It was in the car when the car blew up."

"I did some investigating on Dotty and came up with some names to check out."

"Now?"

"Tomorrow. I'll pick you up at eight."

"I can't get into the bathroom until nine."

"Okay. I'll pick you up at nine-thirty."

"Are you laughing? I can feel you laughing. My life isn't funny!"

"Babe, your life should be a prime-time sitcom."

AT PRECISELY 9:30 I STUMBLED OUT THE DOOR AND stood blinking in the sunlight. I'd managed a shower, and I was fully clothed, but that was where it ended. A half hour isn't a lot of time for a girl to get beautiful. Especially when the girl has a hangover. My hair was pulled back into a ponytail, and I had my lipstick in my jeans jacket pocket. When my hand stopped shaking, and my eyeballs stopped being burning globes, I'd try putting lipstick on.

Ranger rolled up in a shiny black Mercedes sedan and waited at the curb. Grandma was standing behind me on the other side of the door.

"I wouldn't mind seeing him naked," she said.

I slid onto the cream-colored leather seat beside Ranger, closed my eyes, and smiled. The car smelled wonderful, like leather and fries. "God bless you," I said. He had fries and a Coke waiting for me on the console.

"Tank and Lester are checking campgrounds in Pennsylvania and New Jersey. They're doing the closest ones first and then moving out. They're looking for either of the cars, and they're talking to people when possible. We have your list of Evelyn's relatives, but I think they're long shots. Evelyn would worry that they'd get in touch with Mabel. The same goes for Dotty's relatives.

"There were four women Dotty was friendly with at work. I have their names and addresses. I think we should start with them."

"It's nice of you to help me with this. We aren't really employed by anyone. This is just an issue about Annie's safety."

"I'm not doing this for Annie's safety. This is about your safety. We need to get Abruzzi locked up. He's playing with you right now. When he stops enjoying the play he's going to get serious. If the police can't tie him to Soder, Annie might be able to tie him to something. Multiple murders, maybe, if the drawings are from life."

"If we bring Annie in, can we keep her safe?"

"I can keep her safe until Abruzzi is sentenced. Keeping you safe is more difficult. As long as Abruzzi is at large, nothing short of locking you in the Bat Cave for the rest of your life will keep you safe."

Hmm. The Bat Cave for the rest of my life. "You said the Bat Cave has television, right?"

Ranger slid a sideways look my way. "Eat your fries."

BARBARA ANN GUZMAN WAS FIRST ON THE LIST. SHE lived in a tract house in East Brunswick, in a pleasant neighborhood filled with middle-income families. Kathy Snyder, also on the list, lived two doors down. Both houses had attached garages. Neither of the garages had windows.

Ranger parked in front of the Guzman house. "Both women should be at work."

"Are we breaking in?"

"No, we're knocking on the door, hoping we hear kids inside."

We knocked twice, and we didn't hear kids. I squeezed behind an azalea and peeked in Barbara Ann's front window. Lights off, television off, no little shoes laying discarded on the floor.

We walked two houses down to Kathy Snyder. We rang the bell, and an older woman answered.

"I'm looking for Kathy," I said to the woman.

"She's at work," the woman said. "I'm her mother. Can I help you?"

Ranger passed the woman a stack of photos. "Have you seen any of these people?"

"This is Dotty," the woman said. "And her friend. They spent the night with Barbara Ann. Do you know Barbara Ann?"

"Barbara Ann Guzman," Ranger said.

"Yes. Not last night. They were here the night before. A real full house for Barbara Ann."

"Do you know where they are now?"

She looked at the photo and shook her head. "No. Kathy might know. I just saw them because I was walking. I walk around the block every night for a little exercise, and I saw them drive up."

"Do you remember the car?" Ranger asked.

"It was just a regular car. Blue, I think." She looked from Ranger to me. "Is something wrong?"

"The one woman, Dotty's friend, has had some bad luck, and we're trying to help her straighten things out," I said.

The third woman lived in an apartment building in New Brunswick. We drove through the underground garage, methodically going up and down rows, looking for Dotty's blue Honda or Evelyn's gray Sentra. We scored a goose egg on that, so we parked and took the elevator to the sixth floor. We knocked on Pauline Wood's door and got no answer. We tried neighboring apartments, but no one responded. Ranger knocked one last time on Pauline's door and then let himself in. I stayed outside doing lookout. Five minutes later, Ranger was back in the hall, Pauline's door locked behind him.

"The apartment was clean," he said. "Nothing to indicate Dotty was there. No forwarding address for her displayed in a prominent place."

We left the parking garage and drove through town on our way to Highland Park. New Brunswick is a college town with Rutgers at the one end and Douglass College at the other. I graduated from Douglass without distinction. I was in the top ninety-eight per-

cent of my class and damn glad to be there. I slept in
the library and daydreamed my way through history
lecture. I failed math twice, never fully grasping prob-
ability theory. I mean, first off, who cares if you pick
a black ball or a white ball out of the bag? And second, if you're bent over about the color, don't leave
it to chance. Look in the damn bag and pick the color
you want.

By the time I reached college age, I'd given up all
hope of flying like Superman, but I was never able to
develop a burning desire for an alternative occupation.
When I was a kid I read Donald Duck and Uncle
Scrooge comics. Uncle Scrooge was always going off
to exotic places in search of gold. After Scrooge got
the gold, he'd take it back to his money bin and push
his loose change around with a bulldozer. Now this
was my idea of a good job. Go on an adventure. Bring
back gold. Push it around with a bulldozer. How fun
is this? So you can possibly see the reason for my
lack of motivation to get grades. I mean, do you really
need good grades to drive a bulldozer?

"I went to college here," I said to Ranger. "It's
been a bunch of years, but I still feel like a student
when I ride through town."

"Were you a good student?"

"I was a terrible student. Somehow the state managed to educate me in spite of myself. Did you go to
college?"

"Rutgers, Newark. Joined the army after two
years."

When I first met Ranger I would have been surprised by this. Now, nothing surprised me about Ranger.

"The last woman on the list should be at work, but her husband should be at home," Ranger said. "He works food service for the university and goes in at four. The guy's name is Harold Bailey. His wife's name is Louise."

We wound our way through a neighborhood of older homes. They were mostly two-story clapboards with the front porch stretching the width of the house and a single detached garage to the rear. They weren't big, and they weren't small. Many had been badly renovated with fake brick front or add-on front rooms made by enclosing the porch.

We parked and approached the Bailey house. Ranger rang the bell and, just as expected, a man answered the door. Ranger introduced himself and handed the man the photographs.

"We're looking for Evelyn Soder," Ranger said. "We were hoping you might be able to help. Have you seen any of these people in the last couple days?"

"Why are you looking for this Soder woman?"

"Her ex-husband has been killed. Evelyn has been moving around lately, and her grandmother has lost touch with her. She'd like to make sure Evelyn knows about the death."

"She was here with Dotty last night. They came just as I was leaving. They stayed overnight and left in the morning. I didn't see much of them. And I don't know where they were off to today. They were taking the little girls on some sort of field trip. Historical places. That sort of thing. Louise might know more. You could try reaching her at work."

We returned to the car, and Ranger took us out of the neighborhood.

"We're always one step behind," I said.

"That's the way it is with missing children. I've worked a lot of parental abduction cases, and they move around. Usually they go farther from home. And usually they stay in one place longer than a night. But the pattern is the same. By the time information on them comes in, they're usually gone."

"How do you catch them?"

"Persistence and patience. If you stick with it long enough, eventually you win. Sometimes it takes years."

"Omigod, I haven't got years. I'll have to hide in the Bat Cave."

"Once you go into the Bat Cave it's forever, babe."

Eeek.

"Try calling the women," Ranger said. "The work number is in the file."

Barbara Ann and Kathy were cautious. Both admitted that they'd seen Dotty and Evelyn and knew they were also visiting Louise. Both insisted they didn't know where the women were going next. I suspected they were telling the truth. I thought it was possible Evelyn and Dotty were only thinking a day ahead. My best guess was that they'd intended to camp and for some reason that hadn't worked out. Now they were scrambling to stay hidden.

Pauline had been entirely out of the loop.

Louise was the most talkative, probably because she was also the most worried.

"They would only stay the one night," she said. "I know what you're telling me about Evelyn's husband is true, but I know there's more. The kids were exhausted and wanted to go home. Evelyn and Dotty looked exhausted, too. They wouldn't talk about it, but I know they were running away from something. I was thinking it was Evelyn's husband, but I guess that's not it. Holy Mother of God," she said. "You don't suppose they killed him!"

"No," I said, "he was killed by a rabbit. One more thing, did you see the car they were driving? Were they all in one car?"

"It was Dotty's car. The blue Honda. Apparently, Evelyn had a car but it was stolen when they left it at a campground. She said they went out grocery shopping and when they came back the car and everything they owned was gone. Can you imagine?"

I gave her my home phone number and asked her to call if she thought of anything that might be helpful.

"Dead end," I said to Ranger. "But I know why they vacated the campground." I told him about the stolen car.

"The more likely scenario is that Dotty and Evelyn came back after shopping, saw a strange car parked next to Evelyn's, and they abandoned everything," Ranger said.

"And when they didn't return, Abruzzi cleaned them out."

"It's what I'd do," Ranger said. "Anything to slow them down and make things difficult."

We were driving through Highland Park, approaching the bridge over the Raritan River. We were out of leads again, but at least we'd gotten some information. We didn't know where Evelyn was now, but we knew where she'd been. And we knew she no longer had the Sentra.

Ranger stopped for a light and turned to me. "When was the last time you shot a gun?" he asked.

"A couple days ago. I shot a snake. Is this a trick question?"

"This is a serious question. You should be carrying a gun. And you should feel comfortable shooting it."

"Okay, I promise, next time I go out, I'll take my gun with me."

"You'll put bullets in it?"

I hesitated.

Ranger glanced over at me. "You *will* put bullets in it."

"Sure," I said.

He reached out, opened the glove compartment, and took out a gun. It was a Smith & Wesson .38 five-shot special. It looked a lot like *my* gun.

"I stopped by your apartment this morning and picked this up for you," Ranger said. "I found it in the cookie jar."

"Tough guys always keep their gun in the cookie jar."

"Name one."

"Rockford."

Ranger grinned. "I stand corrected." He took a road that ran along the river, and after a half mile he turned into a parking area that led to a large warehouse-type building.

"What's this?" I asked.

"Shooting gallery. You're going to practice using your gun."

I knew this was necessary, but I hated the noise, and I hated the mechanics of the gun. I didn't like the idea that I was holding a device that essentially created small explosions. I was always sure something would go wrong, and I'd blow my thumb clear off my hand.

Ranger got me outfitted with ear protectors and goggles. He laid out the rounds and set the gun on the shelf in my assigned space. He brought the paper target in to twenty feet. If I was ever going to shoot someone, chances were good they'd be close to me.

"Okay, Tex," he said, "let's see what you've got."

I loaded and fired.

"Good," Ranger said. "Let's try it with your eyes open this time."

He adjusted my grip and my stance. I tried again.

"Better," Ranger said.

I practiced until my arm ached, and I couldn't pull the trigger anymore.

"How do you feel about the gun now?" Ranger asked.

"I feel more comfortable. But I still don't like it."

"You don't have to like it."

It was late afternoon when we left the gallery, and we ran into rush hour traffic going back through town. I have no patience for traffic. If I was driving I'd be cussing and banging my head against the steering wheel. Ranger was unfazed, in his zone. Zen calm. Several times I could swear he stopped breathing.

When we hit gridlock approaching Trenton, Ranger took an exit, cut down a side street, and parked in a small lot set between brick storefront businesses and three-story row houses. The street was narrow and felt dark, even during daylight hours. Storefront windows were dirty with faded displays. Black spray-painted graffiti covered the first-floor fronts of the row houses.

If at that very moment someone staggered out of a row house, blood gushing from bullet holes in multiple places on his body, it wouldn't take me by surprise.

I peered out the windshield and bit into my lower lip. "We aren't going to the Bat Cave, are we?"

"No, babe. We're going to Shorty's for pizza."

A small neon sign hung over the door of the building adjoining the lot. Sure enough, the sign said *Shorty's*. The two small windows in the front of the building had been blacked out with paint. The door was heavy wood and windowless.

I looked over my shoulder at Ranger. "The pizza is good here?" I tried not to let my voice waver, but it sounded squeezed and far away in my head. It was the voice of fear. Maybe fear is too strong a word. After the past week maybe fear should be reserved for life-threatening situations. But then again, maybe fear was appropriate.

"The pizza is good here," Ranger said, and he pushed the door open for me.

The sudden wash of noise and pizza fumes almost knocked me to my knees. It was dark inside Shorty's, and it was packed. Booths lined the walls and tables cluttered the middle of the room. An old-fashioned jukebox blasted out music from a far corner. Mostly there were men in Shorty's. The women who were there looked like they could hold their own. The men were in work boots and jeans. They were old and young, their faces lined from years of sun and cigarettes. They looked like they didn't need gun instruction.

We got a booth in a corner that was dark enough not to be able to see bloodstains or roaches. Ranger looked comfortable, his back to the wall, black shirt blending into the shadows.

The waitress was dressed in a white Shorty's T-shirt and a short black skirt. She had big hooters, a lot of brown curly hair, and more mascara than I'd ever managed, even on my most insecure day. She smiled at Ranger like she knew him better than I did. "What'll it be?" she asked.

"Pizza and beer," Ranger said.

"Do you come here a lot?" I asked him.

"Often enough. We keep a safe house in the neighborhood. Half the people in here are local. Half come from a truck stop on the next block."

The waitress dropped cardboard coasters on the scarred wood table and put a frosted glass of beer on each.

"I thought you didn't drink," I said to Ranger. "You know, the-body-is-a-temple thing? And now wine at my apartment and beer at Shorty's."

"I don't drink when I'm working. And I don't get drunk. And the body is only a temple four days a week."

"Wow," I said, "you're going to hell in a handbasket, eating pizza and boozing it up three days a week. I thought I noticed a little extra fat around the middle."

Ranger raised an eyebrow. "A little extra fat around the middle. Anything else?"

"Maybe the beginnings of a double chin."

Truth is, Ranger didn't have fat anywhere. Ranger was perfect. And we both knew it.

He drank some beer and studied me. "Don't you think you're taking a chance, baiting me, when I'm the only thing standing between you and the guy at the bar with the snake tattooed on his forehead?"

I looked at the guy with the snake. "He seems like a nice guy." Nice for a homicidal maniac.

Ranger smiled. "He works for me."

TWELVE

THE SUN WAS SETTING WHEN WE GOT BACK TO THE
car.

"That was possibly the best pizza I've ever had," I
said to Ranger. "Overall, it was a frightening experience, but the pizza was great."

"Shorty makes it himself."

"Does Shorty work for you, too?"

"Yeah. He caters all my cocktail parties."

More Ranger humor. At least, I was pretty sure it
was humor.

RANGER REACHED HAMILTON AVENUE AND GLANCED
over at me. "Where are you staying tonight?"

"My parents' house."

He turned into the Burg. "I'll have Tank drop a car off for you. You can use it until you replace the CR-V. Or until you destroy it."

"Where do you get all these cars from?"

"You don't actually want to know, do you?"

I took a beat to think about it. "No," I said. "I don't suppose I do. If I knew, you'd have to kill me, right?"

"Something like that."

He stopped in front of my parents' house, and we both looked to the door. My mother and my grand-mother were standing there, watching us.

"I'm not sure I feel comfortable about the way your grandma looks at me," Ranger said.

"She wants to see you naked."

"I wish you hadn't told me that, babe."

"Everyone I know wants to see you naked."

"And you?"

"Never crossed my mind." I held my breath when I said it, and I hoped God didn't strike me down dead for lying. I hopped out of the car and ran inside.

Grandma Mazur was waiting for me in the foyer. "The darnedest thing happened this afternoon," she said. "I was walking home from the bakery, and a car pulled up alongside me. And there was a rabbit in it. He was driving. And he handed me one of them post office mailing envelopes, and he said I should give the envelope to you. It all happened so fast. And as soon as he drove away I remembered that it was a rabbit that set fire to your car. Do you think it could be the same rabbit?"

Ordinarily I would have asked questions. What kind of car and did you get the plate? In this case the questions were useless. The cars were always different. And they were always stolen.

I took the sealed envelope from her, carefully opened it, and looked inside. Photos. Snapshots of me, sleeping on my parents' couch. They were taken last night. Someone had let themselves into the house and stood there, watching me sleep. And then photographed me. All without my knowledge. Whoever it was had picked a good night. I'd slept like the dead thanks to the giant margarita and the sleepless night before.

"What's in the envelope?" Grandma wanted to know. "Looks like photographs."

"Nothing very interesting," I said. "I think it was a prank rabbit."

My mother looked like she knew better, but she didn't say anything. By the end of the night we'll have a fresh batch of cookies, and she'll have done all the ironing. That's my mother's form of stress management.

I borrowed the Buick, and I drove to Morelli's house. He lived just outside the Burg, in a neighborhood closely resembling the Burg, less than a quarter mile from my parents'. He'd inherited the house from his aunt, and it turned out to be a good fit. Life is surprising. Joe Morelli, the scourge of Trenton High, biker, babe magnet, barroom brawler, now a semi-respectable property owner. Somehow, over the years, Morelli had grown up. No small feat for a male member of that family.

Bob rushed at me when he saw me at the door. His

eyes were happy, and he pranced around and wagged his tail. Morelli was more contained.

"What's up?" Morelli said, checking out my T-shirt.

"Something very creepy just happened to me."

"Boy, that's a surprise."

"Creepier than normal."

"Do I need a drink before you tell me this?"

I handed him the photos.

"Nice," he said, "but I've seen you sleep on several occasions."

"These were taken last night without my knowledge. A big rabbit stopped Grandma on the street today and told her to give these to me."

He raised his eyes to look at me. "Are you telling me someone let themselves into your parents' house and took these pictures while you were asleep?"

"Yes." I'd been trying to stay calm, but deep inside I was ruined. The idea that someone, Abruzzi himself, or one of his men, had stood over me and watched me sleep had me completely unnerved. I felt violated and vulnerable.

"This guy has a lot of balls," Morelli said. His voice was calm enough when he said it, but the line of his mouth tightened, and I knew he was struggling to control his anger. A younger Morelli would have thrown a chair through a window.

"I don't mean to be critical of the Trenton police," I said, "but wouldn't you think someone could catch this goddamn rabbit? He's riding around, handing out photos."

"Were the doors locked last night?"

"Yes."

"What kind of lock?"

"A dead bolt."

"It doesn't take an expert long to open a dead bolt. Can you get your parents to put a security chain on?"

"I can try. I don't want to scare them with these photos. They love their house, and they feel safe there. I don't want to take that away from them."

"Yes, but you're being stalked by a crazy person."

We were standing in the small front hall, and Bob was pressing against me, snuffling into my leg. I looked down, and there was a big wet spot of Bob drool just above my knee. I scratched the top of his head and ruffled his ears. "I need to get out of my parents' house. Take the action away from them."

"You know you can stay here."

"And endanger you?"

"I'm used to being endangered."

This was true. But this was also the basis for almost every argument we had. And it was the primary reason for our breakup. That and my inability to commit. Morelli didn't want a bounty hunter wife. He didn't want the mother of his children regularly dodging bullets. I guess I can't blame him.

"Thanks," I said. "I might take you up on it. I can also ask Ranger to put me in one of his safe houses. Or I can return to my apartment. If I go back to my apartment I need to have a security system installed. I don't want to come home to any more surprises." Unfortunately, I didn't have the money for a security system. As it was, it didn't matter because I couldn't bring myself to come within fifty feet of the cootie couch.

"What are you going to do tonight?"

"I need to stay in my parents' house and make sure no one breaks in again. Tomorrow I'll move out. I think they'll be safe once I'm gone."

"You're going to stay up all night?"

"Yep. You could come over later if you want, and we could play Monopoly."

Morelli grinned. "Monopoly, hunh? How could I pass that one up? What time does your grandmother go to bed?"

"After the eleven o'clock news."

"I'll be over around twelve."

I fiddled with Bob's ear.

"What?" Morelli asked.

"It's about *us*."

"There's no *us*."

"It feels like there's *some* us."

"This is what I think. I think there's you and me, and sometimes we're together. But there's no *us*."

"That feels a little lonely," I said.

"Don't make this more difficult than it already is," Morelli said.

I packed myself off in the Buick and went in search of a toy store. An hour later, I was done with my shopping, back in the car, heading for home. I stopped for a light on Hamilton, and a split second later, I was rear-ended. Not a big crash. More like a bump. Enough to make the Buick sway, but not enough to push me. My first reaction was my mother's standard reply to anything that was going to make her life more complicated: *Why me?* I doubted there was much damage, but it was going to be a pain in the ass all the same. I yanked the emergency brake on and put the Buick in park. Probably I needed to go out and do the examine-for-dents bullshit. I blew out a sigh and looked in my rearview mirror.

I couldn't see much in the dark, but what I could see wasn't good. I saw ears. Big rabbit ears on the guy in the driver's seat. I swiveled in my seat and squinted out the rear window. The rabbit backed his car up about ten feet and rammed me again. Harder this time. Enough to make the Buick jump forward.

Shit.

I released the brake, put the Buick in gear, and took off, through the red light. The rabbit was close behind. I turned at Chambers Street and ran up and down streets until I slid to a stop in front of Morelli's house. I saw no lights behind me, but that didn't guarantee that the rabbit was gone. He could have cut his lights and parked. I jumped out of the Buick, ran to Morelli's front door, and rang the bell, then I pounded on the door, and then I yelled, "Open up!"

Morelli opened the door, and I jumped inside. "The rabbit is after me," I said.

Morelli stuck his head out and looked up and down the street. "I don't see any rabbits."

"He was in a car. He rear-ended me on Hamilton, and then he chased me here."

"What kind of car?"

"I don't know. I couldn't see in the dark. I could just see his ears sticking up over the wheel." My heart was racing, and I was having a hard time catching my breath. "I'm losing it," I said. "This guy's really pushing my buttons. A rabbit, for crissake! What kind of a mind would think to have me stalked by a rabbit?"

Of course, while I was ranting on about the rabbit and the diabolical mind, I was remembering that it was partially my fault. I was the one who told Abruzzi I liked bunnies.

"We didn't advertise the fact that a rabbit was involved in the Soder murder, so chances of it being a copycat are slim," Morelli said. "If we're going on the assumption that Abruzzi is behind this, then the mind in question is pretty sharp. Abruzzi isn't known for being stupid."

"Just crazy?"

"As crazy as they come. From what I hear, he collects memorabilia and then wears it when he's war gaming. Dresses himself up like Napoleon."

The idea of Abruzzi dressed up like Napoleon got me smiling. He would look ridiculous, second only to the guy in the rabbit suit.

"The rabbit must have been following me from my parents' house," I said to Morelli.

"Where did you go when you left here?"

"I went to buy Monopoly. I got the old-fashioned traditional Monopoly. And I'm going to be the race car."

Morelli took Bob's leash off a hook in the hall and grabbed a jacket. "I'll go back with you, but you have to relinquish the race car to me if Grandma plays. It's the least you can do for me."

•　•　•

AT FOUR O'CLOCK I WOKE UP WITH A START. I WAS
on the couch with Morelli. I'd fallen asleep, sitting
up with his arm around me. I'd lost two games of
Monopoly, and we'd turned to television. The television was off now, and Morelli was slouched back
with his gun on the coffee table next to his cell phone.
Lights were off with the exception of the overhead
light in the kitchen. Bob was sound asleep on the
floor.

"Someone's out there," Morelli said. "I called for
a car."

"Is it the rabbit?"

"I don't know. I don't want to go to the window
and frighten whoever it is away until backup gets
here. They tried the door once, then walked around
back and tried that door."

"I don't hear any sirens."

"They won't come with sirens," he whispered. "I
got Mickey Lauder. I told him to come in an unmarked car and come in on foot."

There was a muffled crash from the back of the
house, and a lot of shouting. Morelli and I ran to the
back and flipped the porch light on. Mickey Lauder
and two uniforms had two people down on the
ground.

"Christ," Morelli said, grinning. "It's your sister
and Albert Kloughn."

Mickey Lauder was grinning, too. He'd dated Valerie in high school. "Sorry," he said, hauling her to
her feet, "I didn't recognize you at first. You've
changed your hair."

"Are you married?" Valerie asked.

"Yeah. Big time. I've got four kids."

"Just curious," Valerie said on a sigh.

Kloughn was still on the ground. "I'm pretty sure she didn't do anything illegal," he said. "She couldn't get in. The doors were locked, and she didn't want to wake anybody. It wouldn't have been breaking and entering, right? You can break into your own house, right? I mean, that's what you have to do if you forget your key, right?"

"I saw you go to bed with the kids," I said to Valerie. "How'd you get out here?"

"The same way you used to sneak out when you were in high school," Morelli said, the grin getting wider. "Out the bathroom window to the back porch roof and then down to the garbage can."

"You must be really hot stuff, Kloughn," Lauder said, still enjoying it. "I could never get her to sneak out for me."

"I don't like to brag or anything," Kloughn said, "but I know what I'm doing."

Grandma came up behind me in her bathrobe. "What's going on?"

"Valerie got busted."

"No kidding?" Grandma said. "Good for her."

Morelli shoved his gun under the waistband of his jeans. "I'm going to get my jacket and have Lauder drop me off at home. You'll be okay now. Grandma can stay up with you. Sorry about Monopoly, but you're a really lousy player."

"I *let* you win because you were doing me a favor."

"Yeah, right."

． ． ．

"I HATE TO INTERRUPT YOUR BREAKFAST," GRANDMA
said to me, "but there's a great big, scary-looking guy
at the door, and he wants to talk to you. He said he's
delivering a car."

That would be Tank.

I went to the door, and Tank handed me a set of
keys. I looked beyond him, to the curb. Ranger had
given me a new black CR-V. Very much like the car
that had gotten blown up. I knew from past experience
it would be upgraded in every way possible. And
probably it had a tracking device stuck in a place I'd
never think to look. Ranger liked to keep tabs on his
cars and his people. A new black Land Rover with a
driver waited behind the CR-V.

"This is for you, too," Tank said, giving me a cell
phone. "It's programmed with your number."

And he was gone.

Grandma looked after him. "Was he from the rental
car company?"

"Sort of."

I returned to the kitchen and drank my coffee while
I checked the answering machine in my apartment. I
had two calls from my insurance company. The first
told me I would be receiving forms by priority mail.
The second told me I was canceled. There were three
calls of nothing but breathing. I assumed this was the
rabbit. The last message was from Evelyn's neighbor,
Carol Nadich.

"Hey, Steph," she said. "I haven't seen Evelyn or
Annie, but something funny is going on here. Give
me a call when you get a chance."

"I'm going out," I said to my mother and grandmother. "And I'm taking my stuff. I'm going to stay with a friend for a couple days. I'm leaving Rex here."

My mother looked up from cutting soup vegetables. "You aren't moving in with Joe Morelli again, are you?" she asked. "I don't know what to tell people. What do I say?"

"I'm not staying with Morelli. Don't tell people anything. There's nothing to tell. If you need to talk to me, you can reach me on my cell phone." I stopped at the door. "Morelli says you should have a security chain put on the doors. He said they're not safe this way."

"What would happen?" my mother said. "We have nothing to steal. This is a respectable neighborhood. Nothing ever happens here."

I carted my bag out to the car, tossed it onto the backseat, and climbed behind the wheel. Better to talk to Carol in person. It took less than two minutes to get to her house. I parked and did a survey of the street. Everything looked normal. I knocked once, and she answered her door.

"Quiet street," I said. "Where is everybody?"

"Soccer games. Every dad and every kid on this street goes to soccer on Saturday."

"So what's weird?"

"Do you know the Pagarellis?"

I shook my head, no.

"They live next door to Betty Lando. Moved in about six months ago. Old Mr. Pagarelli sits out on the porch all the time. He's a widower, living with his son and daughter-in-law. And the daughter-in-law won't let the old guy smoke in the house, so he's always out on the porch. Anyway, Betty said she was talking to him the other day, and he was bragging about how he was working for Eddie Abruzzi. He told Betty that Abruzzi pays him to watch my house. Is that creepy, or what? I mean, what's it to him that Evelyn took off? I don't see what the problem is as long as she makes her rent payment."

"Anything else?"

"Evelyn's car is parked in the driveway. It showed up this morning."

That took some of the wind out of my sails. Stephanie Plum, master detective. I'd driven past Evelyn's car and never noticed. "Did you hear it drive up? Did you see anyone?"

"Nope. Lenny discovered it. He went out for the paper, and he noticed Evelyn's car was here."

"Do you ever hear anyone next door?"

"Only you."

I did a grimace.

"In the beginning there were lots of people looking for Evelyn," Carol said. "Soder and his friends. And Abruzzi. Soder would just walk into the house. I guess he had a key. Abruzzi, too."

I looked over at Evelyn's front door. "You don't suppose Evelyn's in there now?"

"I knocked on the door, and I looked in the back window, and I didn't see anyone."

I moved from Carol's porch to Evelyn's porch, and Carol tagged along behind me. I knocked on the door, hard. I put my ear to the front window. I shrugged my shoulders.

"Nothing going on in there," Carol said. "Right?"

We walked to the back of the house and looked in the kitchen window. As far as I could tell, nothing had been touched. I tried the knob. Still locked. Too bad the window was repaired, I would have liked to get inside. I did another shrug.

Carol and I walked over to the car. We stood four feet away.

"I didn't look in the car," Carol said.

"We should do that," I told her.

"You first," she said.

I sucked in some air and took two giant steps forward. I looked in the car and blew out a sigh of relief. No dead people. No body parts. No rabbits. Although, now that I was closer, the car didn't smell all that terrific.

"Maybe we should call the police," I said.

There have been times in my life when curiosity has pushed aside common sense. This wasn't one of them. The car was sitting in the driveway, unlocked, with the keys dangling in the ignition. It would have been easy for me to pop the trunk and peek inside, but I had no desire to do this. I was pretty sure I knew the reason for the odor. Finding Soder on my couch had been traumatic enough. I didn't want to be the one to find Evelyn or Annie in the trunk of Evelyn's car.

Carol and I sat huddled together on her porch while we waited for the blue-and-white. Neither of us was willing to articulate our thoughts. It was too awful to speculate aloud.

I stood when the police arrived, but I didn't leave

the porch. There were two patrol cars. Costanza was in one of them.

"You're looking white," Costanza said to me. "Do you feel okay?"

I nodded my head. I was afraid to trust my voice.

Big Dog was at the trunk. He had it open, and he was standing hands on hips. "You gotta see this," he said to Costanza.

Costanza walked over and stood next to Big Dog. "Cripes."

Carol and I were holding hands for support. "Tell me," I said to Costanza.

"You sure you want to know?"

I nodded my head yes.

"It's a dead guy in a bear suit."

The world stood still for a moment. "It's not Evelyn or Annie?"

"No. I'm telling you, it's a dead guy in a bear suit. Come look for yourself."

"I'll take your word for it."

"Your grandma's gonna be real disappointed if you don't look at this. Not every day you see a dead guy in a bear suit."

The EMTs rolled in and a couple unmarked cars followed close behind. Costanza stretched some tape around the crime scene.

Morelli parked across the street and strolled over. He looked in the trunk, and then he looked at me. "It's a dead guy in a bear suit."

"That's what they tell me."

"Your grandma's never going to forgive you if you don't take a look at this."

"Do I really want to look at it?"

Morelli studied the body in the trunk. "No, probably not." He walked over to me. "Who owns the car?"

"Evelyn, but nobody's seen her. Carol said the car showed up this morning. Did you draw this case?"

"Nope," Morelli said. "This is Benny's. I'm just sight-seeing. Bob and I were on our way to the park when I heard the call go out."

I could see Bob watching us from the truck. He had his nose pressed to the window, and he was panting.

"I'm okay," I said to Morelli. "I'll call you when I'm done here."

"You have a phone?"

"It came with the CR-V."

Morelli looked at the car. "Rental?"

"Sort of."

"Shit, Stephanie, you didn't get that car from Ranger, did you? No, wait a minute." He held his hands up. "I don't want to know." He looked sideways at me. "Did you ever ask him where he gets all these cars?"

"He said he'd tell me, but then he'd have to kill me."

"Did you ever stop to think he might not be kidding?" He got into his truck, buckled himself in, and cranked the engine over.

"Who's Bob?" Carol asked.

"Bob's the one who's sitting in the truck, panting."

"I'd be panting, too, if I was in Morelli's truck," Carol said.

Benny came over with his pad in his hand. He was in his early forties and probably thinking about retirement in the next couple years. Probably a case like this made retirement even more appealing. I didn't know Benny personally, but I'd heard Morelli talk about him from time to time. From what I heard, he was a good steady cop.

"I need to ask you some questions," Benny said.

I was getting to know these questions by heart.

I sat on the porch with my back to the car. I didn't want to see them haul the guy out of the trunk. Benny sat across from me. I could look beyond Benny and see old Mr. Pagarelli watching us. I wondered if Abruzzi was watching, too.

"You know what?" I said to Benny. "This is getting old."

He looked apologetic. "I'm almost done."

"Not you. This. The bear, the rabbit, the couch, everything."

"Have you ever thought about getting a different job?"

"Every minute of every day." But then, sometimes the job had its moments. "I have to go," I said. "Things to do."

Benny closed his little cop notebook. "Be careful."

That's exactly what I wasn't going to do. I hopped into the CR-V and eased around the emergency vehicles blocking the road. It wasn't quite noon. Lula should still be in the office. I needed to talk to Abruzzi, and I was too chicken to do it all by myself.

I parked at the curb and barreled through the office door. "I want to talk to Eddie Abruzzi," I said to Connie. "Do you have any idea where I might find him?"

"He has an office downtown. I don't know if he'll be there on a Saturday."

"I know where you can find him," Vinnie yelled from his inner sanctum. "He'll be at the track. He goes to the track every Saturday, rain or shine, as long as the horses are running."

"Monmouth?" I asked.

"Yeah, Monmouth. He'll be on the rail."

I looked over at Lula. "Do you feel like going to the track?"

"Hell, yeah. I feel lucky. I might do some betting. My horoscope said I was gonna make good decisions today. Only thing, *you* want to be careful. *Your* horoscope sucked."

This didn't surprise me.

"I see you're driving a new car already," Lula said. "Rental?"

I pressed my lips together.

Lula and Connie exchanged knowing glances.

"Girl, you're gonna *pay* for that car," Lula said. "And I want to know all the details. You better take notes."

"I want measurements," Connie said.

IT WAS A NICE DAY AND THE TRAFFIC WAS STEADY. We were going in the general direction of the shore, and lucky for us, it wasn't July because in July the road would be a parking lot.

"Your horoscope didn't say anything about making good decisions," Lula said. "So I think I'm the one who should be deciding things today. And I'm deciding we should play the ponies and stay far away from Abruzzi. What do you want to talk to him about anyway? What are you going to say to the man?"

"I don't have it totally worked out, but it'll be along the lines of 'fuck off.' "

"Uh-oh," Lula said. "That don't sound like a good decision to me."

"Benito Ramirez fed off fear. I have a feeling Abruzzi is like that, too. I want him to know it's not working." And I want to know what he's after. I want to know why Evelyn and Annie are important to him.

"Benito Ramirez didn't only feed off fear," Lula said. "That was just the first part. That was foreplay. Ramirez liked to hurt people. And he'd hurt you until you were dead . . . or wished you were dead."

I thought about that for the forty minutes it took me to get to the track. The awful part is that I knew it to be true. I knew firsthand. I was the one who discovered Lula after Ramirez was done with her. Finding Steven Soder was a walk in the park compared to finding Lula.

"This is my idea of work," Lula said when I pulled into the lot. "Not everybody's got a good job like us. Sure, we get shot at once in a while, but look here, we're not stuck in some crummy office building today."

"Today is Saturday," I said. "Most people aren't working at all."

"Well, yeah," Lula said. "But we could do this on a Wednesday if we wanted."

My cell phone chirped.

"Put ten dollars to win on Roger Dodger in the

fifth," Ranger said. And he disconnected.

"Well?" Lula asked.

"Ranger. He wants me to bet ten dollars on Roger Dodger in the fifth."

"Did you tell him we were going to the track?"

"No."

"How's he do that?" Lula asked. "How's he know where we are? I'm telling you, he's not human. He's from space or something."

We looked around to see if we were being followed. I hadn't thought to look for a tail on the way down. "Probably he has the car monitored," I said. "Like OnStar, but his system reports to the Bat Cave."

We followed a tidal wave of people through the gate, into the belly of the grandstand. The first race had just been run and the smell of nervous sweat was already permeating the ticket area. The air was thick with collective angst and hope and the frenzied energy that boils at a track.

Lula's eyes were rolling in her head, not sure where to go first, hearing the conflicting call of nachos, beer, and the five-dollar window.

"We need a racing sheet," she said. "How much time do we got? I don't want to miss this race. There's a horse named Decision Maker. That's a sign from God. First my horoscope and then this. I was meant to come here today and bet on this horse. Outta my way. You're getting in my way."

I stood in the middle of the floor and waited for Lula to place her bet. All around me people were talking horses and jockeys, living in the moment, enjoying the diversion. I, on the other hand, wasn't allowed the diversion. I couldn't get my mind off Abruzzi. I was being stalked. My emotions were being manipulated. My security was threatened. And I was angry. I was up to here with it. Lula was absolutely right about Benito Ramirez and his sadistic cruelty. And she was probably right that talking to Abruzzi was a bad idea. But I was going to do it anyway. I couldn't help myself. Of course, I had to find him first. And that wasn't going to be as easy as I originally thought. I'd forgotten how big the area was at the rail, how many people congregated there.

The bell sounded to close the windows, and Lula rushed over to me. "I got it. I just got it in time. We got to hurry up and get seats. I don't want to miss this. I just know this horse is going to win. He's a long shot, too. We're going out to dinner tonight. I'm treating."

We found seats in the grandstand and watched the horses come in. If I'd had my own CR-V there would have been minibinoculars in the glove compartment. Unfortunately, the minibinoculars were now a melted glob of glass and slag, probably compressed to the thickness of a dime.

I systematically worked my way through the crowd at the rail, trying to find Abruzzi. The horses took off, and the crowd surged forward, shouting, waving programs. It was impossible to see anything other than a blur of color. Lula was screaming and jumping up and down next to me.

"Go, you motherfucker," she was yelling. "Go, go, go, you dumb sonovabitch!"

I wasn't sure what to wish for. I wanted her to win,

but I was afraid if she won, she'd be impossible with the horoscope stuff.

The horses streaked across the finish line, and Lula was still jumping. "Yes," she was screaming. "Yes, yes, yes!"

I looked over at her. "You won, right?"

"You bet your ass I won. I won big. Twenty to one. I must have been the only genius in this whole freaking place who bet on that four-legged wonder. I'm going to get my money. Are you coming with me?"

"No. I'm going to wait here. I want to look for Abruzzi now that the crowd is thinning."

THIRTEEN

PART OF THE PROBLEM WAS THAT I WAS SEEING everyone at the rail from the back. Difficult enough to recognize someone you know intimately this way. Almost impossible to recognize someone you've only seen briefly on two occasions.

Lula plunked down into the seat next to me. "You're not going to believe this," she said. "I just looked into the eyes of the devil." She had her ticket clutched tight in her hand, and she made the sign of the cross. "Holy mother of God. Look here. I'm crossing myself. What's with that? I'm Baptist. Baptist don't do this cross shit."

"Eyes of the devil?" I asked.

"Abruzzi. I ran right into Abruzzi. I was coming

from collecting my money, and I just placed my bet, and I bumped right into him like it was destiny. He looked down at me, and I looked into those eyes, and I almost messed my pants. It's like all my blood turns cold when I look into those eyes."

"Did he say anything?"

"No. He smiled at me. It was awful. It was that smile that's just a slash in his face and doesn't go to his eyes. And then calm as anything, he turned around and walked away."

"Was he alone? What was he wearing?"

"He was with that Darrow guy again. I think Darrow must be muscle. And I don't know what he was wearing. It's like my brain gets paralyzed when I get five feet from Abruzzi. I just get sucked into those creepy eyes." Lula gave a shiver. "Yeesh," she said.

At least I knew Abruzzi was here. And I knew he was with Darrow. I started working my way through the rail crowd again. I was beginning to recognize people. They tended to go away to bet, but then they gravitated back to their favorite spot on the rail.

They were Jersey people, the younger guys dressed in T-shirts and khakis and jeans, the older guys wearing Sansabelt polyester slacks and three-button knit golf shirts. Their faces were animated. Jersey doesn't hold much back. And their bodies were padded with a good protective layer of deep-fried fish and sausage sandwich fat.

From the corner of my eye I saw Lula make the sign of the cross again.

Lula caught me looking at her. "It's a comfort,"

Lula said. "I think the Catholics might have hit on something here."

The third race started, and Lula rocketed out of her seat. "Go, Ladies' Choice," she screamed. "Ladies' Choice! Ladies' Choice!"

Ladies' Choice won by a nose, and Lula looked stunned. "I won again," she said. "There's something wrong here. I never win."

"Why did you pick Ladies' Choice?"

"It was the obvious one. I'm a lady. And I had to make a choice."

"You think you're a lady?"

"Fuckin' A," Lula said.

This time, I followed her out of the grandstand to the window. She was moving carefully, looking around, trying to avoid another meeting with Abruzzi. I was looking around for the opposite reason.

Lula stopped and went rigid. "There he is," she said. "Over there at the fifty-dollar window."

I saw him, too. He was third in line. Darrow was behind him. I could feel every muscle in my body go into contraction. It was like I was squinting from my eyeballs clear down to my sphincter.

I marched over and got right up into Abruzzi's face. "Hey," I said, "remember me?"

"Of course," Abruzzi said. "I have your picture in a frame on my desk. Do you know you sleep with your mouth open? It's actually very sensuous."

I went still, hoping not to show emotion. Truth is, he knocked the air out of my lungs. And he sent a stab of revulsion into me that sickened my stomach. I'd expected he'd say something about the photos. I hadn't expected this. "I guess you need to pull these idiot pranks to compensate for the fact that you're not having any success at locating Evelyn," I said. "She's got something you want and you can't get your hands on it, can you?"

Now it was Abruzzi's turn to go still. For a single terrifying moment I thought he was going to hit me. Then his composure returned, and the blood rushed back into his face. "You're a stupid little bitch," he said.

"Yep," I said. "And I'm your worst nightmare." Okay, it was sort of a hokey movie line, but I've *always* wanted to say it. "And I'm not impressed with the rabbit thing. It was clever the first time when you carted Soder into my apartment, but it's getting tired."

"You said you liked bunnies," Abruzzi said. "Don't you like them anymore?"

"Get a life," I said. "Find yourself a new hobby."

And I turned on my heel and stalked off.

Lula was waiting at the mouth of the tunnel that led to our seats. "What'd you say to him?"

"I told him to let it ride on Peaches' Dream in the fourth."

"The hell you did," Lula said. "Not often you see a man turn white like that."

By the time I got to my seat my knees were knocking together, and my hands were shaking so bad I was having a hard time hanging onto my program.

"Jeez," Lula said, "you aren't having a heart attack or anything, are you?"

"I'm okay," I said. "It's the excitement of the horse racing."

"Yeah, I figured that was it."

A hysterical giggle escaped from my mouth. "It's not like Abruzzi scares me."

"Sure, I know that," Lula said. "Nothing scares you. You're a big badass bounty hunter."

"Damn right," I said. And then I concentrated on not hyperventilating.

"WE SHOULD DO THIS MORE OFTEN," LULA SAID, GETting out of my car, unlocking the Trans Am.

She was parked on the street in front of the office. The office was closed, but the new bookstore in the house next door was open. Lights were on, and I could see Maggie Mason unpacking boxes in the window.

"I had a setback in the last race," Lula said, "but aside from that I had a very good day. I just let it ride. Next time we could go to Freehold, and then we don't have to worry about running into *you know who*."

Lula drove off, but I stayed. I was like Evelyn now. On the run. No place safe to settle. For lack of something better, I went to the movies. Halfway through the movie I got up and left. I got into my car, and I went home. I parked in the lot, and I didn't allow myself to hesitate behind the wheel. I got out of the CR-V, beeped it locked, and walked straight to the back door that led to the lobby. I took the elevator to the second floor, marched down the hall, and unlocked the door to my apartment. I took a deep breath and stepped inside. It was very quiet. And dark.

I flipped the lights on ... every single light I

owned. I walked room to room, avoiding the cootie couch. I went back to the kitchen, removed six cookies from the bag of frozen chocolate chip cookies, and put them on a cookie sheet. I popped them into the oven and stood there, waiting. Five minutes later, the house smelled like homemade cookies. Bolstered by cookie fumes, I marched into the living room and looked at the couch. The couch looked fine. No stains. No dead body imprint.

You see, Stephanie, I said to myself. The couch is okay. No reason to be creeped out by the couch.

Hah! An invisible Irma whispered in my ear. Everyone knows you can't *see* death cooties. Take my word for it, that couch has the biggest, fattest death cooties that ever existed. That couch has the mother of all death cooties.

I tried to sit on the couch but I couldn't bring myself to do it. Soder and the couch were fixed together in my mind. Sitting on the couch was like sitting on Soder's dead, sawed-in-half lap. The apartment was too small for both me *and* the couch. One of us was going to have to go.

"Sorry," I said to the couch. "Nothing personal, but you're history." I put my weight behind one end, and I pushed the couch across the living room, into the small entrance foyer in front of the kitchen, out the front door, and into the hall. I positioned it against the wall between my apartment and Mrs. Karwatt's apartment. Then I ran back into my apartment, closed my door, and did a sigh. I knew there were no such things as death cooties. Unfortunately, that's an intellectual fact. And death cooties are an emotional reality.

I took the cookies out of the oven, put them on a plate, and carted them off to the living room. I zapped the television on and found a movie. Irma hadn't said anything about death cooties on the remote, so I assumed death cooties didn't stick to electronic devices. I pulled a dining room chair over to the television, ate two of the cookies, and watched the movie.

Halfway through the movie, the doorbell rang. It was Ranger. Dressed in his usual black. Full utility belt, looking like Rambo. Hair tied back. He stood there in silence when I opened the door. The corners of his mouth tipped slightly into the promise of a smile.

"Babe, your couch is in the hall."

"It has death cooties."

"I knew there'd be a good explanation."

I shook my head at him. "You're such a show-off." Not only had he placed me at the track, his horse had paid off five to one.

"Even superheroes need to have fun once in a while," he said, looking me over, brushing past me, walking into the living room. "It smells like you're marking your territory with chocolate chip cookies."

"I needed something to chase away the demons."

"Any problems?"

"Nope." Not since I pushed the couch into the hall. "So what's up?" I said. "You look like you're dressed for work."

"I had to secure a building earlier this evening."

I'd once been with him when his team secured a

building. It involved throwing a drug dealer out a third-story window.

He took a cookie off the plate on the floor. "Frozen?"

"Not anymore."

"How'd it go at the track?"

"I ran into Eddie Abruzzi."

"And?"

"We had words. I didn't find out as much as I'd hoped, but I'm convinced Evelyn has something he wants."

"I know what it is," Ranger said, eating his cookie.

I stared at him openmouthed. "What is it?"

He smiled. "How bad do you want to know?"

"Are we playing?"

He slowly shook his head no. "This isn't play." He backed me against the wall, and he leaned into me. His leg slid between mine, his lips brushed lightly across my lips. "How bad do you want to know, Steph?" he asked again.

"*Tell me.*"

"It'll get added to the debt."

Like I was going to worry about that now? I was in way over my credit limit weeks ago! "Are you going to tell me, or what?"

"Remember I told you Abruzzi is a war gamer? Well, he does more than game. He collects memorabilia. Old guns, army uniforms, military medals. And he doesn't just collect them. He wears them. Mostly when he games. Sometimes when he's with women, I'm told. Sometimes when he's settling a bad debt. Word on the street is that Abruzzi is missing a medal.

Supposedly the medal belonged to Napoleon. The story being told is that Abruzzi tried to buy the medal, but the guy who owned it wouldn't sell it, so Abruzzi killed him and took the medal. Abruzzi kept the medal on his desk at his house. He wore it when he gamed. Believed it made him invincible."

"And this is what Evelyn has? The medal?"

"That's what I hear."

"How did she get it?"

"I don't know."

He moved against me and desire skittered through my stomach and burned low in my belly. He was hard *everywhere*. His thigh, his gun ... *everything* was hard.

He lowered his head and kissed my neck. He touched his tongue to the place he just kissed. And then he kissed it again. His hand slid under my T-shirt, his palm heating my skin, his fingers at the base of my breast.

"Pay-up time," he said. "I'm collecting on the debt."

I almost collapsed onto the floor.

He took my hand and tugged me toward the bedroom. "The movie," I said. "The best part of the movie is coming up." In all honesty, I couldn't remember a single thing about the movie. Not the name or anyone in it.

He was standing close, his face inches from mine, his hand at the back of my neck. "We're going to do this, babe," he said. "It's going to be good." And then he kissed me. The kiss deepened, became more demanding, more intimate.

I had my hands splayed over his chest, and I felt the toned muscle under my hands, felt his heart beating. So he has a heart, I thought. That's a good sign. He must be at least *part* human.

He broke from the kiss and pushed me into the bedroom. He kicked his boots off, dropped his gun belt, and he stripped. The light was low, but it was enough to see that what Ranger promised in SWAT clothes was kept when the clothes were shed. He was all firm muscle and smooth dark skin. His body was in perfect proportion. His eyes were intense and focused.

He peeled my clothes off and wrangled me onto the bed. And then suddenly he was inside me. He once told me that time spent with him would ruin me for all other men. When he said it, I thought it was an outrageous threat. I no longer thought it outrageous.

We lay together for a while when we were done. Finally he ran his hand the length of my body. "It's time," he said.

"*Now* what?"

"You didn't think the debt would be paid that easily, did you?"

"Uh-oh, is this the part with the handcuffs?"

"I don't need handcuffs to enslave a woman," Ranger said, kissing my shoulder.

He kissed me lightly on my lips and then dipped his head to kiss my chin, my neck, my collarbone. He moved lower, kissing the swell of my breast and my nipple. He kissed my navel and then my belly, and then he put his mouth to my . . . *omigod!*

• • •

HE WAS STILL IN MY BED THE NEXT MORNING. HE was pressed next to me, his arm holding me close. I woke to the sound of the alarm on his watch. He shut the alarm off and rolled away to check the pager that had been placed on the nightstand, next to his gun.

"I have to go, babe," he said. And he was dressed. And he was gone.

Oh shit. What did I do? I just did *it* with the Wizard. Holy crap! Okay, calm down. Let's examine this more sanely. What just happened here? We did *it.* And he left. The leaving seemed a smidgen abrupt, but then it was Ranger. What did I expect? And he hadn't been abrupt last night. He'd been . . . amazing. I sighed and heaved myself out of bed. I showered and dressed and went into the kitchen to say good morning to Rex. Only there was no Rex. Rex was living with my parents.

The house felt empty without Rex, so I packed myself off to my parents'. It was Sunday and there was the added incentive of doughnuts. My mother and grandmother always bought doughnuts on their way home from church.

The horse kid was galloping through the house in her Sunday School dress. She stopped galloping when she saw me and her face grew thoughtful. "Have you found Annie yet?"

"No," I said. "But I talked to her mom on the phone."

"Next time you talk to her mom you should tell her Annie's missing stuff at school. Tell her I got put in the Black Stallion reading group."

"You're telling another whopper," Grandma said. "You're in the Blue Bird reading group."

"I don't want to be a blue bird," Mary Alice said. "Blue birds are poopy. I want to be a black stallion." And she galloped away.

"I love that kid," I said to Grandma.

"Yep," Grandma said. "She reminds me a lot of you when you were that age. Good imagination. It comes from my side of the family. Except it skipped a generation with your mother. Your mother and Valerie and Angie are blue birds through and through."

I helped myself to a doughnut and poured out a cup of coffee.

"You look different," Grandma said to me. "I can't put my finger on it. And you've been smiling ever since you walked in."

Damn Ranger. I noticed the smile when I brushed my teeth. It wouldn't go away! "Amazing what a good night's sleep can do for you," I said to Grandma.

"I wouldn't mind having a smile like that," Grandma said.

Valerie came to the table, looking morose. "I don't know what to do about Albert," she said.

"Not got a two-bathroom house?"

"He lives with his mother, and he has less money than I do."

No surprises there. "Good men are hard to find," I said. "And when you find them, there's always something wrong with them."

Valerie looked in the doughnut bag. "It's empty. Where's my doughnut?"

"Stephanie ate it," Grandma said.

"I only had one!"

"Oh," Grandma said, "then maybe it was me. I had three."

"We need more doughnuts," Valerie said. "I have to have a doughnut."

I grabbed my bag and hiked it onto my shoulder. "I'll get more. I could use another one, too."

"I'll go with you," Grandma said. "I want to ride in your shiny black car. I don't suppose you'd let me drive?"

My mother was at the stove. "Don't you *dare* let her drive. I'm holding you responsible. If she drives and gets in an accident, you're going to be the one visiting her in the nursing home."

We went to Tasty Pastry on Hamilton. I worked there when I was in high school. Gave away my virginity there, too. Behind the eclair case, after-hours, with Morelli. I'm not sure how it happened. One minute I was selling him a cannoli and next thing I knew I was on the floor with my pants down. Morelli's always been good at talking the pants off women.

I parked in the small lot on the side of Tasty Pastry. The after-church rush was over, and the lot was empty. There were seven parking slots that went nose in to the red brick wall of the bakery, and I parked square in the middle slot.

Grandma and I went into the bakery and picked out another dozen doughnuts. Probably overkill, but better to have too many than to be doughnut deprived.

We came out of the bakery, and we were approaching Ranger's CR-V when a green Ford Explorer careened into the lot and came to a screeching halt next to us. The driver had a rubber Clinton mask over his face, and the passenger seat was occupied by the rabbit.

My heart went *ka-thunk* in my chest, and I got a rush of adrenaline. "Run," I said, shoving Grandma, plunging my hand into my bag to find my gun. "Run back to the bakery."

The guy in the rubber mask and the guy in the rabbit suit were out of the car before it stopped rolling. They rushed at Grandma and me with guns drawn and herded us between the two cars. The rubber mask guy was of average height and build. He was wearing jeans and running shoes and a Nike jacket. The rabbit was wearing the big rabbit head and street clothes.

"Against the car, and hands where I can see them," the mask guy said.

"Who are you supposed to be?" Grandma asked. "You look like Bill Clinton."

"Yeah, I'm Bill Clinton," the guy said. "Get against the car."

"I never understood that part about the cigar," Grandma said.

"*Get against the car!*"

I backed against the car and my mind was racing. Cars were moving on the street in front of us, but we were hidden from sight. If I screamed I doubted I'd be heard by anyone, unless someone walked by on the sidewalk.

The rabbit got up close to me. "*Thaaa id ya raa raa da haaar id ra raa.*"

"What?"

"*Haaar id ra raa.*"

"We can't figure out what you're saying, on account of you're wearing that big stupid rabbit head," Grandma said.

"*Raa raa,*" the rabbit said. "*Raa raa!*"

Grandma and I looked over at Clinton.

Clinton shook his head in disgust. "I don't know what he's saying. What the hell's *raa raa?*" he asked the rabbit.

"*Haaar id ra raa.*"

"Christ," Clinton said. "Nobody can understand you. Haven't you ever tried to talk in that thing before?"

The rabbit gave Clinton a shove. "*Ra raa,* you fraaakin' *aar* ho."

Clinton flipped the rabbit the bird.

"*Jaaaark,*" the rabbit said. And then he unzipped his pants and pulled out his wanger. He waggled his wanger at Clinton. And then he waggled it at Grandma and me.

"I remember them as being bigger than that," Grandma said.

The rabbit yanked and pulled at himself and managed to get half a hard-on.

"*Rogga. Ga rogga,*" the rabbit said.

"I think he's trying to tell you this is a preview," Clinton said. "Something to look forward to."

The rabbit was still working it. He'd found his rhythm, and he was really whacking away.

"Maybe you should help him out," Clinton said to me. "Go ahead. Touch it."

My lip curled back. "What are you nuts? I'm not touching it!"

"I'll touch it," Grandma said.

"*Kraaa,*" the rabbit said. And his wanger wilted a little.

A car turned off the street, into the lot, and Clinton gave the rabbit a shot in the arm. "Let's roll."

They backed up, still holding us at gunpoint. Both men jumped into the Explorer and took off.

"Maybe we should have got some cannoli," Grandma said. "I got a sudden taste for cannoli."

I loaded Grandma into the CR-V and drove her back to the house.

"We saw that rabbit again," Grandma told my mother. "The one who gave me the pictures. I think he must live by the bakery. This time he showed us his ding-a-ling."

My mother was justifiably horrified.

"Was he wearing a wedding band?" Valerie asked.

"I didn't notice," Grandma said. "I wasn't looking at his hand."

"You were held at gunpoint and sexually assaulted," I said to Grandma. "Weren't you frightened? Aren't you upset?"

"They weren't real guns," Grandma said. "And we were in the parking lot to the bakery. Who would be serious about something like that in a bakery parking lot?"

"They were real guns," I said.

"Are you sure?"

"*Yes.*"

"Maybe I'll sit down," Grandma said. "I thought that rabbit was just one of those exhibitionists. Remember Sammy the Squirrel? He was always dropping his drawers in people's backyards. Sometimes we'd give him a sandwich after."

The Burg has had its share of exhibitionists, some mentally challenged, some drunk beyond reason, some just out for a good time. For the most part, the attitude is eye-rolling tolerance. Once in a while someone drops his drawers in the wrong backyard and ends up with an ass filled with buckshot.

I called Morelli and told him about the rabbit. "He was with Clinton," I said. "And they weren't getting along all that great."

"You should file a report."

"There's only one body part I'd ever recognize on this guy, and I don't think you've got it in the mug books."

"Are you carrying a gun?"

"Yes. I didn't have time to get to it."

"Put it on your hip. It's illegal to carry concealed anyway. And it wouldn't be a bad idea to actually put a couple bullets in it."

"I *have* bullets in it." Ranger put them in. "Have they identified the guy in the trunk yet?"

"Thomas Turkello. Also known as Thomas Turkey. Muscle for hire out of Philadelphia. My guess is he was expendable, and better to snuff him than take a chance on him talking. The rabbit is probably inner circle."

"Anything else?"

"What would you want?"

"Abruzzi's fingerprint on a murder weapon."

"Sorry."

I was reluctant to disconnect, but I didn't have anything else to say. The truth is, I had a hollow feeling in my stomach that I hated to put a name to. I was mortally afraid it was loneliness. Ranger was fire and magic, but he wasn't real. Morelli was everything I wanted in a man, but he wanted me to be something I wasn't.

I hung up and retreated to the living room. If you sat in front of the television in my parents' house, you weren't expected to talk. Even if asked a direct question, the viewer had the discretion of feigning hearing loss. Those were the rules.

Grandma and I were side by side on the sofa, watching the Weather Channel. Hard to tell which of us was more shell-shocked.

"I guess it's a good thing I didn't touch it," Grandma said. "Although, I gotta admit, I *was* kind of curious. It wasn't real pretty, but it was big toward the end there. Have you ever seen one that big?"

The perfect time to invoke the television no-answer privilege.

After a couple minutes of weather I went back to the kitchen and had my second doughnut. I collected my things and I headed out. "I'm going," I said to Grandma. "All's well that ends well, right?"

Grandma didn't answer. Grandma was zoned out to the Weather Channel. There was a high pressure area moving across the Great Lakes.

I went back to my apartment. This time I had my gun in my hand before I got out of the car. I crossed the lot and entered the building. I paused when I got to my door. This was always the tricky part. Once I was in the apartment I felt fairly secure. I had a security chain and a bolt besides the deadlock. Only Ranger could get in unannounced. Either he walked through the door ghost style, or else he vaporized himself like a vampire and slid under the jamb. I guess there might be a mortal possibility, but I didn't know what it was.

I unlocked my door and searched through my apartment like the movie version of a CIA operative, skulking from room to room, gun drawn, crouched position, ready to fire. I was crashing open doors and jumping around. Good thing no one was there to see me because I knew I looked like an idiot. The good part was, I didn't find any rabbits with their tools hanging out. Compared to rape by the rabbit, spiders and snakes seemed like small change.

Ranger called ten minutes after I got into my apartment.

"Are you going to be home for a while?" he asked. "I want to send someone over to set up a security system."

So the man of mystery reads minds, too.

"My man's name is Hector," Ranger said. "He's on his way."

Hector was slim and Hispanic, dressed in black. He had a gang slogan tattooed onto his neck and a single tear tattooed under his eye. He was in his early twenties, and he only spoke Spanish.

Hector had my door open and was making a final adjustment when Ranger arrived. Ranger gave a barely audible greeting to Hector in Spanish and glanced at the sensor that had just been installed in my doorjamb.

Then Ranger looked at me, giving away nothing of his thoughts. Our eyes held for a few long moments, and Ranger turned back to Hector. My Spanish is limited to burrito and taco, so I couldn't understand the exchange between Ranger and Hector. Hector was talking and gesturing, and Ranger was listening and questioning. Hector gave Ranger a small gizmo, picked up his tool chest, and left.

Ranger crooked his finger at me, giving me the *come here* sign. "This is your remote. It's a keypad, small enough to hook to your car key. You have a four-digit code to open and close your door. If the door has been violated the remote will tell you. You're not attached to a watchdog. There's no alarm. This is designed to give you easy access and to tell you if someone's broken into your apartment, so you have no more surprises. You have a steel fire door, and Hector's installed a floor bolt. If you lock yourself in, you should be safe. There's not much I can do about your windows. The fire escape is a problem. It's less of a problem if you keep your gun on your nightstand."

I looked down at the remote. "Does this go on the tab?"

"There's no tab. And there's no price for what we give each other. Not ever. Not financial. Not emotional. I have to get back to work."

He stepped away to leave, and I grabbed him by the front of his shirt. "Not so fast. This isn't television. This is my life. I want to know more about this no-emotional-price thing?"

"It's the way it has to be."

"And what's this job you have to get back to?"

"I'm running a surveillance operation for a government agency. We're independent contractors. You aren't going to grill me on details, are you?"

I released his shirt and blew out a sigh. "I can't do this. This isn't going to work."

"I know," Ranger said. "You need to repair your relationship with Morelli."

"We needed a time-out."

"I'm being a good guy right now because it suits my purposes, but I'm an opportunist, and I'm attracted to you. And I'll be back in your bed if the Morelli time-out goes on for too long. I could make you forget Morelli if I put my mind to it. That wouldn't be good for either of us."

"Yeesh."

Ranger smiled. "Lock your door." And he was gone.

I locked my door, and I set the floor bolt. Ranger had successfully taken my mind off the masturbating rabbit. Now if I could just get my mind to stop thinking about Ranger. I knew everything Ranger said was true, with the possible exception of forgetting Morelli. It wasn't easy to forget Morelli. I'd put a lot of effort into it over the years, but had never been successful.

My phone rang, and someone made kissy sounds to me. I hung up, and it rang again. More kissy sounds. When it rang a third time I pulled the plug.

A half hour later, someone was at my door. "I know you're in there," Vinnie yelled. "I saw the CR-V in the parking lot."

I unlocked the floor bolt, the door bolt, the security chain, and the dead bolt.

"Jesus Christ," Vinnie said when I finally opened the door. "You'd think there was something valuable in this rat trap."

"*I'm* valuable."

"Not as a bounty hunter, you aren't. Where's Bender? I've got two days to produce Bender, or I pay the money to the court."

"You're here to tell me that?"

"Yeah. I figured you needed some reminding. I've got my mother-in-law at my house today, driving me nuts. I thought this would be a good time to get Bender. I tried to call you, but your phone isn't working."

What the hell, I didn't have anything else to do. I was sitting here trapped in my apartment with my phone disconnected.

I left Vinnie to wait in the entrance hall, and I went in search of my gun belt. I returned with the black nylon web holster strapped to my leg and my .38 loaded and ready for quick draw.

"Whoa," Vinnie said, clearly impressed. "You're finally serious."

Right. Serious about not getting porked by a rabbit. We cruised out of the lot with me driving and Vinnie working the radio. I turned toward the center of town, keeping one eye on the road ahead and one eye on the rearview mirror. A green SUV came up behind me. He cut over a double line and passed me. The guy in the Clinton mask was behind the wheel, and the big ugly rabbit was riding shotgun. The rabbit turned and popped up through the sun roof and looked back at me. His ears were whipping around in the wind, and he was holding his head on with both hands.

"It's the rabbit," I yelled. "Shoot him! Take my gun and shoot him!"

"What are you, nuts?" Vinnie said. "I can't shoot an unarmed rabbit."

I was struggling, trying to get my gun out of the holster, trying to drive at the same time.

"*I'm* going to shoot him then. I don't care if I get sent to jail. It'll be worth it. I'm going to shoot him in his stupid rabbit head." I wrenched the gun out of the holster, but I didn't want to shoot through Ranger's windshield. "Take the wheel," I yelled to Vinnie. I opened the window, leaned out, and got off a shot.

The rabbit instantly retreated into the car. The SUV accelerated and turned left, onto a side street. I waited for traffic to pass, and then I turned left, also. I saw them ahead of me. They were turning and turning until we went full circle, and we were back on State. The SUV pulled up at a convenience store, and the two men took off on foot, around the brick building. I slid to a stop beside the Explorer. Vinnie and I jumped from the CR-V and ran after the men. We chased them for a couple blocks, they cut through a yard, and they disappeared.

Vinnie was bent at the waist, sucking air. "Why are we chasing a rabbit?"

"It's the rabbit who firebombed my CR-V."

"Oh yeah. Now I remember. I should have asked

sooner. I would have stayed in the car. Jesus, I can't believe you got off a shot hanging out the window. Who do you think you are, the Terminator? Christ, your mother would have my nuts if she knew you did that. What were you thinking?"

"I got excited."

"You weren't excited. You were berserk!"

FOURTEEN

WE WERE IN A NEIGHBORHOOD OF LARGE OLD houses. Some of them had been renovated. And some were waiting for renovation. Some had been turned into apartment buildings. Most of the houses were on good-size lots and sat back from the road. The rabbit and his partner had disappeared around the side of one of the apartment houses. Vinnie and I prowled around the house, standing still from time to time, listening, hoping the rabbit would give himself away. We checked between cars parked in the driveway, and we looked behind shrubs.

"I don't see them," Vinnie said. "I think they're gone. Either they slipped past us and doubled back to their car, or else they're holed up in this house."

We both looked at the house.

"Do you want to search the house?" Vinnie asked.

It was a big Victorian. I'd been in houses like this before, and they were filled with closets and hallways and closed doors. Good houses for hiding. Bad houses for searching. Especially for a chickenshit like me. Now that I was out in the air, sanity was returning. And the longer I was out walking around, the less I wanted to find the rabbit.

"I think I'll pass on the house."

"Good call," Vinnie said. "Easy to get your head blown off in a house like this. Of course, that wouldn't figure into the equation for you, because you're so freaking nuts. You've gotta stop watching those old Al Capone movies."

"You should talk. What about the time you shot up Pinwheel Soba's house? You just about destroyed it."

Vinnie's face creased into a smile. "I got lost in the moment."

We walked back to the car with guns still drawn, staying alert to sounds and movement. Half a block from the convenience store, we saw smoke billowing from the other side of the brick building. The smoke was black and acrid, smelling like burning rubber. The sort of smoke you get when a car catches fire.

Sirens were wailing in the distance, and I had another one of those parakeet-flying-away feelings. Dread in the pit of my stomach. It was followed by a rush of calm that signaled the arrival of denial. It couldn't possibly be happening. Not another car. Not *Ranger's* car. It had to be *someone else's* car. I started making deals with God. Let it be the Explorer, I suggested to God, and I'll be a better person. I'll go to church. I'll eat more vegetables. I'll stop abusing the shower massage.

We turned the corner and, sure enough, Ranger's car was burning. Okay, that's it, I told God. All deals are *off*.

"Holy crap," Vinnie said. "That's your car. That's the second CR-V you've burned up this week. This might set a new record for you."

The clerk was standing outside, watching the spectacle. "I saw the whole thing," he said. "It was a big rabbit. He rushed into the store and got a can of barbecue starter fuel. And then he poured it in the black car and lit a match to it. Then he drove away in the green SUV."

I holstered my gun, and I sat on the cement apron in front of the store. Bad enough the car was totaled, my bag had been in it. My credit cards, my driver's license, my lip gloss, my defense spray, and my new cell phone were all gone. And I'd left the keys in the ignition. And the keypad to my security system was hooked onto the key ring.

Vinnie sat next to me. "I always have a good time when I go out with you," Vinnie said. "We should do this more often."

"Do you have your cell phone on you?"

Morelli was the first number I dialed, but Morelli wasn't home. I hung my head. Ranger was next on the list.

"Yo," Ranger said when he answered.

"Small problem."

"No kidding. Your car just went off the screen."

"It sort of burned up."

Silence.

"And you know that keypad you gave me? It was in the car."

"Babe."

VINNIE AND I WERE STILL SITTING ON THE CURB when Ranger arrived. Ranger was dressed in jeans and a black T-shirt and boots, and he looked almost normal. He glanced at the smoldering car, then he looked at me and shook his head. The head shake was actually more the *suggestion* of a head shake. I didn't want to try to guess the thought that prompted the head shake. I didn't imagine it would be good. He spoke to one of the cops and gave him a card. Then he collected Vinnie and me and brought us back to my apartment building. Vinnie got into his Caddie and took off.

Ranger smiled and gestured to the gun on my hip. "Looking good, babe. Did you shoot anyone today?"

"I tried."

He gave a soft laugh, crooked his arm around my neck, and kissed me just above my ear.

Hector was waiting for us in the hall. Hector looked like he should be wearing an orange jumpsuit and leg irons. But hey, what do I know? Probably Hector is a real nice guy. Probably he doesn't know that a teardrop under the eye signifies a gang kill. And even if he *does* know, it's only *one* teardrop, so it's not like he's a *serial* killer, right?

Hector gave Ranger a new keypad, and he said something in Spanish. Ranger said something back, they did one of those complicated handshakes, and Hector left.

Ranger beeped my door open and went in with me. "Hector's already been through. He said the apartment is clean." He put the keypad on the kitchen counter. "The new keypad is programmed exactly like the last."

"Sorry about the car."

"It was just a matter of time, babe. I'll write it off as entertainment." He glanced at the readout on his pager. "I have to go. Make sure you engage the floor bolt when I leave."

I kicked the bolt into place, and I paced around in my kitchen. Pacing is supposed to be calming, but the more I paced, the more annoyed I became. I needed a car for tomorrow, and I wasn't going to take another car from Ranger. I didn't like being entertainment. Not automotive entertainment. Not sexual entertainment.

Ah hah! a voice inside me said. Now we're getting somewhere. This pacing you're doing isn't about the car. This is about the sex. You're all bummed out because you got boinked by a man who wanted nothing more than physical sex. *Do you know what you are?* the voice asked. *You're a hypocrite.*

So? I said to the voice. And? What's your point?

I thrashed through my cupboards and refrigerator looking for a Tastykake. I knew there were none left, but I looked anyway. Another exercise in futility. My specialty.

Okay. Fine. I'll go out and buy some. I grabbed the keypad Ranger left for me, and I stomped out of the apartment. I slammed the door shut, punched in the code, and realized I was standing out there with nothing but a keypad. No car keys. Unnecessary, of course, because I didn't have a car. Also, I was without money and credit cards. Large sigh. I needed to go back inside and rethink this.

I punched in the code and tried the door. The door wouldn't open. I put the code in again. Nothing. I didn't have a key. All I had was the damn stupid keypad. No reason to panic. I had to be doing something wrong. I went through it again. It wasn't that complicated. Punch in the numbers and the door unlocks. Maybe I was remembering the numbers wrong. I tried a couple other combinations. No luck.

Piece of shit technology. I hate technology. Technology *sucks*.

Okay, take it easy, I told myself. You don't want a repeat performance of the car window shoot-out. You don't want to go gonzo over a silly keypad. I took a couple deep breaths, and I fed the numbers into the keypad one more time. I grabbed the doorknob and pulled and twisted, but the door wouldn't open.

"Goddamn!" I threw the keypad down on the floor and jumped up and down. *"Damn, damn, damn!"* I kicked the keypad all the way to the far end of the hall. I ran down the hall, unholstered my gun, and shot the keypad. *BAM!* The keypad jumped, and I shot it again.

An Asian woman opened the door across the hall. She looked out at me, gave a gasp, pulled back inside, and closed and locked her door.

"Sorry," I called out to her, through the door. "I got carried away."

I retrieved the mangled keypad and skulked back to my half of the hall.

My next door neighbor, Mrs. Karwatt, was in her doorway. "Are you having a problem, dear?" she asked.

"I'm locked out of my apartment." Fortunately, Mrs. Karwatt kept a key.

Mrs. Karwatt gave me the spare key, I inserted it in the lock, and the door wouldn't open. I followed Mrs. Karwatt into her house, and I used her phone to call Ranger.

"The frigging door won't open," I said.

"I'll send Hector."

"No! I can't understand Hector. I can't talk to him." And he scares the bejeezus out of me.

Twenty minutes later, I was sitting in the hall with my back to the wall, and Ranger and Hector showed up.

"What's wrong?" Ranger asked.

"The door won't open."

"Probably just a programming glitch. Do you have the keypad?"

I dropped the keypad into his hand.

Ranger and Hector looked down at the keypad. They looked up at each other, exchanged raised eyebrows, and smiled.

"I think I see the problem," Ranger said. "Someone's shot the shit out of this keypad." He turned it over in his hand. "At least you were able to hit it. Nice to know the target practice paid off."

"I'm good at close range."

It took Hector twenty seconds to open my door and ten minutes to remove the sensors.

"Let me know if you want the system put back in," Ranger said.

"I appreciate the thought, but I'd rather walk blind-folded into an apartment filled with alligators."

"Do you want to try your luck with another car? We could raise the stakes. I could give you a Porsche."

"Tempting, but no. I'm expecting an insurance check tomorrow. As soon as I get it, I'll have Lula drive me to a dealer."

Ranger and Hector took off, and I locked myself into my apartment. I'd worked out a lot of aggression shooting the keypad, and I felt much more mellow now. My heart was only skipping a beat once in a while, and the eye twitch was hardly noticeable. I ate the last lump of frozen cookie dough. It wasn't a Tastykake, but it was pretty good, all the same. I zapped the television on and found a hockey game.

"UH-OH," LULA SAID THE NEXT MORNING. "WAS that a taxi that brought you to the office? What happened to Ranger's car?"

"It burned up."

"Say what?"

"And my bag was in it. I need to go shopping for a new handbag."

"I'm the woman for the job," Lula said. "What time is it? Are the stores open yet?"

It was ten o'clock, Monday morning. The stores

were open. I'd reported my melted credit cards. I was
ready to roll.

"Hold on," Connie said. "What about the filing?"

"The filing's just about all done," Lula said. She
took a stack of files and shoved them into a drawer.
"Anyway, we aren't gonna be long. Stephanie always
gets the same boring bag. She goes straight to the
Coach counter and gets one of them big-ass black
leather shoulder bags, and that's the end of that."

"Turns out that my driver's license burned up, too,"
I said. "I was hoping you might also give me a ride
to the DMV."

Connie did a big eye roll. "Go."

IT WAS NOON WHEN WE GOT TO QUAKER BRIDGE
Mall. I bought my shoulder bag, and then Lula and I
tested out some perfume. We were on the upper level,
walking toward the escalators on our way to leave for
the lot, and a familiar shape loomed in front of me.

"You!" Martin Paulson said. "What is it with you?
I can't get away from you."

"Don't start with me," I said. "I'm not happy with
you."

"Gee, that's too bad. I almost really care. What are
you doing here today? Looking for somebody new to
brutalize?"

"I didn't brutalize you."

"You knocked me down."

"You *fell* down. Twice."

"I told you I have a bad sense of balance."

"Look, just get out of my way. I'm not going to
stand here and argue with you."

"Yeah, you heard her," Lula said. "Get out of her way."

Paulson turned to better see Lula, and apparently he was caught off guard by what he saw, because he lost his balance and fell backward, down the escalator. There were a couple people in front of him, and he knocked them over like bowling pins. They all landed in a heap on the floor.

Lula and I scrambled down the escalator to the pile of bodies.

Paulson seemed to be the only one who was hurt. "My leg's broken," he said. "I bet you anything my leg's broken. I keep telling you, I have a problem with equilibrium. Nobody ever listens to me."

"There's probably a good reason why no one listens to you," Lula said. "You look like a big bag of wind, if you ask me."

"It's all your fault," Paulson said. "You scared the hell out of me. They should get the fashion police out after you. And what's with the yellow hair? You look like Harpo Marx."

"Hunh," Lula said. "I'm outta here. I'm not standing here getting insulted. I got to get back to work anyway."

We were in the car at the exit to the parking lot, and Lula stopped short. "Hold on. Do I have my shopping bags in the backseat?"

I turned and looked. "No."

"Damn! I must have dropped them when that sack of monkey doodie pushed me."

"No problem. Pull up to the door, and I'll run in and get them."

Lula drove to the entrance, and I retraced our steps, back to the middle of the mall. I had to walk past Paulson to get to the escalator. The EMTs had him on a stretcher and were getting ready to wheel him out. I took the escalator to the second level and found the shopping bags laying on the floor by the bench, right where Lula had left them.

Thirty minutes later, we were back at the office, and Lula had her bags spread out on the couch. "Uh-oh," she said. "We got one too many bags. You see this here big brown bag? It's not mine."

"It was on the floor with the other bags," I said.

"Oh boy," Lula said. "Are you thinking what I'm thinking? I don't even want to look in that bag. I got a bad feeling about that bag."

"You were right about the bad feeling," I said, looking into the bag. "There are a pair of pants in here that could only belong to Paulson. Plus a couple shirts. Oh crap, there's a box all wrapped up in happy birthday kid's wrapping paper."

"My suggestion is you throw that bag in the Dumpster, and you go wash your hands," Lula said.

"I can't do that. The guy just broke his leg. And there's a kid's birthday present in here."

"No big deal," Lula said. "He can go onto the Internet and steal some more stuff and get another present."

"This is my fault," I said. "I took Paulson's bag. I need to get it back to him."

There are several hospitals in the Trenton area. If Paulson was taken to St. Francis, I could walk up the street and give him his bag before he was discharged.

And there was a good chance Paulson was at St. Francis because it was the closest hospital to his home.

I called the switchboard and had them check with ER. I was told Paulson was indeed in ER, and they expected him to be there a while longer.

I wasn't looking forward to seeing Paulson, but it was a nice spring day, and it felt good to be outside. I decided I'd walk to the hospital, and then I'd walk to my parents' and mooch dinner and say hello to Rex. I had my new bag over my shoulder, and I was feeling confident because my gun was in my bag. Plus new lip gloss. Am I a professional, or what?

I swung along Hamilton for a couple blocks and then cut off just before the hospital's main entrance and took the side street to the emergency entrance. I found the nurse in charge and asked her to give the bag to Paulson.

So now I was off the hook, the bag was no longer my responsibility. I'd gone the extra mile to get it back to Paulson, and I left the hospital feeling all elated with my own goodness.

My parents lived behind the hospital, in the heart of the Burg. I walked past the parking garage and paused at the intersection. It was midafternoon, and there were few cars on the roads. Schools were still in session. Restaurants were empty.

A lone car rolled down the street and paused at the stop sign. A car was parked at the curb to my left. I heard a foot scrape against gravel. I turned my head at the sound. And the rabbit popped up from behind the parked car. He was fully suited this time.

"*Boo!*" he said.

I gave an involuntary shriek. He'd caught me by surprise. I shoved my hand into my bag in search of my gun, but a second person was suddenly in front of me, grabbing at my shoulder strap. It was the guy in the Clinton mask. If I could have gotten to my gun, I would gladly have shot them. And if it had been a single man, I might have been able to get to my gun. As it was, I was overpowered.

I went down kicking and screaming and clawing with both men on top of me. The streets were deserted, but I was making a lot of noise and there were houses nearby. If I yelled loud enough and long enough I knew I'd be heard. The car in the intersection wheeled around and rolled to a stop inches away from us.

The rabbit opened the back door and tried to drag me into the car. I was spread-eagle in the car door opening, hanging on with my fingernails, screaming my head off. The Clinton mask guy tried to grab my legs, and when he came in close I kicked out and caught him under the chin with my CAT. The guy staggered backward and keeled over. *Crash!* Flat on his back on the sidewalk.

The driver was out of the car now. He was wearing a Richard Nixon mask, and I was pretty sure I recognized the build. I was pretty sure it was Darrow. I wriggled away from the rabbit. Hard to hold onto things when you're wearing a rabbit suit with rabbit paws. I tripped on the curb and went down on one knee. I scrambled up and took off, running for all I was worth. The rabbit ran after me.

There was a car in the intersection, and I streaked

past it yelling. My voice felt hoarse, and I was probably croaking more than yelling. The knee was torn out of my jeans, my arm was scratched and bleeding, and my hair was in my face, wild and tangled from rolling on the ground with the rabbit. I barely glanced at the car, noting only that it was silver. I could hear the rabbit behind me. My lungs were burning, and I knew I couldn't outrun him. I was too scared to think ahead. I was blindly running down the street.

I heard the screech of wheels and a car motor getting gunned. Darrow, I thought. Coming to get me. I turned to look, and I saw it wasn't Darrow behind me. It was the silver car that had been in the intersection. It was a Buick LeSabre. And my mother was at the wheel. She ran flat-out into the rabbit. The rabbit did a flip off the car in an explosion of fake fur and landed in a crumpled heap at the side of the road. The Darrow-driven car slid to a stop beside the rabbit. Darrow and the other rubber mask guy got out, scooped the rabbit up, dumped him into the backseat, and took off.

My mother was stopped a few feet from me. I limped to the car, she popped the lock, and I got in.

"Holy Mary, mother of God," my mother said. "You were being chased by Richard Nixon, Bill Clinton, and a rabbit."

"Yeah," I said. "Good thing you came along when you did."

"I ran over the rabbit," she wailed. "I probably killed him."

"He was a bad rabbit. He deserved to die."

"He looked like the Easter bunny. I killed the Easter bunny," she sobbed.

I pulled a tissue out of my mother's purse and handed it to her. Then I looked through the purse more thoroughly. "You have any Valium in here? Any Klonapin or Ativan?"

My mother blew her nose and put the car in gear. "Do you have any idea what it's like for a mother to drive down the street and see her daughter being chased by a rabbit? I don't know why you can't have a normal job. Like your sister."

I rolled my eyes. My sister again. Saint Valerie.

"And she's dating a nice man," my mother said. "I think he has honorable intentions. And he's a lawyer. He'll make a good living someday." My mother drove back to the intersection, so I could retrieve my shoulder bag. "And what about you," she wanted to know. "Who are you dating?"

"Don't ask," I said. I wasn't dating anyone. I was fornicating with Batman.

"I'm not sure what I should do next," my mother said. "Do you think I should report this to the police? What would I say to them? I mean, how would it sound? I was on my way to Giovichinni's for lunch meat when I saw a rabbit chasing my daughter down the street, so I ran over him, but now he's gone."

"Remember when I was a kid, and we were all going to the movies, and Daddy hit the dog on Roebling? We got out and looked for the dog, but we couldn't find him. He just ran off somewhere."

"I felt terrible about that."

"Yeah, but we went to the movies anyway. Maybe we should just go get the lunch meat."

"It *was* a *rabbit*," my mother said. "And he had no business being in the road."

"Exactly."

We drove to Giovichinni's in silence and parked in front of the store. We both got out and looked at the front of the Buick. There was some rabbit fur stuck to the grille, but aside from that the LeSabre looked okay.

While my mother was talking to the butcher, I stole off and called Morelli on the outside pay phone. "This is a little awkward," I said, "but my mother just ran over the rabbit."

"Ran over?"

"As in *roadkill*. We're not sure what to do about it."

"Where are you?"

"Giovichinni's, buying lunch meat."

"And the rabbit?"

"Gone. He was with two other guys. They scooped him up off the road and drove away with him."

There was a long silence on the phone. "I'm fucking speechless," Morelli finally said.

An hour later, I heard Morelli's truck pull up in front of my parents' house. He was in jeans and boots and a cotton crew with the sleeves pushed up. The crew was loose enough to hide the gun that was always at his waist.

I'd showered and fixed my hair, but I didn't have fresh clothes to change into, so I was still in the torn, bloodstained jeans and dirt-smudged T-shirt. I had a ragged cut on my knee, a large scrape on my arm, and another on my cheek. I met Morelli on the porch and closed the door behind me. I didn't want Grandma Mazur joining us.

Morelli gave me the long, slow lookover. "I could kiss that cut on your knee and make it all better."

A skill acquired from years of playing doctor.

We sat side by side on the step, and I told him about the rabbit at the bakery and the attempted abduction at the intersection. "And I'm almost sure Darrow was driving," I said.

"Do you want me to have him brought in?"

"No. I couldn't positively ID him."

Morelli's face broke into a smile. "Your mother really ran the rabbit over?"

"She saw him chasing me. And she ran him over. Threw him about ten feet into the air."

"She likes you."

I nodded yes. And my eyes filled.

A car drove by. Two men.

"That could be them," I said. "Two of Abruzzi's guys. I try to be vigilant, but the cars are always different. And I only know Abruzzi and Darrow. The others have always had their faces covered. I have no good way of knowing when I'm being stalked. And it's worse at night when all I can see are lights coming and going."

"We're working overtime, trying to find Evelyn, canvassing the neighborhoods for witnesses, but so far there hasn't been a break. Abruzzi's got himself well protected."

"Do you need to talk to my mom about the rabbit thing?"

"Were there any witnesses?"

"Only the two guys in the car."

"We don't usually write up accidents involving rabbits. This *was* a *rabbit,* right?"

MORELLI DECLINED DINNER. I COULDN'T BLAME HIM. Valerie had Kloughn home with her, and the table was standing room only.

"Isn't he the cute one," Grandma whispered to me in the kitchen. "Just like the Pillsbury Doughboy."

After dinner I got my dad to drive me home.

"What do you think of this clown?" he asked on the way. "He seems to be sweet on Valerie. Do you think there's any chance this could turn into something?"

"He didn't get up and leave when Grandma asked him if he was a virgin. I thought that was a good sign."

"Yeah, he hung in there. He must really be desperate if he's willing to get involved with this family. Has anyone told him the horse kid belongs to Valerie?"

I figured there wasn't a problem with Mary Alice. Kloughn probably had empathy for a kid who was different. What Kloughn might not understand was Valerie in the fluffy pink slippers. Probably we should make sure he never sees the slippers.

It was almost nine when my dad dropped me off. The parking lot was filled and lights were on in all the apartment windows. The seniors were settled in

for the night, victims of failing night vision and television addiction. By nine o'clock they were happy
campers, having self-medicated with tumblers of
booze and *Diagnosis Murder*. At 10:00 they'd pop a
little white pill and hurl themselves into hours of sleep
apnea.

I approached my front door and decided I'd been
hasty in rejecting Ranger's security system. It would
be nice to know if someone was waiting for me inside.
I had my gun shoved into the waistband of my jeans.
And I had a plan outlined in my head. My plan was
to open the door, take the gun in hand, flip all the
lights on, and do another embarrassing imitation of a
television cop.

The kitchen was easy to cover. Nothing there. The
living room and dining room were next. Again, easy
to take in. The bathroom was more tense. I had the
shower curtain to contend with. I needed to remember
not to close the shower curtain. I ripped the shower
curtain open and let out a whoosh of air. No one dead
in my tub.

At first glance, my bedroom was fine. Unfortunately, I knew from past experience that the bedroom
was filled with hiding places for all sorts of nasty
things, like snakes. I looked under the bed and in all
my drawers. I opened my closet door and let out another whoosh of air. Nobody here. I'd gone through
the entire apartment and not found anyone, dead or
alive. I could lock myself in and feel perfectly safe.

I was leaving the bedroom when it hit me. A visual
memory of something odd. Something out of place. I
returned to my closet and opened the door. And there

it was, hanging with the rest of my clothes, smashed between my suede jacket and a denim shirt. The rabbit suit.

I snapped on rubber gloves, removed the rabbit suit from my closet, and deposited it in the elevator. I didn't want another full-scale crime-scene investigation assault on my apartment. I used the pay phone in the lobby to put in an anonymous call to the police about the suit in the elevator. And then I returned to my apartment and slid *Ghostbusters* into the DVD player.

Halfway through *Ghostbusters* I got a call from Morelli. "You wouldn't happen to know anything about the rabbit suit in your elevator, would you?"

"Who me?"

"Off the record, out of morbid curiosity, where did you find it?"

"It was hanging in my closet."

"Christ."

"Do you suppose this means the rabbit no longer needs the suit?" I asked.

I DIALED RANGER FIRST THING THE NEXT MORNING. "About that security system," I said.

"Are you still having visitors?"

"I found a rabbit suit in my closet last night."

"Anybody in it?"

"Nope. Just the suit."

"I'll send Hector."

"Hector scares the hell out of me."

"Yeah, me, too," Ranger said. "But he hasn't killed anybody in over a year now. And he's gay. You're probably safe."

FIFTEEN

THE NEXT CALL WAS FROM MORELLI. "I JUST GOT into work, and I heard an interesting piece of information," Morelli said to me. "Do you know Leo Klug?"

"No."

"He's a butcher at Sal Carto's Meat Market. Your mother probably gets her kielbasa there. Leo is about my height but heavier. He has a scar running the length of his face. Black hair."

"Okay. I know who you mean. I was in there a couple weeks ago, picking up some sausage, and he waited on me."

"It's pretty well known here that Klug has done some contract butchering."

"You're not talking about cows."

"Cows are the day job," Morelli said.

"I have a feeling I'm not going to like the direction of this conversation."

"Lately, Klug has been hanging out with a couple guys who work for Abruzzi. And this morning, Klug turned up dead, the victim of a hit-and-run."

"Omigod."

"He was found on the side of the road half a block from the butcher shop."

"Any idea who hit him?"

"No, but statistics are high for a drunk driver."

We pondered that for a moment.

"Probably your mother should run the LeSabre through a car wash," Morelli said.

"Holy crap. My mother killed Leo Klug."

"I didn't hear that," Morelli said.

I got off the phone and made some coffee. I scrambled an egg and popped a piece of bread into the toaster. Stephanie Plum, domestic goddess. I sneaked out into the hall, swiped Mr. Wolesky's paper, and read it with my breakfast.

I was returning the paper when Ranger and Hector stepped out of the elevator.

"I know where she is," Ranger said. "I just got a call. Let's roll."

I cut my eyes to Hector.

"Don't worry about Hector," Ranger said.

I grabbed my bag and a jacket and ran to keep up with Ranger. He was driving the bug-eyed truck again. I hauled myself up to seat level and buckled in.

"Where is she?"

"Newark Airport. Jeanne Ellen was returning with her FTA, and she saw Dotty and Evelyn and the kids in the waiting area one gate over. I had Tank check on their flight. It was scheduled to take off at ten but it's been delayed an hour. We should be able to get there in time."

"Where were they going?"

"Miami."

Traffic was heavy through Trenton. It eased up for a while and then got heavy again on the Turnpike. Fortunately, the flow on the Turnpike was steady. Good Jersey traffic. The kind that gets your adrenaline going. Bumper to bumper at eighty miles an hour.

I looked at my watch when we took the airport exit. It was almost 10:00. A few minutes later, Ranger swung into the Delta passenger drop-off and stopped at the curb. "It's getting tight," he said. "You go ahead while I park. If you have a gun on you, you have to leave it in the truck."

I gave him my gun and took off. I checked the departures monitor when I entered the terminal. The flight was now on time. Still leaving from the same gate. I cracked my knuckles while I stood in line at the security check. I was so close to Evelyn and Annie. It would be a killer headache if I missed them here.

I passed through security and followed the signs to the gate. I was moving down the corridor, and I was looking at everyone. I scanned ahead, and I saw Evelyn and Dotty and the kids, two gates away. They were sitting, waiting. Nothing unusual about them. A couple moms and their kids, going to Florida.

I quietly approached them and sat in the empty seat next to Evelyn. "We need to talk," I said.

They seemed only mildly surprised. As if nothing could surprise them much anymore. They both looked tired. Their clothes looked slept in. The kids were amusing each other, being loud and obnoxious. The sort of kids you see all the time in airports. Strung out.

"I meant to call you," Evelyn said. "I would have called when we got to Miami. You should tell Grammy I'm okay."

"I want to know why you're running. And if you don't tell me I'm going to make problems for you. I'm going to stop you from leaving."

"*No.*" Evelyn said. "Please don't do that. It's important that we catch this plane."

The first boarding announcement went out.

"The Trenton police are looking for you," I said. "You're wanted for questioning for two murders. I can call security and have you brought back to Trenton."

Evelyn's face went white. "He'll kill me."

"Abruzzi?"

She nodded.

"Maybe you should tell her," Dotty said. "We haven't got much time."

"When Steven lost the bar to Abruzzi, Abruzzi came over to the house with his men and he *did* something to me."

I felt myself instinctively suck in some air. "I'm sorry," I said.

"It was his way of making us afraid. He's like a cat with a mouse. He likes to play before he kills. And he likes to dominate women."

"You should have gone to the police."

"He would have killed me before I got to testify. Or worse, he might have done something to Annie. The legal system moves too slow with a man like Abruzzi."

"Why is he after you now?" Ranger had already told me the answer, but I wanted to hear it from Evelyn.

"Abruzzi is a war nut. He plays war games. And he collects medals and things. And he had one medal that he kept on his desk. I guess it was his favorite medal because it belonged to Napoleon.

"Anyway, when Steven and I got divorced the court gave Steven visitation rights. He got Annie every Saturday. A couple weeks ago Abruzzi had a birthday party at his house for his daughter, and he demanded that Steven bring Annie."

"Was Annie friends with Abruzzi's daughter?"

"No. It was just Abruzzi's way of asserting his power. He's always doing things like that. He calls the people around him his *troops*. And they have to treat him like the Godfather or Napoleon or some big general. So he gave this party for his daughter and the troops were all supposed to attend with their kids.

"Steven was considered one of the troops. He lost the bar to Abruzzi, and it was like Abruzzi owned him after that. Steven didn't like losing the bar, but I think he liked belonging to Abruzzi's family. Made him feel like a big shot to be associated with someone everyone was afraid of."

Until he got sawed in half.

"Anyway, while the party was going on, Annie wandered into Abruzzi's office, spotted the medal on Abruzzi's desk, and took it back to the party to show the rest of the children. No one paid much attention and, somehow, the medal got stuffed into Annie's pocket. And she brought it home."

There was a second boarding call and from the corner of my eye I could see Ranger standing at a distance, watching.

"Keep going," I said. "There's still time."

"As soon as I saw the medal I knew what it was."

"Your ticket out?"

"*Yes*. As long as I was in Trenton, Abruzzi would own Annie and me. And I had no money to leave. No job skills. And worse, there was the divorce agreement. But the medal was worth a lot of money. Abruzzi used to brag about it all the time.

"So I packed up and left. I was out of the house an hour after the medal walked in. I went to Dotty for help because I didn't know where else to go. Until I sold the medal I didn't have any money."

"Unfortunately, it takes time to sell a medal like that," Dotty said. "And it had to be done quietly."

A tear slid down Evelyn's cheek. "I made a mess of it for Dotty. Now she's dragged into it and can't get out."

Dotty was keeping watch over the pack of kids. "It'll work out okay," she said. But she didn't look like she believed it.

"What about the pictures Annie drew in her pad?" I asked. "They were pictures of people getting shot. I thought maybe she witnessed a murder."

"If you look more closely you'll see the men are wearing medals. She drew the pictures while I was packing. Everyone who came into contact with Abruzzi, even children, knew about war and killing and medals. It was an obsession."

I suddenly felt very defeated. There was nothing here for me. No witness to a murder. No one who could help remove Abruzzi from my life.

"We have a buyer waiting for us in Miami," Dotty said. "I sold my car to get these tickets."

"Can you trust this buyer?"

"He seems to be okay. And I have a friend meeting us at the airport. He's a pretty sharp guy, and he's going to oversee the transaction. I think the transaction is pretty simple. We hand over the medal. Some expert examines it. And Evelyn gets a suitcase filled with money."

"Then what?"

"We'll probably have to stay hidden. Start a new life somewhere. If Abruzzi gets caught or killed, we can come home."

I had no reason to detain them. I thought they'd made some bad choices, but who was I to judge? "Good luck," I said. "Keep in touch. And call Mabel. She worries about you."

Evelyn jumped up and hugged me. Dotty gathered the kids together, and they all toddled off to Miami.

Ranger came over and slung an arm around me. "They told you a sob story, didn't they?"

"Yep."

He smiled and kissed me on the top of my head. "You really should think about getting into a different line of work. Grooming kitty cats, maybe. Or floral design."

"It was very convincing."

"Did the little girl witness a murder?"

"No. She stole a medal that was worth a suitcase full of money."

Ranger raised his eyebrows and grinned. "Good for her. I like to see enterprise in kids."

"I haven't got a murder witness. And the bear and the rabbit are dead. I think I'm fucked."

"Maybe after lunch," he said. "My treat."

"You mean *lunch* is your treat?"

"That, too. I know a place here in Newark that makes Shorty's look like a sissy joint."

Oh boy.

"And by the way, I checked your thirty-eight when you left it in the truck. You only have two bullets in it. I have this sinking feeling that the gun will go back to the cookie jar when you empty the cylinder."

I smiled at Ranger. I can be mysterious, too.

RANGER PAGED HECTOR WHEN WE WERE ON OUR way home, and Hector was in front of my apartment, waiting for us when we stepped out of the elevator. He handed the new keypad to Ranger, and he smiled at me and made a gun with his fist and forefinger. "*Bang,*" he said.

"Pretty good," I said to Ranger. "Hector's learning English."

Ranger flipped me the keypad, and he left with Hector.

I let myself into my apartment, and I stood in my kitchen. Now what? Now I had to hang out and wonder when Abruzzi would come for me. What form would it take? And how awful would it be? Awful beyond my imaginings, probably.

If I was my mother I'd be ironing. My mother ironed under stress. Stay far away from my mother when she is ironing. If I was Mabel I'd be baking. What about Grandma Mazur? That was an easy one. The Weather Channel. So what do I do? I eat Tastykakes.

Okay, there's my problem. I haven't got any Tastykakes. I'd had a burger with Ranger, but I'd skipped dessert. And now I needed a Tastykake. Without a Tastykake I was left to sit here and worry about Abruzzi. Unfortunately, I had no way of taking myself out to Tastykake Land because I didn't have a car. I was still waiting for the stupid insurance check to arrive.

Hey, hold the phone. I could *walk* to the convenience store. Four blocks. Not the sort of thing a Jersey girl ordinarily did, but what the hell. I had my gun back in my bag with two bullets ready and waiting. That was a confidence builder. I would have shoved it under the waistband of my jeans like Ranger and Joe, but there wasn't room. Probably I should restrict myself to just *one* Tastykake.

I locked up and took the stairs to the first floor. I didn't live in a fancy building. It was kept clean, and it was adequately maintained. It had been built without frills. And for that matter, without quality. Still, it was enduring. It had a back door and a front door and both doors opened to a small foyer. The stairs and the elevator also opened to the foyer. Mailboxes banked one wall. The floor was tiled. Management had added a potted palm and two wingback chairs in an attempt to compensate for the lack of a swimming pool.

Abruzzi was sitting in one of the wingback chairs. His suit was impeccable. His shirt was a brilliant white. His face was expressionless. He motioned to the wingback next to him. "Sit down," he said. "I thought we should have a conversation."

Darrow was motionless at the door.

I sat in the chair, and I took the gun out of my bag, and I aimed it at Abruzzi. "What would you like to talk about?"

"Is that gun supposed to frighten me?"

"It's a precaution."

"Not good military strategy for a meeting of surrender."

"Which one of us is supposed to be surrendering?"

"You, of course," he said. "You're soon to be taken as a prisoner of war."

"News flash. You need serious psychiatric help."

"I've lost troops because of you."

"The rabbit?"

"He was a valued member of my command."

"The bear?"

Abruzzi gave a distracted wave of his hand. "The bear was hired help. He was sacrificed for your benefit and my protection. He had an unfortunate habit of gossiping to people outside my family."

"Okay, how about Soder. Was he troops?"

"Soder failed me. Soder had no character. He was a coward. He couldn't control his own wife and daughter. He was a useless liability. Just like his bar. The insurance on the bar was worth more than the bar itself."

"I'm not sure what part I play in all this."

"You're the enemy. You chose to be on Evelyn's side in this game. As I'm sure you know, Evelyn has something I want. I'll give you a last chance to survive. You can help me get back what's rightfully mine."

"I don't know what you're talking about."

Abruzzi looked down at my gun. "Two bullets?"

"That's all I need." Oh man, I couldn't believe I just said that. I hoped Abruzzi left first because I probably just wet the chair.

"It's war, then?" Abruzzi asked. "You should reconsider. You won't like what's going to happen to you. No more fun and games."

I didn't say anything.

Abruzzi stood and walked out the door. Darrow followed.

I sat in the chair for a while with the gun in my hand, waiting for my heart rate to drop back to normal. I stood up and checked the chair seat. Then I checked *my* seat. Both dry. It was a miracle.

Walking four blocks for a Tastykake had lost some of its appeal. Maybe it would be better to set my affairs in order. Aside from establishing a legal guardian

for Rex, the only open end in my life was Andy
Bender. I went upstairs to my apartment, and I called
the office.

"I'm going after Bender," I said to Lula. "Do you
want to ride shotgun?"

"No way, Jose. You'd have to put me in a full
contamination suit before I'd go anywhere near that
place. Even then, I wouldn't go. I'm telling you,
God's got something going on there. He's got plans."

I hung up with Lula, and I called Kloughn.

"I'm going after Bender," I said to him. "Do you
want to ride along?"

"Oh darn. I can't. I'd like to. You know how much
I'd like to do that. But I can't. I just got a big case.
A car crash, right in front of the Laundromat. Well,
okay, it wasn't exactly in *front* of the Laundromat. I
had to run a few blocks to get to it in time. But I
think there's going to be some good injury."

Maybe this is for the best, I told myself. Maybe at
this point in time I'm better off doing the job alone.
Maybe I would have been better off alone *always*.
Unfortunately, I still don't have handcuffs. And
what's worse, I don't have a car. What I have is a
gun with two bullets.

So I chose the only alternative left to me. I called
a cab.

"WAIT HERE FOR ME," I TOLD THE DRIVER. "I WON'T
be long."

He cut his eyes to me, and then he looked out at
the projects. "Good thing I know your father, or I
wouldn't sit here idling my engine. This isn't exactly
an upscale neighborhood."

I had my gun in the black nylon webbed holster, strapped to my leg. I left my bag in the cab. I walked to the door and knocked.

Bender's wife answered.

"I'm looking for Andy," I told her.

"You're kidding, right?"

"I'm serious."

"He's dead. I thought you would have heard."

For a moment my mind went blank. My second reaction was disbelief. She was lying. Then I looked beyond her and realized the apartment was clean, and there was no sign of Andy Bender. "I didn't hear," I said. "What happened?"

"Remember how he had the flu?"

I nodded.

"Well, it killed him. Turned out he had one of those superbugs. After you left, he got a neighbor to take him to the hospital, but it went into his lungs and that was that. It was an act of God."

All the hair stood up on my arm. "I'm sorry."

"Yeah, right," she said. And she closed the door.

I walked back to the cab and slunk into the back-seat.

"You're awful white," the driver said. "Are you okay?"

"Something bizarre just happened, but I'm fine. I'm getting used to bizarre things."

"Now what?"

"Take me to Vinnie's."

I BURST INTO THE BONDS OFFICE. "YOU'RE NOT GOING to believe this," I said to Lula. "Andy Bender is dead."

"Get *out*. Are you shitting me?"

The door to Vinnie's inner office whipped open. "Were there witnesses? Cripes, you didn't shoot him in the back, did you? My insurance company *hates* that."

"I didn't shoot him at all. He died from the flu. I was just at his apartment. His wife told me he was dead. From the flu."

Lula did the sign of the cross. "I'm glad I learned about this cross thing," she said.

Ranger was at Connie's desk. He had a file in his hand, and he was smiling. "Did you just get out of a cab?"

"Maybe."

The smile widened. "You went after an FTA in a cab."

I rested my hand on my gun and blew out a sigh. "Don't give me a hard time. I'm not having a great day, and as you know, I've got two bullets left. I might end up using them on one of us."

"Do you need a ride home?"

"Yes."

"I'm your man," Ranger said.

Connie and Lula fanned themselves behind his back.

I climbed into the truck and looked around.

Ranger cut his eyes to me. "Are you looking for someone?"

"Abruzzi. He threatened me again."

"Do you see him?"

"No."

It's not a long drive from the office to my apartment building. A couple miles. Progress is slowed by lights and occasionally traffic, depending on the time of day. I would have liked the drive to be longer today. I felt safe from Abruzzi when I was with Ranger.

Ranger turned into my lot and parked. "There's a man in the SUV by the Dumpster," Ranger said. "Do you know him?"

"No. He doesn't live in the building."

"Let's talk to him."

Ranger and I got out of the truck, walked to the SUV, and Ranger rapped on the driver's side window.

The driver rolled the window down. "Yeah?"

"Waiting for someone?"

"What's it to you?"

Ranger reached in, grabbed the guy by the front of his jacket, and pulled him halfway through the window.

"I'd like you to take a message to Eddie Abruzzi," Ranger said. "Can you do that for me?"

The driver nodded.

Ranger released the driver and stepped back. "Tell Abruzzi he's lost the war, and he should move on."

We both had guns drawn, and we kept them steady on the SUV until it was out of sight.

Ranger looked up at my window. "We're going to stand here for a minute to give the rest of the team time to get out of your apartment. I don't want to have to shoot anybody. I'm on a tight schedule today. I don't want to get hung up filling out police forms."

We waited five minutes and then went into the building and took the stairs. The second-floor hall was empty. The keypad reported that security had been breached on my apartment. Ranger went in first and walked through. The apartment was empty.

The phone rang just as Ranger was leaving. It was Eddie Abruzzi and he wasted no time with me. He asked for Ranger.

Ranger put him on the speakerphone.

"Stay out of this," Abruzzi said. "This is a private matter between the girl and me."

"Wrong. As of this moment, you're out of her life."

"So you're choosing sides?"

"Yeah, I'm choosing sides."

"You leave me no choice then," Abruzzi said. "I suggest you look out the window, into the parking lot." And he disconnected.

Ranger and I walked to the window and looked out. The SUV was back. It pulled up to Ranger's truck with the bug-eyed lights, the guy in the passenger side lobbed a package into the truck bed, and the truck was instantly engulfed in flames.

We stood there for a few minutes, watching the spectacle, listening to the sirens get closer.

"I liked that truck," Ranger said.

BY THE TIME MORELLI ARRIVED IT WAS AFTER SIX and the remains of the truck were being hauled onto a flatbed. Ranger was finishing up police paperwork. He looked over at Morelli and gave him a nod of acknowledgment.

Morelli stood very close to me. "Do you want to tell me about this?" he asked.

"Off the record?"

"Off the record."

"We had a tip that Evelyn was at Newark Airport. We drove to Newark and caught her before she boarded. After hearing her story I decided she needed to get on the plane, so I let her go. I had no reason to detain her anyway. I just wanted to know what this was about. When we got back, Abruzzi's men were waiting. There were some words, and they torched the truck."

"I need to talk to Ranger," Morelli said. "You're not going anywhere, are you?"

"If I could borrow your truck I'd get a pizza. I'm starved."

Morelli gave me his keys and a twenty. "Get two. I'll call it in to Pino's for you."

I pulled out of the lot and headed for the Burg. I turned at the hospital, and I checked my rearview mirror. I was being careful now. I was trying not to let my fear surface but it was boiling inside me. I kept telling myself it was only a matter of time before the police got something on Abruzzi. He was too flagrant. He was too wrapped up in his own craziness, playing the game. There were too many people involved. He'd killed the bear and Soder to keep them quiet, but there were others. He couldn't kill everyone.

I didn't see anyone turn with me, but that was no guarantee. If more than one car is used it's sometimes hard to spot a tail. Just to be safe, I had my gun out when I parked in the lot. I had just a short distance to go. Once I was inside I'd be okay. There were always a couple cops in Pino's. I swung down from the truck and started for the door to the bar. I took two steps and a green van appeared from nowhere. It

glided to a stop, the window rolled down, and Valerie
looked out at me, her mouth duct-taped shut, her eyes
wild with fear. There were three other men in the van,
including the driver. Two of them wore full rubber
masks: Nixon and Clinton again. Plus there was a guy
in a paper bag with two eyes torn out. I guess the
budget only covered two rubber masks. The Bag held
a gun to Valerie's head.

I didn't know what to do. I was frozen. Mentally
and physically paralyzed.

"Drop the gun," the Bag said. "And slowly walk
to the van, or I swear to God, I'll kill your sister."

The gun fell out of my hand. "Let her go."

"After you get in."

I reluctantly moved forward, and Nixon shoved me
into the backseat. He duct-taped my mouth and
wrapped tape around my hands. The van roared off,
out of the Burg, across the river into Pennsylvania.

After ten minutes we were on a dirt road. Houses
were small and sporadic, stuck into patches of woods.
The van slowed and then stopped on the shoulder. The
Bag opened the door and shoved Valerie out. I saw
her hit the ground and roll, off the shoulder, into the
brush at the side of the road. The Bag pulled the door
shut and the van took off.

Minutes later the van turned into a driveway and
stopped. We all got out and went into a small clap-
board bungalow. It was pleasantly decorated. Not expensive stuff, but comfortable and clean. I was
directed to a kitchen chair and told to sit. A short
while after I took my place, a second car crunched on
the dirt and gravel outside. The bungalow door

opened, and Abruzzi walked in. He was the only man not in a mask.

He took a chair opposite me. We were close enough that our knees touched, and I could feel the heat from his body. He reached out and ripped the tape from my mouth.

"Where is she?" he asked me. "Where is Evelyn?"

"I don't know."

He hit me with an openhanded slap to the face that caught me off guard and knocked me off my chair. I was in shock when I hit the floor, too stunned to cry, too frightened to protest. I tasted blood, and I blinked tears away.

The guy in the Clinton mask hauled me up by my armpits and set me back on the chair.

"I'm going to ask you again," Abruzzi said. "I'm going to keep asking you until you tell me. Each time you don't answer I'm going to give you pain. Do you like pain?"

"I don't know where she is. You give me too much credit. I'm not that good at finding people."

"Ah, but you're friends with Evelyn, aren't you? Her grandmother lives next door to your parents. You've known Evelyn all your life. I think you know where she is. And I think you know why I want to find her." Abruzzi got up and went to the stove. He turned the gas on, got a poker from the fireplace, and held it into the flame. He tested the poker with a drop of water. The water sizzled and evaporated. "What first?" Abruzzi said. "Should we poke out an eye? Should we do something sexual?"

If I told Abruzzi Evelyn was in Miami, he'd go

down there and find her. Probably he'd kill her and Annie. And probably he'd kill me, too, no matter what I said.

"Evelyn is on her way across the country," I said. "She's driving."

"That's the wrong answer," Abruzzi said. "I know she boarded a plane for Miami. Unfortunately, Miami is a big place. I need to know where she's staying in Miami."

The Bag held my hands on the tabletop, the guy in the Nixon mask cut my sleeve away, then held my head, and Abruzzi held the hot poker to my bare arm. Someone screamed. I guess it was me. And then I fainted. When I came around I was on the floor. My arm felt like fire, and the room smelled like pot roast cooking.

The Bag dragged me to my feet and set me on the chair again. The most horrifying part to all this was that I honestly didn't know where Evelyn was staying. No matter how much they tortured me, I couldn't tell them. They'd have to torture me until I was dead.

"Okay," Abruzzi said. "One more time. Where is Evelyn?"

There was the sound of a motor revving outside, and Abruzzi paused to listen. The guy in the Nixon mask went to the window, and suddenly lights blazed through the curtains, and the green van crashed through the picture window in the front of the house. There was a lot of dust and confusion. I was on my feet, not sure where to go, when I realized Valerie was driving the van. I wrenched the side door open, threw myself inside, and yelled at her to *go*. She put the van into reverse, backed out of the house at about forty miles per hour, and careened out of the driveway.

Valerie still had her mouth and hands duct-taped together, but it wasn't slowing her down. She barreled down the dirt road, hit the highway, and skidded onto the bridge approach. My fear now was that she'd dump us into the river if she didn't slow down. There were chunks of wallboard stuck to the windshield wipers, the windshield was cracked, and the front of the van was smashed.

I ripped the tape off Valerie's mouth, and she let out a howl. Her eyes were still wild, and her nose was running. Her clothes were torn and dirt-smudged. I yelled at her to ease off the gas, and she started to cry.

"Jesus Christ," she said between sobs. "What the hell kind of a life do you lead? This isn't real. This is fucking television."

"Wow, Val, you said *fuck*."

"Damn fucking right. I'm fucking freaked out. I can't believe I found you. I just started walking. I thought I was walking back to Trenton, but I got turned around somehow. And then I saw the van. And I looked in the window and saw them burning you. And they'd left the keys hanging in the ignition. And . . . and I'm going to throw up." She screeched to a stop at the side of the road, opened the door, and heaved.

I took over the driving after that. I couldn't take Valerie home in her present condition. My mother would have a plotz. I was afraid to go to my apartment. I didn't have a phone, so I couldn't get in touch with Ranger. That left Morelli. I turned into the Burg on the way to Morelli's house, and on a long shot, went a block out of my way and drove past Pino's.

Morelli's truck was still there, plus Ranger's Mercedes and the black Range Rover. Morelli, Ranger, Tank, and Hector were in the lot. I pulled the van in next to Morelli's truck, and Valerie and I tumbled out.

"He's in Pennsylvania," I said. "In a house on a dirt road. He would have killed me, but Valerie drove the van into the house and somehow we got out."

"It was fucking awful," Valerie said, teeth chattering. "I was so fucking scared." She looked down at her wrists, still wrapped in duct tape. "My wrists are taped together," she said, as if it was the first she noticed.

Hector produced a knife and slit the tape, first on me and then on Valerie.

"How do you want to do this?" Morelli asked Ranger.

"Take Steph and Valerie home," Ranger said.

Ranger looked at me, and our eyes held for a moment. Then Morelli slid an arm around me and eased me up, into his truck. Tank boosted Val up next to me.

Morelli took us to his house. He made a phone call and some clean clothes appeared. His sister's, I imagine. I was too tired to ask. We cleaned Val up and took her home to my parents. We made a fast stop at the hospital emergency room to have my burn bandaged, and then we went back to Morelli's house.

"Stick a fork in me," I said to Morelli, "I'm done."

Morelli closed and locked his front door and turned the lights off. "Maybe you should consider taking a less dangerous job, like human cannonball or crash test dummy."

"You were worried about me."

"Yeah," Morelli said, gathering me into him. "I was worried about you." He held me close and rested his cheek on my head.

"I haven't got any jammies with me," I said to Morelli.

His lips skimmed my ear. "Cupcake, you're not going to need any."

I WOKE UP IN MORELLI'S BED WITH MY ARM BURNING like mad and my upper lip swollen. Morelli had me tucked in next to him. And Bob was on the other side of me. The alarm was buzzing on the clock beside the bed. Morelli reached out and knocked the clock off the nightstand.

"Gonna be one of those days," he said.

He rolled out of bed and a half hour later he was dressed and in the kitchen. He was wearing running shoes and jeans and a T-shirt. He stood at the counter while he had coffee and toast. "Costanza called while you were in the bathroom," he said, sipping his coffee, watching me over the rim of his mug. "One of the patrols found Eddie Abruzzi about an hour ago. He was in his car, in the farmer's market parking lot. Looks like he killed himself."

I stared at Morelli blank-faced. Not able to believe what I just heard.

"He left a note," Morelli said. "It said he was depressed over some business deals."

There was a long silence between us.

"It wasn't a suicide, was it?" I phrased it as a question, when it was actually a statement.

"I'm a cop," Morelli said. "If I thought it was anything other than a suicide I'd have to look into it."

Ranger killed Abruzzi. I knew it as sure as I was standing there. Morelli knew it, too.

"Wow," I said softly.

Morelli looked at me. "Are you okay?"

I nodded yes.

He drank the last of his coffee, and he put the mug in the sink. He pulled me in tight against him and he kissed me.

I said *wow* again. More feeling this time. Morelli really knew how to kiss.

He took his gun from the kitchen counter and holstered it at his waist. "I'll take the Ducati today and leave you the truck. And when I get off work we should talk."

"Oh boy. More talk. That never gets us anywhere."

"Okay, maybe we shouldn't talk. Maybe we should just have sweaty sex."

Finally, a sport I could enjoy.